# ORIGIN

Pinnacle Thrillers by J. A. KONRATH

*The List*

*Origin*

# ORIGIN

## J. A.
## KONRATH

**PINNACLE BOOKS**
Kensington Publishing Corp.
www.kensingtonbooks.com

PINNACLE BOOKS are published by

Kensington Publishing Corp.
119 West 40th Street
New York, NY 10018

All Kensington titles, imprints, and distributed lines are available at special quantity discounts for bulk purchases for sales promotions, premiums, fund-raising, educational, or institutional use. Special book excerpts or customized printings can also be created to fit specific needs. For details, write or phone the office of the Kensington sales manager: Kensington Publishing Corp., 119 West 40th Street, New York, NY 10018, attn: Sales Department; phone 1-800-221-2647.

ISBN-13: 978-0-7860-4275-3
ISBN-10: 0-7860-4275-3

First Pinnacle premium mass market printing: December 2018

10 9 8 7 6 5 4 3 2 1

Printed in the United States of America

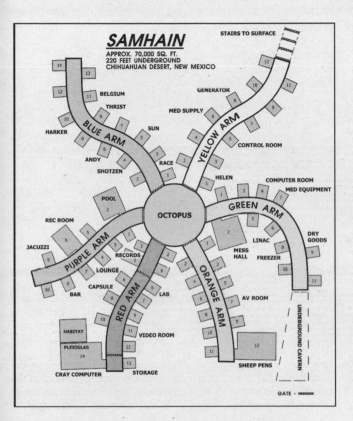

*And when the thousand years are ended,*
*Satan will be loosed from his prison.*

—Revelation 20:7

# PANAMA

**November 15, 1906**

"Where is it?" Theodore Roosevelt asked John Stevens as the two men shook hands. Amador, Shonts, and the rest of the welcoming party had already been greeted and dismissed by the President, left to wonder what had become of Roosevelt's trademark grandiosity.

Fatigue from his journey, they later surmised.

They were wrong.

The twenty-sixth President of the United States was far from tired. Since Stevens's wire a month previous, Roosevelt had been electrified with worry.

The canal project had been a tricky one from the onset—the whole Nicaraguan episode, the Panamanian revolution, the constant bickering in Congress—but nothing in his political or personal past had prepared him for this development. After five days of travel aboard the battleship *Louisiana*, his wife, Edith, sick and miserable, Roosevelt's nerves had become so tightly stretched they could be plucked and played like a mandolin.

"You want to see it *now*?" Stevens asked, wiping

the rain from a walrus mustache that rivaled the President's. "Surely you want to rest from your journey."

"Rest is for the weak, John. I have much to accomplish on this visit. But first things first. I must see the discovery."

Roosevelt bid quick apologies to the puzzled group, sending his wife and three Secret Service agents ahead to the greeting reception at Tivoli Crossing. Before anyone, including Edith, could protest, the President had taken Stevens by the shoulder and was leading him down the pier.

"You are storing it nearby," Roosevelt stated, confirming that his instructions had been explicitly followed.

"In a shack in Cristobal, about a mile from shore. I can arrange for horses."

"We shall walk. Tell me again how it was found."

Stevens chewed his lower lip and lengthened his stride to keep in step with the commander in chief. The engineer had been in Panama for over a year, at Roosevelt's request, heading the canal project.

He wasn't happy.

The heat and constant rain were intolerable. Roosevelt's lackey Shonts was pompous and annoying. Though yellow fever and dysentery were being eradicated through the efforts of Dr. Gorgas and the new sanitation methods, malaria still claimed dozens of lives every month, and labor disputes had become commonplace and increasingly complicated with every new influx of foreign workers.

Now, to top it all off, an excavation team had discovered something so horrible that it made the enormity of the canal project look trivial by comparison.

"It was found at the East Culebra Slide in the Cut," Stevens said, referring to the nine-mile stretch of land that ran through the mountain range of the Continental Divide. "Spaniard excavation team hit it at about eighty feet down."

"Hard workers, Spaniards," Roosevelt said. He knew the nine thousand workers they had brought over from the Basque provinces were widely regarded as superior to the Chinese and West Indians because of their tireless efforts. "You were on the site at the time?"

"I was called to it. I arrived the next day. The . . . *capsule*, I suppose you could call it, was taken to Pedro Miguel by train."

"Unopened?"

"Yes. After I broke the seal on it and saw the contents . . ."

"Again, all alone?"

"By myself, yes. After viewing the . . . well, immediately afterward I wired Secretary Taft . . ." Stevens trailed off, his breath laboring in effort to keep up with the frantic pace of Roosevelt.

"Dreadful humidity," the President said. He attempted to wipe the hot rain from his forehead with a damp handkerchief. "I had wished to view the working conditions in Panama at their most unfavorable, and I believe I certainly have."

They were quiet the remainder of the walk, Roosevelt taking in the jungle and the many houses and buildings that Stevens had erected during the last year. *Remarkable man*, Roosevelt mused, but he'd expected nothing less. Once this matter was decided, he was looking forward to the tour of the canal effort. There was so much that interested him. He was anxious to see one of the famed hundred-ton Bucyrus steam shovels that so outperformed the ancient French excavators. He longed to ride in one. Being the first President to ever leave the States, he certainly owed the voters some exciting details of his trip.

"Over there. To the right."

Stevens gestured to a small shack nestled in an outcropping of tropical brush. There was a sturdy padlock hooked to a hasp on the door, and a sign warning in several languages that explosives were contained therein.

"No one else has seen this," Roosevelt confirmed.

"The Spaniard team was deported right after the discovery."

Roosevelt used the sleeve of his elegant white shirt to clean his spectacles while Stevens removed the padlock. They entered the shed and Stevens shut the door behind them.

It was stifling in the small building. The President immediately felt claustrophobic in the dark, hot room, and had to force himself to stand still while Stevens sought the lantern.

Light soon bathed the capsule sitting before them.

It was better than twelve feet long, pale gray, with carvings on the outside that resembled Egyptian hieroglyphics to Roosevelt. It rested on the ground, almost chest high, and appeared to be made of stone. But it felt like nothing the President had ever touched.

Running his hand across the top, Roosevelt was surprised by how smooth, almost slippery, the surface was. Like an oily silk, but it left no residue on the fingers.

"How does it open?" he asked.

Stevens handed his lamp to Roosevelt and picked up a pry bar hanging near the door. With a simple twist in a near-invisible seam the entire top half of the capsule flipped open on hidden hinges like a coffin.

"My dear God in heaven," the President gasped.

The thing in the capsule was horrible beyond description.

"My sentiments exactly," Stevens whispered.

"And it is . . . alive?"

"From what I can judge, yes. Dormant, but alive."

Roosevelt's hand ventured to touch it, but the man who charged up San Juan Hill wasn't able to summon the nerve.

"Even being prepared for it, I still cannot believe what I am seeing."

The President fought his repulsion, the cloying heat adding to the surreality of the moment. Roosevelt detected a rank, animal smell, almost like a musk, coming out of the capsule.

The smell of the . . . *thing*.

He looked it over, head to foot, unable to turn away. The image seared itself into his mind, to become the source of frequent nightmares for the remainder of his life.

"What is the course of action, Mr. President? Destroy it?"

"How can we? Is it our right? Think what this means."

"But what if it awakens? Could we contain it?"

"Why not? This is the twentieth century. We are making technological advancements on a daily basis."

"Do you believe the public is ready for this?"

"No," Roosevelt said without hesitation. "I do not believe the United States, or the world, even in this enlightened age, would be able to handle a discovery of this magnitude."

Stevens frowned. He didn't believe any good could come of this, but as usual he had trouble going toe-to-toe with Roosevelt.

"Speak your mind, John. You have been living with this for a month."

"I believe we should burn it, Mr. President. Then sink its ashes in the sea."

"You are afraid."

"Even a man of your standing, sir, must admit to some fear gazing at this thing."

"Yes, I can admit to being afraid. But that is because we fear what we do not understand. Perhaps with understanding . . ."

Roosevelt made his decision. This would be taken back to the States. He'd lock it away someplace secret and recruit the top minds in the world to study it. He instructed Stevens to have a crate built and for it to be packed and boarded onto the *Louisiana*—no, better make it the *Tennessee*. If Mother found out what was aboard her ship she might die of fright.

"But if the world sees this . . ."

"The world will not. Pay the workers off and have them work at night without witnesses. I expect the crate to be locked as this shed was, and the key given to me. Worry no more about this, John, it is no longer your concern."

"Yes, Mr. President."

Roosevelt clenched his teeth and forced himself to stick out his hand to touch the thing—a brief touch that he would always recall as the most frightening experience of his life. He covered the fear with a bully Roosevelt *harrumph* and a false pout of bravado.

"Now let us lock this up and you can show me that canal you are building." Stevens closed the lid, but the smell remained.

The twenty-sixth President of the United States walked out of the shed and into the rain. His hands were shaking. He made two fists and shoved them into his pockets. The rain speckled his glasses, but he made no effort to clean them off. His whole effort was focused on a silent prayer to God that he'd made the right decision.

# CHAPTER 1

*Present day*

"*You have reached Worldwide Translation Services. For English, press one.*

"*Por español . . .*"

*BEEP.*

"*Welcome to WTS, the company for your every translation and interpretation need. Our skilled staff of linguists can converse in over two dozen languages, and we specialize in escort, telephone, consecutive, simultaneous, conference, sight, and written translations. For a list of languages we're able to interpret, press one. For Andrew Dennison, press two. For a . . .*" *BEEP.*

The business phone rang. Andy glanced at the clock next to the bed. Coming up on 3:00 A.M. Chicago time. But elsewhere in the world they were eating lunch.

If he didn't pick up, it would be forwarded to voice mail.

Unfortunately, voice mail didn't pay his bills.

"WTS, this is Andrew Dennison."

"Mr. Dennison, this is the President of the United States. Your country needs you."

Andy hung up. He remembered being a kid, sleeping

over at a friend's house, making prank calls. It seemed so funny back then.

He closed his eyes and tried to return to the dream he'd been having. Something to do with Susan, his ex-girlfriend, begging for him to come back. She'd told him that would only happen in his dreams, and she'd proven herself right.

The phone rang again.

"Look, kid. I've got your number on the caller ID, so I know you're calling from . . ."

He squinted at the words WHITE HOUSE on the phone display.

"Mr. Dennison, in exactly five seconds two members of the Secret Service will knock on your door."

There was a knock at the door.

Andy jackknifed to a sitting position.

"Those are Agents Smith and Jones. They're to escort you to a limousine waiting downstairs."

Andy took the cordless over to his front door, squinted through the peephole.

Standing in the hallway were two men in black suits.

"Look, Mr.—uh—President, if this is some kind of tax thing . . ."

"Your particular skills are required in a matter of national security, Mr. Dennison. I'll brief you in New Mexico."

"This is a translation job?"

"I can't speak any more about it at this time, but you must leave immediately. You'll be paid three times your normal rate, plus expenses. My agents can explain in further detail. We'll talk when you arrive."

The connection ended. Andy peered through his

peephole again. The men looked like Secret Service. They had the blank stare dead to rights.

"Do you guys have ID?" he asked through the door.

They held up their IDs.

Andy swallowed, and swallowed again. He considered his options and realized he really didn't have any.

He opened the door.

"As soon as you're dressed, Mr. Dennison, we can take you to the airport."

"How many days should I pack for?"

"No need to pack, sir. Your things will be forwarded to you."

"Do you know what language I'm going to be using? I've got books, computer programs . . ."

"Your things will be forwarded."

Andy had more questions, but he didn't think asking them would result in answers. He dressed in silence.

The limo, while plush, wasn't accessorized with luxuries. No wet bar. No television. No phone. And the buttons for the windows didn't work.

Andy wore his best suit, Brooks Brothers gray wool, his Harvard tie, and a pair of leather shoes from some Italian designer, which cost three hundred dollars and pinched his toes.

"So where in New Mexico am I going?" Andy asked the agents, both of whom rode in the front seat.

They didn't reply.

"Are we going to O'Hare or Midway?" No answer.

"Can you guys turn on the radio?"

The radio came on. Oldies. Andy slouched back in his seat as Mick Jagger crooned.

Chicago whipped by him on both sides, the streets

full of people even at this late hour. Summer in the city was around the clock. The car stopped at a light and three college-age girls, drunk and giggling, knocked on his one-way window and tried to peer inside. They were at least a decade too young for him.

The limo's destination turned out to be Midway, the smaller of Chicago's two airports. Rather than enter the terminal, they were cleared through the perimeter fence and pulled directly out onto the runway. They parked in front of a solitary hangar, far from the jumbo jets. Andy was freed from the limo and led silently to a Learjet. He boarded without enthusiasm. He'd been on many jets, to many places more exotic than New Mexico.

Andy was bursting with curiosity for his current situation, but sleep was invading his head. It would probably turn out to be some silly little international embarrassment, like a Pakistani ambassador who hit someone while drunk driving. What was the Hindko word for *intoxication*? He couldn't remember, and since they didn't let him take his books, he had no way to look it up.

At a little past 4:00 A.M. the pilot boarded and introduced himself with a strong handshake, but didn't offer his name. He had no answers for Andy either.

Andy slept poorly, on and off, for the next few hours.

He awoke during the landing, the jolt nudging him alert when the wheels hit the tarmac. After the plane came to a stop, the pilot announced they'd arrived at their destination, Las Cruces International Airport. Andy rubbed some grit from his eyes and stretched in his seat, waiting for the pilot to open the hatch.

The climate was hot and dry, appropriate for the desert. The pilot informed Andy to remain on the runway and then walked off to the terminal.

Andy waited in the powerful sun, the only human being in sight, his rumpled suit soon clinging to him like a close family. A minute passed. Two. A golden eagle rode a thermal in the distance, circling slowly. Andy wondered when his ride would arrive. He wondered why this town was called The Crosses. He wondered what the hell was so important that the leader of the free world woke him up at 3:00 A.M. and flew him out here.

From the opposite end of the runway an army Humvee approached. Andy noticed the tags: Fort Bliss. The driver offered him a thermos of coffee and then refused further conversation.

They drove west on Interstate 10 and turned onto highway 549, heading into the desert. Traffic went from infrequent to nonexistent, and after they passed the Waste Isolation Pilot Plant—a large complex fenced off with barbed wire—they turned off road and followed some dirt trail that Andy could barely make out.

The Florida Mountains loomed in the distance. Sagebrush and tumbleweeds dotted the landscape. Andy even saw the skull of a steer resting on some rocks. This was the authentic West, the West of Geronimo and Billy the Kid. Andy had been to several deserts in his travels: the Gobi in China, the Rub' al-Khali in Saudi Arabia, the Kalahari in South Africa . . . but this was his first visit to the Chihuahuan Desert. It left him as the others had—detached. Travel meant work, and Andy never had a chance to enjoy any of the places he'd visited around the world.

The Humvee stopped abruptly and Andy lurched in his seat.

"We're here," the driver said.

Andy craned his neck and looked around. Three hundred and sixty degrees of desert, not a building nor a soul in sight.

"You're kidding."

"Please get out of the Humvee, sir. I'm supposed to leave you here."

"Leave me here? In the desert?"

"Those are my orders."

Andy squinted. There was nothing but sand and rock for miles and miles.

"This is ridiculous. I'll die out here."

"Sir, please get out of the Humvee."

"You can't leave me in the middle of the desert. It's insane." The driver drew his pistol.

"Jesus!"

"These are my orders, sir. If you don't get out of the Humvee, I've been instructed to shoot you in the leg and drag you out. One . . ."

"I don't believe this."

"Two . . ."

"This is murder. You're murdering me here."

"Three."

The driver cocked the gun and aimed it at Andy's leg. Andy threw up his hands. "Fine! I'm out!"

Andy stepped out of the Humvee. He could feel the heat of the sand through the soles of his shoes.

The driver holstered his weapon, hit the gas, and

swung the Humvee around. It sped off in the direction it had come. Andy watched until it shrank down to nothing.

He turned in a complete circle, feeling the knot growing in his belly. The only thing around him was scrub brush and cacti.

"This is not happening."

Andy searched the sky for any helicopters that might be flying in to pick him up. The sky was empty, except for a fat desert sun that hurt his eyes. Andy couldn't be sure, but the air seemed to be getting hotter. By noon it would be scorching.

He looked at his watch and wondered how long he could go without water. The very idea of it made his tongue feel thick. A day, maybe two at most. It would take at least two days to walk back to the airport. He decided to follow the truck tracks.

"Andrew Dennison?"

Andy spun around, startled. Standing twenty yards away was a man. He wore loose-fitting jeans and a blue polo shirt, and he approached Andy in an unhurried gait. As the figure came into sharper focus, Andy noticed several things at once. The man was old, maybe seventy, with age spots dotting his bald dome and deep wrinkles set in a square face. But he carried himself like a much younger man, and though his broad shoulders were stooped with age, he projected an apparent strength. *Military*, Andy guessed, and upper echelon as well.

Andy walked to meet the figure, trying not to appear surprised that he'd just materialized out of nowhere.

The thoughts of vultures and thirst were replaced by several dozen questions.

"I'm General Regis Murdoch. Call me Race. Welcome to Project Samhain."

Race offered a thick and hairy hand, which Andy nervously shook. It felt like shaking a two-by-four.

"General Race, I appreciate the welcome, but I think I've been left out of the loop. I don't know . . ."

"All in good time. The President wants to fill you in, and you're to meet the group."

"Where?" Andy asked, looking around.

The general beamed. "Almost a hundred years old, and still the best hidden secret in the United States. Right this way."

Andy followed Race up to a pile of rocks next to a bush. Close inspection revealed that they'd been glued, or maybe soldered, to a large metal plate which spun on a hinge. The plate swiveled open, revealing a murky stairwell leading into the earth.

"Cutting edge stuff in 1906, now kind of dated." Race smiled. "But sometimes the old tricks are still the best."

Race prompted Andy down the sandy iron staircase and followed after closing the lid above them. The walls were concrete, old and crumbling. Light came from bare bulbs hanging overhead every fifteen steps.

*Only a few hours ago I was asleep in my bed*, Andy thought.

"Don't worry," Race said. "It gets better."

After almost two hundred steps down they came to a large metal door with a wheel in the center, like a submarine hatch. Race stopped in front of the door and cleared his throat. He leaned closer to Andy, locking eyes with him.

"Three hundred million Americans have lived during the last century, and you are only the forty-third to ever enter this compound. During your time here and for the rest of your life afterward, you're going to be sworn to absolute secrecy. Failure to keep this secret will lead to your trial and inevitable execution for treason."

"Execution," Andy repeated.

"The Rosenbergs were numbers twenty-two and twenty-three. You didn't buy that crap about selling nuclear secrets, did you?"

Andy blinked. "I'm in an episode of *The X-Files*."

"That old TV show? They wish they had what we do."

Race opened the door and bade Andy to enter. They'd stepped into a modern hospital. Or at least, that's what it looked like. Everything was white, from the tiled floors and painted walls to the fluorescent lights recessed into the ceiling. A disinfectant smell wafted through the air, cooled by air-conditioning. They walked down a hallway, the clicking of Andy's expensive shoes amplified to an almost comic echo. It could have been a hundred other buildings Andy had been in before, except this one was several hundred feet underground and harbored some kind of government secret.

Andy asked, "This was built in 1906?"

"Well, it's been improved upon as the years have gone by. Didn't get fluorescent lights till 1938. In '49 we added the Orange Arm and the Purple Arm. We're always replacing, updating. Just got a Jacuzzi in '99, but it's on the fritz."

"How big is this place?"

"About seventy-five thousand square feet. Took two years to dig it all out. God gets most of the credit though. Most of this space is a series of natural caves. Not nearly the size of the Carlsbad Caverns two hundred miles to the east, but enough for our purpose."

"Speaking of purpose . . ."

"We're getting to that."

The hallway curved gradually to the right and Andy noted that the doors were all numbered in yellow paint with the word YELLOW stenciled above them. Andy guessed correctly that they were in the Yellow Arm of the complex, and was happy that at least one thing made sense.

"What's that smell?" Andy asked, noting that the pleasant scent of lemon and pine had been overtaken by a distinct farmlike odor.

"The sheep, over in Orange 12. They just came in last week, and they stink like, well, sheep. We think we can solve the problem with HEPA filters, but it will take some time."

"Sheep," Andy said. He wondered, idly, if he'd been brought here to interpret their bleating.

The hallway they were taking ended at a doorway, and Race ushered Andy through it and into a large round room that had six doors along its walls. Each door was a different color.

"Center of the complex. The head of the Octopus, so to speak. I believe you've got a call waiting for you."

In the middle of the room was a large round table, circled with leather executive-type office chairs. Computer monitors, electronic gizmos, and a mess of cords and papers haphazardly covered the tabletop as if they'd been dropped there from a great height.

Race sat Andy down in front of a screen and tapped a few commands on a keyboard. The President's head and shoulders appeared on the flat-screen monitor, and he nodded at Andy as if they were in the same room.

"Video phone, got it in '04." Race winked.

"Mr. Dennison, thank you for coming. You've done your country a great service."

The President looked and sounded like he always did: fit, commanding, and sincere. Obviously he'd had a chance to sleep.

"Where do I talk?" Andy asked Race.

"Right at the screen. There's a mike and a camera housed in the monitor." Andy leaned forward.

"Mr. President, I'd really like to know what's going on and what I'm supposed to be doing here."

"You were chosen, Andy, because you met all of the criteria on a very long list. We need a translator, one with experience in ancient languages. You've always had a gift for language. My sources say you were fluent in Spanish by age three, and by six years old you could also speak French, German, and some Russian. In grade school you were studying the Eastern tongues, and you could speak Chinese by junior high."

*Only Mandarin*, Andy thought. He couldn't speak Cantonese until a few years later.

"You graduated high school in three years and were accepted to Harvard on scholarship. You spent four years at Harvard, and wrote and published your thesis on giving enunciation to cuneiform, at age nineteen.

"When you left school in 1986 you lived on money

left to you by your parents, who died in a fire three years before. After the money ran out you got a job at the United Nations in New York. You were there less than a year before being fired. During a Middle East peace talk you insulted the Iraqi ambassador."

"He was a pervert who liked little girls."

"Iraq was our ally at the time."

"What does that have to do with—"

The President held up a hand, as he was so accustomed to doing with reporters.

"I'm not sitting in a seat of judgment, Andy. But you're entitled to know why you were chosen. After the UN fired you, you started your own freelance translation service, WTS. You've been making an average living, one that allows you to be your own boss. But business has been slow lately, I assume because of the Internet."

Andy frowned. In the beginning, the World Wide Web had opened up a wealth of information for a translator, giving him instant access to the greatest libraries in the world. But, of course, it gave everyone else access to those libraries too. Along with computer programs that could translate both the written and the spoken word.

"So you know I'm good at my job, and you know I could use the money."

"More than that, Andy. You're single, and you aren't currently seeing anyone. You don't have any relatives. Business is going poorly and you're behind on your Visa and your Discover Card payments, and you've just gotten your second warning from the electric company.

Your unique mind, so active and curious years ago, hasn't had a challenge since college.

"You didn't talk to the media after the incident at the UN, even though reporters offered you money for the story. That's important, because it shows you can keep your mouth shut. In short, by bringing you in on this project, you don't have anything to lose, but everything to gain."

"Why aren't I comforted that the government knows so much about me?"

"Not the government, Andy. Me. No one else in Washington is aware of you, or of Project Samhain. Only the incumbent President knows what goes on there in New Mexico. It was passed on to me by my predecessor, and I'll pass it on to my successor when I leave office. This is the way it's been since President Theodore Roosevelt commissioned construction of this facility in 1906."

Andy didn't like this at all. His curiosity was being overtaken by a creepy feeling.

"This is all very interesting, but I don't think I'm your man."

"I also know about Myra Thackett and Chris Simmons."

Andy's mouth became a thin line. Thackett and Simmons were two fictitious employees that Andy pretended to have under salary at WTS. Having phantom people on the payroll reduced income tax and was the only way he'd been able to keep his business afloat.

"So this is a tax thing after all."

"Again, only I know about it, Andy. Not the IRS. Not the FBI. Just me. And I can promise you that

Ms. Thackett and Mr. Simmons will never come back to haunt you if you help us here."

"What exactly"—Andy chose his words carefully—"do you want from me?"

"First you must swear, as a citizen of the United States, to never divulge anything you see, hear, or learn at Project Samhain, under penalty of execution. Not to a friend. Not even to a wife. My own wife doesn't even know about this."

Not seeing an alternative, Andy held up his right hand, as if he were testifying in court.

"Fine. I swear."

"General Murdoch will provide the details, he knows them better than I. Suffice it to say, this may be the single most important project this country, maybe even the world, has ever been involved with. I wish you luck, and God bless." The screen went blank.

"It's aliens, isn't it?" Andy turned to Race. "You've got aliens here."

"Well, no. But back in '47 we had a hermit who lived in the mountains—he found our secret entrance and got himself a good look inside. Before we could shut him up he was blabbing to everyone within earshot. So we faked a UFO landing two hundred miles away in Roswell to divert attention." Andy rubbed his temples.

"You want some aspirin?" Race asked. "Or breakfast, maybe?"

"What I want, after swearing under the penalty of execution, is to know what the hell I'm doing here."

"They say an image is worth a thousand words. Follow me."

Race headed to the Red door and Andy loped behind.

The Red Arm hallway looked exactly like the Yellow Arm; white and sterile with numbered doors, this time with the word RED stenciled on them. But after a few dozen yards Andy noted a big difference. Race had to stop at a barrier that blocked the hallway. It resembled a prison door, with thick vertical steel bars set in a heavy frame.

"Titanium," Race said as he pressed some numbers on a keypad embedded in the wall. "They could stop a charging rhino."

There was a beep and a metallic sound as the door unlocked. The door swung inward, and Race held it open for Andy, then closed it behind him with a loud clang. It made Andy feel trapped. They came up on another set of bars fifty yards farther up.

"Why two sets?" Andy asked. "You have a rhino problem here?"

"Well, it's got horns, that's for sure."

Race opened the second gate and the Red Arm came to an abrupt end at doors Red 13 and Red 14.

"He was found in Panama in 1906, by a team digging the canal," Race said. "For the past hundred years he's been in some kind of deep sleep, like a coma. Up until last week. Last week he woke up."

"He?"

"We call him Bub. He's trying to communicate, but we don't know what he's saying."

Andy's apprehension increased with every breath. He had an irrational urge to turn around and run. Or maybe it wasn't so irrational.

"Is Bub human?" Andy asked.

"Nope." Race grinned. The general was clearly

enjoying himself. *Didn't have visitors too often*, Andy guessed.

"So what is he?"

"See for yourself."

Race opened door Red 14, and Andy almost gagged on the animal stench. This wasn't a farm smell. This was a musky, sickly, sweet-and-sour, big-carnivore smell.

Forcing himself to move, Andy took two steps into the room. It was large, the size of a gymnasium, the front half filled with medical equipment. The back half had been partitioned off with a massive translucent barrier, glass or plastic. Behind the glass was . . . "Jesus Christ," Andy said.

Andy's mind couldn't process what he was seeing. The teeth. The eyes. The claws.

This thing wasn't supposed to exist in real life.

"*Biix a beel*," Bub said.

Andy flew past Race, heading for the hallway.

"I promise not to tell anyone."

"Mr. Dennison . . ."

Andy met up with the titanium bars and used some of his favorite curses from several different languages. His palms were soaked with sweat, and he'd begun to hyperventilate.

Race caught up, placing a hand on his shoulder.

"I apologize for not preparing you, but I'm an old man with so little pleasure in my life, and it's such a hoot watching people see Bub for the first time." Andy braced the older man.

"Bub. Beelzebub. You've got Satan in there."

"Possibly. Father Thrist thinks it's a lower-level

demon like Moloch or Rahab, but Rabbi Shotzen concedes it may be Mastema."

"I'd like to leave," Andy said, attempting to sound calm. "Right now."

"Don't worry. He's not violent. I've even been in the dwelling with him. He's just scary-looking, is all. And that Plexiglas barrier is rated to eight tons. It's as safe as visiting the monkey house at the zoo."

Andy tried to find the words.

"You're a lunatic," he decided.

"Look, Andy, I've been watching after Bub for over forty years. We've had the best of the best in the world here—doctors, scientists, holy men, you name it. We've found out so much, but the rest is just theory. Bub's awake now and trying to communicate. You're the key to that. Don't you see how important this is?"

"I'm . . ." Andy began, searching his mind for a way to put it.

Race finished the thought for him. "Afraid. Of course you're afraid. Any damn fool would be, seeing Bub. We've been taught to fear him since we were born. But if I can paraphrase Samuel Butler, we don't know the devil's side of the story, because God wrote all the books. Just think about what we can learn here."

"You're military," Andy accused. "I'm sure the weapons implications of controlling the Prince of Darkness aren't lost on you."

Race lost his friendly demeanor, his eyes narrowing.

"We have an opportunity here, Mr. Dennison. An opportunity that we haven't had since Christ walked the earth. In that room is a legendary creature, and the things that he could teach us about the world, the universe, and creation itself stagger the imagination. You've been chosen to help us, to work with our team in getting some answers. Many would kill for the chance."

Andy folded his arms. "You expect me to believe not only that the devil is harmless and just wants to have a chat, but that the biggest government conspiracy in the history of the world has only good intentions?"

Race's face remained impassive for a few seconds longer, and then he broke out laughing.

"Damn, that does sound hard to swallow, don't it?"

Andy couldn't help but warm a bit at the man's attitude. "General Murdoch . . ."

"Race. Call me Race. And I understand. I've been part of the project so long the whole thing is the norm to me. You need to eat, rest, think about things. We'll grab some food and I'll show you your room."

"And if I want to leave?"

"This isn't a prison, son. I'm sure you weren't the only guy on the President's list. You're free to go whenever you please, so long as you never mention this to anyone."

Andy took a deep, calming breath and the effects of the adrenaline in his system began to wear off. Race opened the gate and they began their trek back down the hallway.

"The world really is going to hell, isn't it?" Andy said.

Race grinned. "Sure is. And we've got a front-row seat."

# CHAPTER 2

Breakfast was light but nourishing, consisting of banana muffins, sausage, and coffee. The coffee was the only thing fresh. The food, like all food in the compound, was frozen and then microwaved. Race told Andy that refrigeration had been possible since the compound was created, but the small group of people who lived here didn't warrant the constant trips to refresh supplies. Instead, two huge freezers were stocked several times a year with everything from cheese and bread to Twinkies and Snickers. Milk, an item that didn't freeze well, was available vacuum-packed.

"How many people are here right now?" Andy asked, stirring more sugar into his coffee.

They sat on orange chairs at a Formica table with a sunflower pattern. Green 2—or the mess hall as Race called it—doubled as both a dining area and a kitchen. The decor, save for the microwaves, was pure 1950s cafeteria.

"Eight, including you. The holies, the priest and the rabbi, leave for brief periods every so often. Everyone else is here for the long haul. Believe it or not, except for the isolation and the fact that you don't see the great outdoors, this is almost like a resort. We've got a sauna, a four-lane swimming pool, a full library, even a racquetball court."

"Who foots the bill for all of this if only the President knows about it?"

"Social Security. Now you know why the benefits are so low."

Andy used his fist to stifle a yawn. The food was settling well and he suddenly realized how tired he was.

"I'll show you to your room," Race said. "If you haven't had a chance yet, take the time to make a list of things you need from your apartment: clothes, books, whatever. I know you've got some things already en route, toiletries and such, but anything else you might need, just holler. That goes for things you might need for research too. We have a blank check here, no questions asked. Back in the '60s, as a joke, two guys asked for a Zamboni. Came the next day. Sure pissed off President Johnson. That man could curse like no one I've ever met."

"I'm still not convinced I'm staying."

"That's fine, but it's a funny thing about Bub. We've had people scream, faint dead away, become downright hysterical the first time they see him. But we've never had one leave without finishing their job. Curiosity is a powerful motivator."

*It also killed the cat*, Andy thought.

They left the mess hall and headed down the Blue Arm via the Octopus. As they walked, the door to Blue 5 opened and a woman came out into the hallway. She was petite, and the lab coat she wore was too big for her even though the sleeves had been rolled up. Her hair was blue-black and cut into a bob, perfectly framing a triangular Asian face.

Andy was immediately entranced. It had been a long time since he'd been in the presence of a beautiful woman. The last was his ex-girlfriend Susan. Pre-Susan, he'd dated a lot. His looks were okay, but the ability to speak in dozens of languages was something women really liked. Post-Susan, he'd been a desert island. She'd taken more than just his heart. She'd taken his confidence as well.

"Dr. Jones, this is Andy Dennison, the translator. Andy, this is Dr. Sunshine Jones, our resident veterinarian."

"Hi," Andy said, smiling big. "You know, when I was a kid I had a retriever named Sunshine. I loved that dog."

Dr. Jones stared at him, her face made of marble.

"Not that I'm comparing you to a dog," Andy said quickly. "But it's a small world, both you and my dog having the same, uh, name." She didn't respond. Andy's smile deflated.

Race, who watched the exchange with barely concealed amusement, cut in to give Andy a hand.

"Mr. Dennison was called in at three this morning. He just met Bub an hour ago. You could say he had the typical reaction."

"Hey, I'm from Chicago," Andy said, trying to recover. "I'm not bothered by too much."

"Is that so?" Dr. Jones said. Her voice lacked the faintest trace of good nature. "Bub's next feeding is at noon. Maybe you'd like to lend a hand?"

"Sure."

Dr. Jones nodded, then walked down the Blue Arm to the Octopus. Andy waited until she'd gone through the door before commenting.

"Very intense lady."

"She's been here a week, since Bub woke up, and I haven't seen her smile once. Does a helluva job though. She's the one who figured out Bub's, uh, nutritional requirements."

"Which are?"

"Remember those sheep you smelled?"

Andy frowned, the banana muffins doing a flip in his stomach.

"Well," Race said. "Here's your room."

Race opened the door to Blue 6. Andy gave it a quick glance over. It was set up like a hotel suite: bed, desk, TV, dresser, washroom. The only thing missing was a view.

"Our water heater is on the fritz, so all we got is lukewarm for the time being. That phone on the nightstand is in-house only. All the rooms in Samhain got 'em. Hit the pound sign and then the number of the arm followed by the room number. Blue Arm is number one, Yellow Arm, number two—there's a list next to the phone. I'm in Blue 1, so just hit pound-one-one to get me. Or hit star-one-hundred and go live over the house speakers."

Andy yawned, knowing he wouldn't remember any of that.

"The only outside line is in the control room," Race continued, "and for obvious reasons that's restricted.

If you need to get a message to the rest of the world, you have to go through me."

Andy looked at the bed and felt his will drain away.

"Do I get a wake-up call?"

"I believe you've already got one in the form of Dr. Jones. I know a thing or two about being macho, but I'm not sure you should witness a feeding just yet, even to impress the cute doctor."

"It's that bad?"

"I've seen action in two wars, son, and it's that bad."

Andy took Race's outstretched hand and mumbled a thank-you, though he wasn't really sure what he was thankful for. He was three items into his list of necessities when he fell asleep.

A buzzing woke him up. Andy wasn't sure where he was, and when he remembered, he couldn't figure out what the noise meant. It turned out to be his phone, humming like an angry bee.

He lifted the receiver.

"Mr. Dennison? This is Dr. Jones."

Andy blinked and said good morning. The clock on the dresser said 12:07, so it was technically afternoon, but that didn't enter into his sleep-addled head.

"Can you meet me at Orange 12, say, in fifteen minutes?"

"Sure. Orange 12."

The doctor hung up. Andy rubbed his eyes and extended the motion into scratching his chin. Stubble. He sat up in bed. Thought about the demon. Felt his heart begin to race.

*Pretend it's just another translation job*, he told himself.

A suitcase that he recognized as his own was sitting next to the bathroom door. When he calmed down, he opened the case to find clothing and sundries, packed neater than he'd ever been able to. His electric razor was in a zippered pocket, and he took that and his toothbrush kit into the bathroom with him.

After a shave and a brush he hopped into and out of a tepid shower, using soap in his hair because he hadn't bothered to look for shampoo. Five minutes later he was dressed in some khakis and a light blue denim shirt. After a brief indecision he left two buttons open at the neck rather than one, and was then out the door and headed for the Orange Arm.

When he reached the center of the compound—the Octopus as Race had called it—he found two men sitting at the center table. Both were at least thirty years his senior. The one on the left wore round Santa Claus glasses on an equally round face. He had a balding head and a gray goatee, and his large green sweater was tight on his rotund body. The other man was his comic opposite; long and gaunt, cheeks sunken rather than cherubic, scowl lines instead of smile lines. He looked uncomfortable in his jeans, whereas his companion looked at home in his.

Andy recalled Bert and Ernie from *Sesame Street*.

They were in an intense conversation when Andy entered, and his arrival didn't warrant an interruption.

"As usual," the chubby one said in a voice deep and full, "you're narrowing your concept of Christian hell to church teachings, with Dante, Milton, and Blake thrown in for good measure. But the concept of an underworld goes back to Mesopotamia almost four thousand years ago, which predates both Christianity and Judaism."

The thin man sighed as if the world rested on his shoulders. "I'm aware of Mesopotamia, as I am of Egyptian, Zarathustrian, Grecian, and Roman beliefs in hell." He had a thin, reedy voice that matched his appearance. "I'm also aware of the complexities of explaining the presence of evil in a divinely created universe. But it seems to make more sense to have an embodiment of evil in the form of Satan than a dualistic God who is both forgiving and wrathful."

"Fa!" the fat one said, raising up his hands and rolling his eyes. "Enough with Yahweh's dark shadow. From the second century BC, my people have believed in a distinct malevolent deity, in this case Mastema, who was created by ha-Shem to do His dirty work, namely, punishing sin. It can be read that Mastema, not Adonai, was the one behind the trials of Job. The same Mastema who tempted the prophets Moses and Jesus."

The thin one winced. "I hate it when you call Jesus a prophet."

"You must be the holies," Andy said. It was the first opportunity he'd had to get a word in.

"What makes more sense?" The fat man turned to Andy. Andy guessed correctly that he was Rabbi Shotzen. "The devil as a fallen angel, or the devil as a purposeful creation of God to be an alternative to His light?"

"I'm an atheist," Andy said.

There was a moment of silence.

"How can you refuse your own eyes?" asked Father Thrist. "You saw Bub, correct?"

"Yeah."

"Well, he's unmitigated proof that God must exist. For there to be devils, there must be hell, and if there's hell, there's a heaven and a God."

Andy decided he didn't want to get drawn into this conversation.

"I saw a thing that looked like what we call a devil. I can't draw any more conclusions than that."

"Another Thomas," Thrist said to Shotzen. "Here we have, in captivity, one of Satan's minions, and everyone who sees him doubts. Why not set him free? The world wouldn't tremble with fear, as predicted. Bub would probably go on the talk show circuit and then become a sponsor for soft drinks."

The agitated priest turned to Andy again and pointed a finger, a gesture he seemed comfortable making. "Satan's greatest feat is to convince us he doesn't exist. He doesn't want us to believe in him, and that makes it easier for him to spread his evil. Lucifer is the Master of Lies."

"I disagree, Father," Shotzen cut in. "God wants us to know the devil exists. It's his infernal existence that steers us toward the path of truth and light."

Andy headed for the Orange door, content to leave the philosophical demands of the situation in other hands. The discussion continued without him; in fact, Andy guessed they hadn't even noticed he'd left.

The Orange Arm looked newer than the rest of the facility, with brighter paint and shinier tile, but the smell was barnyard fresh. Andy wrinkled his nose.

Dr. Jones was waiting for him in front of Orange 12, holding a clipboard that commanded her attention. She didn't look up at Andy as he approached.

"I'm ready for lunch," Andy said. He tried on a small grin.

She walked into Orange 12 without replying. Andy followed. The room was large, almost the size of Bub's habitat. Several empty pens were off to the right, and to the left side was a fenced area where almost two dozen sheep milled about. For all his travels, Andy had never seen a sheep before, and was surprised at how big they were. They were waist high and fat, like a bunch of gray marshmallows on toothpick legs.

"Is that actual grass they're on?" Andy asked.

"Astroturf. My idea of turning this part of the complex into a biosphere was rejected as too complicated. The turf wears well and is easy to clean."

"It looks like they're eating parts of it."

"Yeah, I told them that would happen. Come on."

Dr. Jones went to a set of lockers near the pens and removed a leather harness that resembled the reins for a horse. The reins were handed to Andy, and the doctor reached back into the locker and took out a half-dozen boxes of Cap'n Crunch cereal. She walked up to the fence and rang a large cowbell hanging from a pole. All of the animals turned to look.

"They eat hay, but they love breakfast cereal. To get

them to approach I have to bribe them. The problem is they're skittish. Every time they come to get the treat, one of them is taken away."

Dr. Jones began opening boxes and pouring them into the trough inside the fence. The sheep watched for a minute before the first of them approached. He stuck his face in the crunchy treat and began snacking. Dr. Jones patted him on the head.

"You want the harness?" Andy asked.

"No, this is Wooly. He's the Judas sheep. He always comes first, and then the others follow. If we snagged him, they'd all be too afraid to come the next time."

Wooly grunted his agreement, sucking up the cereal like a vacuum. Soon he was joined by two others, muscling their way in. Dr. Jones grabbed one of them by the scruff of the neck, gathering up wool in her fist. It appeared rough, but the animal didn't seem to notice and continued its binge.

When the cereal was gone, Dr. Jones deftly slipped the harness over the sheep's head, tightening the straps with her free hand. She held the reins in her armpit and opened the last box of cereal, luring her captured animal over to the gate. Several of the other sheep followed, and Wooly snorted his disapproval at being left out.

"Shoo the others away while I open the gate," Dr. Jones told Andy.

Andy, feeling quite the dork, flapped his hands around and made hissing noises. The sheep just stared at him, and out of the corner of his eye he thought he saw the stoic Dr. Jones smirk.

"Go on, sheep! Go! Move it! Go on!"

The herd slowly backed off, and Dr. Jones opened the gate and led her captive to one of the pens. Once it was safely locked in she went to fetch her clipboard.

Andy gave the sheep a pat on the head and stared into its alien eyes with their elongated pupils. Bub's eyes. He shuddered, realizing he didn't want to see the demon again so soon.

With a tape measure Dr. Jones checked the sheep's length and its height at the shoulder. She noted the measurements and then pressed some buttons on a digital display next to the pen. It registered the sheep's weight. She jotted this down as well.

"So, do people call you Sunny?"

"Not if they want me to reply."

*Ouch*, Andy thought. *How can someone so cute be so cold?*

"I thought all vets were supposed to be cheerful. Something to do with their love of animals."

She gave him a blank stare and then began to examine the sheep's teeth.

"What do you go by, then?"

"Sun. People call me Sun."

"Sun. It's unique."

"My mother was Vietnamese. She fell in love with an American soldier, who brought her to this country before Saigon fell. Sunshine was one of the first English words she learned. She didn't know any better."

"Oh, I think she did. It matches your cheerful disposition."

Sun was now looking into the sheep's eyes, holding their lids open. The sheep protested the inspection by twisting away.

"Wait a second," Andy said, snapping his fingers. "You're Vietnamese."

"Don't say it," Sun warned.

But Andy, a grin stretched across his face, couldn't resist. "You're a Vietnam vet."

Sun's face became even harder, something Andy hadn't thought possible.

"Never heard that one before. Open the pen there."

Andy lifted the latch on the gate and Sun led the sheep out of the pen and over to the entrance door.

"I've visited Vietnam twice," Andy said. "Beautiful place. All of those war movies make it look like hell, but it's actually very tranquil, don't you think?"

"I wouldn't know. I've never been there. I'm an American." Andy decided to shut up.

They led the sheep through the hallway and into the Octopus, where the rabbi and the priest were still arguing.

"Here comes another one, wretched thing." Rabbi Shotzen pointed to the sheep with his chin.

Father Thrist frowned. "I don't understand why you can't kill the sheep humanely first." He crossed his arms, obviously uncomfortable.

"Bub only takes 'em live, guys," Sun answered. "You know that."

The rabbi said, "What about some kind of painkiller? Morphine, perhaps?"

"We don't know how that would affect Bub's unique anatomy."

"How about a cigarette at least? A last meal?"

"He had Cap'n Crunch," Andy offered.

"You gentlemen are more than welcome to perform the last rites, if you wish," Sun said.

Again, Andy caught the faintest hint of a smirk.

"Sacrilege," the rabbi said. But he approached the sheep and held its head, speaking a few words of Hebrew.

"Perhaps Bub can be trained in the ways of shohet," Andy said. "Then he can eat according to shehita."

If Shotzen was impressed by Andy's knowledge of his people's tongue, he didn't show it. Instead the chubby holy man shook his head in disagreement.

"Bub won't eat kosher meat. He's trefah, a blood drinker."

The rabbi went back to his seat. Sun walked the sheep to the Red door.

Father Thrist refused to look.

"Rabbi Shotzen says that prayer every time we feed Bub a sheep," Sun told Andy when they entered the Red Arm.

"It wasn't a prayer. The rabbi simply apologized to the sheep, because it wasn't going to be killed by a proper butcher, according to the Jewish laws of slaughtering animals humanely."

Sun punched in the code for the first gate, and Andy made sure he noted the five-digit number. The titanium bars swung open, but the sheep didn't want to budge.

"She smells him," Sun said. She took a black swatch of cloth from her coat pocket and slipped it over the animal's eyes. "They're calmer when they can't see."

With some firm tugging and a sniff of cereal, the sheep moved forward.

"You're a vet, you're supposed to take care of animals. Doesn't this bother you, marching one off to death?"

Sun sighed. "Have you ever eaten a hamburger?"

"Sure, but . . ."

"Bub's a carnivore, like a lion, like a shark, like you and me. As much as everyone around here is shocked by Bub's eating habits, if they ever visited a slaughterhouse they'd be a thousand times more repulsed."

"But you're a vet."

"I'm a vet who eats hamburgers. I also spent six months in Africa studying lions."

Andy said *hello* in four African tribal languages.

She wasn't impressed.

They came to the second door, and Andy punched in the numbers on the panel. Nothing happened.

"Two different codes," Sun said. "You can't have a secret government compound without security overkill."

The sheep tried to bolt at the sound of the heavy door clanging open, but Sun had a tight grip on the reins.

Andy stopped at Red 14 and grasped the door handle but he didn't turn it right away. The moment stretched.

"You don't have to go in," Sun said. "I just needed you to help in Orange 12."

She was giving him a graceful way out, but he knew her opinion of him would drop even further if he took it.

Andy turned the knob and entered.

The smell hit him again, heady and musky, almost making Andy gag. This time the room wasn't empty. Standing among the medical equipment was a man in a lab coat. He was tall and intense-looking, with a thin line for a mouth and wide expressive eyes. His hair was light gray, short and curly. Andy put him at about forty, but he could have gone eight years either way.

"Oh good, feeding time," the man said.

"Dr. Frank Belgium, this is Andy Dennison," Sun said. "He's the translator."

"Good good good, we're in need of one. Attack the mystery from all angles, the more the better. Yes yes yes."

"Frank's a molecular biologist." Sun said it as if that were explanation for Dr. Belgium's weird speech patterns and birdlike movements. "How's the sequencing going, Frank?"

"Slow slow slow. Our boy—yes, he is a boy, even though there isn't any evidence of external genitalia— his bladder empties through the anus, like a bird. He has eighty-eight pairs of chromosomes. We're looking at over a hundred thousand different genes, about quadruple what humans have. Billions of codons. Even the Cray is having a hard time isolating sequences. Nothing yet, but a link will show up, I'm sure it will."

"All life on earth, from flatworms to elephants, share some DNA sequences," Sun explained. "Dr. Belgium believes Bub also shares several of these chains."

Dr. Belgium nodded several times. "Bub's got the same four bases as all life, the same twenty amino acids. Even taking into account his . . . *different* anatomical layout, I believe he's terrestrial, that is, he has earthly relatives somewhere. We're trying matches with goats, rams, bats, gorillas, humans, crocodiles, pigs, everything that he looks like he may be a part of, to fit him into the animal kingdom . . . but now it's feeding time, so let's see if we can witness another miracle, shall we?"

Sun led the sheep past Andy and over to Bub's habitat. Andy, who'd been avoiding looking in that direction, forced himself to watch.

At first, Bub wasn't visible. The dwelling was filled with a running stream and trees and bushes and grass, as deep as a basketball court and about thirty feet high. The foliage was so dense in parts that even a creature Bub's size could apparently hide in it.

"All fake," Dr. Belgium said. "Fake brush, fake rocks, fake stream. It's supposed to resemble the area where he was found, in Panama. I don't think he's fooled."

"Where is he?" Andy asked, cautiously approaching the Plexiglas shield. He squinted at the trees, trying to make out anything red.

Bub dropped from directly above, the ground shaking as he landed just three feet in front of Andy.

Andy yelled and jumped backward, falling onto his ass.

Sun laughed. "Did you forget he could fly?"

Andy didn't notice Sun's amusement. Bub was crouching before him, his black wings billowing out behind him like a rubber parachute.

Andy's mouth went dry. The demon was the most amazing and horrifying thing he'd ever seen.

Hoofs big as washtubs.

Massively muscled black legs, with knees that bent backward like the hindquarters of a goat.

Claws the size of manhole covers, ending in talons that looked capable of disemboweling an elephant.

Bub approached the Plexiglas and cocked his head to the side, as if contemplating the new arrival. It was a bear's head, with black ram horns, and rows of jagged triangular teeth.

Shark's teeth.

His snout was flat and piggish, and he snorted, fogging up the glass. His elliptical eyes—black, bifurcated pupils set into corneas the color of bloody urine—locked on Andy with an intensity that only intelligent beings could manage.

He was so close, Andy could count the coarse red hairs on the demon's broad chest. The animal smell swirled up the linguist's nostrils, mixed with odors of offal and fecal matter.

Bub raised a claw and placed it on the Plexiglas.

"*Hach wi' hew*," Bub said.

Andy yelled again, crab-walking backward and bumping into the sheep.

The sheep bleated in alarm.

Bub, as if commanded, backed away from the window. His giant, rubbery wings folded over once, twice, and then tucked neatly away behind his massive back. He walked over to a large tree and squatted there, waiting.

Sun led the sheep past the Plexiglas and to a doorway on the other side of the room. They entered, and a minute later a small hatch opened inside the habitat, off to Bub's left.

Andy mentally screamed at Sun, *Don't open that door!* even though the opening was far too narrow for Bub to fit through.

Bub watched as the sheep walked into his domain. The door closed behind it.

The sheep shook off its blindfold and looked around its new environment.

Upon seeing Bub it let forth a very human-sounding scream.

In an instant, less than an instant, Bub had sprung from his spot by the tree and sailed through the air almost twenty feet, his wings fully outstretched. He snatched up the sheep in his claws, an obscene imitation of a bat grabbing a moth.

Andy turned away, expecting to hear chomping and bleating. When none came, he ventured another look.

Bub was back by the tree, sitting on his haunches. The sheep was cradled in his enormous hands, as a child might hold a gerbil. But the sheep was unharmed. In fact, Bub was stroking it along its back, and making soft sounds.

*Sheep sounds.*

"He's talking to the sheep," Dr. Belgium said. "He's going to do it. Here comes the miracle."

Andy watched as the sheep ceased in its struggle. Bub continued to pet the animal, his hideous face taking on a solemn cast. There was silence in the room. Andy realized he'd been holding his breath.

The movement was sudden. One moment Bub was rubbing the sheep's head, the next moment he twisted it backward like a jar top.

There was a sickening crunch, the sound of wet kindling snapping. The sheep's head lolled off to the side at a crazy angle, rubbery and twitching.

Andy felt an adrenaline surge and had to fight not to run away.

"Now here it comes," Dr. Belgium said, his voice a whisper.

Bub held the sheep close to his chest and closed his elliptical eyes. A minute of absolute stillness passed.

Then one of the sheep's legs jerked.

"What is that?" Andy asked. "A reflex?"

"No," Sun answered. "It's not a reflex."

The leg jerked again. And again. Bub set down the sheep, which shook itself and then got to its feet.

"Jesus," Andy gasped.

The sheep took two steps and blinked. What made the whole resurrection even more unsettling was the fact that the sheep's head hung limply between its front legs, turned completely around so it looked at them upside down.

Andy's fear changed to awe. "But it's dead. Isn't it dead?"

"We're not sure," Sun said. "The lungs weren't moving a minute ago, but now they are."

"But he broke its neck. Even if it was alive, could it move with a broken neck?"

The sheep attempted to nibble at some grass with his head backward.

"I guess it can," Sun said.

"Amazing," Dr. Belgium said. "Amazing amazing amazing."

"Shouldn't you get the sheep?" Andy asked. "Run some tests?"

"Go right ahead," Sun said. "The door's over there."

"Probably not a good idea to go in there before Bub's eaten," Dr. Belgium said.

Andy said, "Can't you tranquilize him or something? Race said he went into the habitat before."

"Twice, against my insistence, but only to get some stool samples and to fix a clog in the artificial stream. Both times Bub ignored him. Even Race isn't insane enough to go in there and take his food away. And I'm not going to tranquilize Bub until we know more about his physiology. We don't know what tranquilizers would do to him."

Bub barked a sound, similar to a cough. The sheep trotted around in a circle, head swinging from side to side, trying to bleat with a broken neck.

Bub coughed again.

Or was it a laugh?

The sheep swung its head around at Bub and screamed. Bub reached out and grabbed the sheep. The grab was rough, all pretense of tenderness gone. Holding a hind leg in each claw, he ripped the sheep in half and began to feast on the innards.

Andy's stomach climbed up his throat and threatened to jump out. He put a hand over his mouth and turned away, the munching and gobbling sounds filling the large room.

"From amazing to horrible," Dr. Belgium said, returning to his computer station.

"He eats everything," Sun said, putting the reins in her coat pocket. "The skull, bones, hide, even intestines. Doesn't waste a crumb. The perfect carnivore."

Andy threw up, seeing the banana muffins for the second time that day. He apologized and fled the room, his brain scrambling to remember the code number for the gate. He managed, but got stuck when he reached the second one.

This was insane. This whole project was insane. Andy felt no curiosity at all—only terror, revulsion, and anger at being suckered into this mess. He gave the bars a shake and a swift kick, swearing in several different languages.

Sun came up behind him and punched in the correct code.

"Thanks," Andy mumbled.

He took off down the hall, barely noticing the deep frown of concern on Sun's face.

# CHAPTER 3

**D**r. Sun Jones wasn't pleased with herself. She had to stop alienating every man who showed the slightest bit of interest in her. It wasn't healthy.

But then she hadn't felt healthy in quite some time.

Physically, Sun knew she had more strength and stamina than anyone else in the compound. Even in Africa she'd adhered to her daily exercise regimen of sit-ups and push-ups, receiving more than a few quizzical stares from the indigenous wildlife. Physically, she was a well-tuned machine.

Emotionally, it was a different story.

Sun walked down the arm to Red 3 and let herself in. The lights were already on, bright and harsh and making the large space seem more like an operating theater than a records repository.

Filling the room were dozens of file cabinets, ranging in style from antique oak to modern stainless steel, arranged rank and file like library aisles. Off in the corner was a small desk, piled high with the papers she'd been recently reviewing.

Sun sat in a chair twice her age and tried to focus on the massive amount of work ahead of her. She'd discovered the records room on her second day here, and had been spending all of her free time trying to organize the astounding amount of data it contained.

Everything about the project was filed here, from the 1907 payroll ledger of the Spanish team who dug the compound (and was then deported back to Spain), up to the arrival of last month's food shipment. Invoices, reports, inventories, letters, dossiers, presidential mandates, and even recipes for chicken cacciatore were all haphazardly mixed together with little thought to common sense.

At one time there may have been some order to the room. Helen Murdoch, Race's ill wife, had put an end to that. Sun didn't know the details, but Dr. Belgium had mentioned that years ago Helen had "*torn Red 3 apart*," and cleanup had consisted of simply shoving things back into cabinets.

Sun had wanted to ask Helen about that, and even went so far as to visit her in her room, but the woman was too far gone to remember anything.

*Sad.*

The obvious answer—hire a team to organize everything into a database—had been thought of but deemed unrealistic. Manpower was the only thing the project lacked. The more people involved, the more likely there would be a security leak, so employment at Samhain was kept bare bones.

Sun had taken it upon herself to make the task hers. She'd been hired to study Bub in his habitat, based on her experience with large predators. It turned out to be amazingly dull, even though Bub was an extraordinary specimen. Watching a pride of roaming lions was a learning experience. Watching a lion at the zoo was sleep-inducing. Bub simply sat around, as if waiting for something. The only time he became lively was at his feedings, and even that had little variation. The records room gave her an opportunity to be useful.

Sun had no office experience to speak of, but she had good organization skills, and after only one week her effort was paying off. She'd been chronologically sorting the mountains of paperwork into two main sections, SAMHAIN and BUB. Each of these main topics had a dozen subsections, which would undoubtedly be broken down even further.

The work was slow going, made even more so by Sun's inquisitive nature; all too often she would find something particularly fascinating and drift off task. Like the Rosenberg file.

It traced the hiring of an independent engineering firm called G & R to improve upon the compound's emergency generator in 1951. The hirees, one Julius Rosenberg and one David Greenglass, snooped where they shouldn't have and actually tried to blackmail President Truman.

Truman didn't go for it, and the two, along with Rosenberg's wife, Ethel, were executed for treason on less-than-authentic charges.

No one had blabbed since.

Sun thought Race was simply trying to scare her with that story when she'd first arrived. Now she had no illusions that her oath of secrecy was as serious as they come. Strangely, it didn't matter to her one bit.

Sun had no one to tell.

While the political history was interesting, Sun was

even more intrigued by the thousands of tests done on Bub since his arrival a hundred years ago.

Forty-some people had worked at Samhain, encompassing over a dozen professions, from botanist to phrenologist. More often than not, those who were chosen stayed for the rest of their lives. Samhain had been both their home and their life's work, and as far as she knew Sun was the only person who had ever seen it. It was both inspiring and depressing.

The files Sun had been recently reviewing were from the 1970s, most of them concerning a series of experiments done by two men named Meyer and Storky. The duo performed a staggering number of tests on Bub, up until Meyer's death from Kaposi's sarcoma in 1979. So dedicated were they to research that Meyer had a linear accelerator sent to Samhain when he was diagnosed, and took his radiation treatments on-site so they could continue their experiments without interruption.

Some of their finds were extraordinary.

Bub was impervious, it seemed, to extreme cold. They'd placed several refrigeration units in Red 13, the room Bub was kept in while he was comatose, and gradually lowered the temperature to four below zero degrees Celsius. Bub's internal body temperature didn't drop a single degree, and his heart rate and breathing remained consistent.

The two then moved in some heaters and cranked it up to over two hundred degrees. An egg fried on the table next to Bub, but he didn't fry. The demon's skin got hot, but his internal temperature didn't fluctuate more than a degree.

Meyer and Storky also discovered that Bub could

breathe just about anything. It had been known since the '40s that Bub's complex respiratory system, which included four lungs, two diaphragms, and two organs that resembled air bladders, processed nitrogen and oxygen and excreted a combination of methane and nitrous oxide. Through experimentation they showed that Bub could process pure nitrogen, or pure oxygen, or carbon dioxide, helium, hydrogen, propane, and even chlorine gas, and was able to break it down to nourish his cells.

They stopped short at nerve gas, even though President Nixon gave them the okay.

Sun read all of this with great interest, but the interest was slowly giving way to something else.

Paranoia.

Bub was resistant to all disease, fungal, viral, and bacterial. His body attacked any invader, whether it be bubonic plague, herpes zoster, ringworm, or even Dutch elm disease, surrounded it with what were assumed to be antibodies, and expelled the intruder from his anus in a crystalline pellet. Meyer even went so far as to inject him with enough anthrax to wipe out a large city. Bub excreted it within twenty minutes.

He wasn't invulnerable to physical harm, but damn near close. Ever since the first doctor drew some of Bub's blood and watched in amazement as the needle mark repaired itself moments later, it had been known that the demon possessed rapidly accelerated healing ability. Meyer and Storky must have been amazed by this, because they spent no less than three years conducting experiments on the anomaly. They poked, gouged, sliced, burned, scraped, and subjected every part of Bub to chemical attack.

Bub could repair all harm, even plugs taken from flesh and bone, within seconds. It happened so fast that they brought in a 35 mm film camera to shoot the miracle in slow motion.

Meyer theorized that Bub's endocrine system was extremely advanced. The endocrine system in humans was capable of instantaneous reaction, such as a burst of adrenaline in a dangerous situation. Bub's had developed to the point where it had taken over the healing functions, knitting wounds instantly. Nixon had given the go-ahead to fully amputate one of Bub's limbs, but Meyer and Storky only went as far as a fingertip.

It grew back, longer and sharper than before.

Sun thought of Hercules and the Hydra. Every time Hercules cut off a head, the Hydra grew two more.

Meyer and Storky also tried to accurately gauge Bub's age. They took a sample of Bub's horn and tried to carbon-date it. All living things take in carbon-14, which is created in the earth's atmosphere when the sun's rays strike nitrogen gas. It combines with oxygen to form $CO_2$. As long as the organism is alive, it has a constant new supply of C-14. But in dead tissue, the C-14 begins to decay into nitrogen-14, with a half-life of about 5,730 years. Since Bub's horn—made of keratinlike hair and feathers—was dead tissue, it seemed ideal for the task.

Something wasn't right, apparently, because the amount of N-14 found in the sample would have put Bub's age at over 200,000 years. Obviously impossible. Meyer hypothesized that since Bub breathed and was able to process nitrogen, that somehow accounted for the high N-14 count. Sun, who never excelled at chemistry, found that explanation suspicious, but easier to believe than the idea that Bub was older than mankind itself.

Along with a record of Bub's medical history, Sun was also sorting through the hundreds and thousands of pictures taken since the project's beginning. Everything and everyone involved in Samhain over the last century had been photographed, filmed, recorded, and videotaped, and more than half of the file cabinets in Red 3 were filled to the brim with visual media.

Somewhere, buried in all of this mess, was the answer she was looking for.

Sun didn't share Dr. Belgium's belief that Bub was some strange, prehistoric missing link. She also didn't share the view of the holies, who believed Bub was a true demon, a spawn of hell.

Sun had a different theory, one she wasn't willing to share yet. Not without proof. Given that the average tenure here was twenty-two years, Sun figured she'd find it eventually. In twenty-two years a person could find anything.

Maybe even peace.

She finished sorting the files in front of her and then moved on to the next cabinet. It was crammed full of serum and tissue analyses. Sun picked up a thick folder containing an in-depth report on the physical properties of Bub's early stool samples. It didn't surprise her to find out that they contained ample amounts of radioactivity.

The demon was so damn tough, even his droppings were nuclear.

She gave the file a cursory flip-through and dropped it in the BUB pile.

"Attention, this is Race."

Sun reflexively looked up at the intercom speaker near the door.

"We have a new arrival, Andrew Dennison, and I think it would be a good time to have a group powwow to get him up to speed on the project. The mess hall, in five. Refreshments will be served." Race chuckled and cut out.

Sun placed her hands on her lower back and stretched, the vertebrae crackling like a bag of chips. She left the lights on in Red 3 and headed for the Octopus. Her thoughts drifted to Andy Dennison, not for the first time.

Sun thought he was cute, in a nonthreatening teddy bear kind of way. He was trying hard to be amusing. The complete opposite of Steven, who was so self-assured and serious. She compared all men to Steven, and they all came up lacking. That was one of the reasons she'd been celibate since his death.

Everyone else seemed like a step down.

So what was it about this new guy that intrigued her? Must be hormonal, she decided. She had been completely alone in Africa. Andy was the first man her age she'd had a conversation with in close to a year.

Maybe she should let down her guard a notch, stop acting so hard-nosed. Would it kill her to be personable? He obviously found her attractive. She should be flattered rather than irritated.

But then, she should be a lot of things.

Sun walked through the Octopus and went down the

Green Arm. Before entering the mess hall she absently reached for her purse to check her hair in her makeup compact. The gesture annoyed her; she hadn't carried a purse or a compact in a long time.

She settled for finger-combing her bangs back, and went into the cafeteria. The holies were already there, locked in their usual intense debate. Dr. Belgium was measuring coffee to put into the automatic maker, his actions as meticulous and precise as they were in the lab. Andy was leaning against the water cooler, hands in his pockets. Sun caught his eye and tried to look sympathetic. He gave her a shy smile back and walked over to her.

"Sorry about . . ."

"No need," Sun interrupted. "We've all been there."

"I haven't thrown up since doing keg stands in college."

"Where did you go to school?"

"Oh. Harvard."

He said it as if it embarrassed him. Sun had met plenty of Harvard men, and they usually wore it like a badge of honor. *Interesting.*

"How about you?" Andy asked.

"Johns . . . uh, Iowa State."

"Were you going to say Johns Hopkins? I didn't know they offered veterinary medicine."

Sun thought fast. "I lived in Maryland, took some undergrad classes there. Transferred to Iowa."

If he'd caught her lie she couldn't tell.

"Is that what you always wanted to be? A vet?"

"Yeah." Another lie. "Did you always want to be a linguist?"

"I never really thought about it. It's something I've always been good at."

"Do you like it?"

"I don't know. I guess I do, or why would I do it, right? Do you like being a vet?"

"Yes," Sun said, happy to say something honest. "I don't beat myself up if my patients die."

Andy smiled. He had a pleasant smile, she thought. She smiled back, surprised at how good it felt.

"I'm still not sure if I want to stay," Andy said. "This isn't a normal translating job for me. I don't know if I can do it."

"It's okay to be afraid."

"I'd bet you've never been afraid of anything in your entire life."

"Not true. When I was seven, a bat got in my bedroom. Harmless, couldn't have been bigger than a tennis ball. But the way it flew; in a figure eight, unbelievably fast, inches from my face on every pass—it terrified me. Then it landed on my head, got tangled up in my hair. I was so scared I couldn't move. Took about five minutes to get up the guts to scream. Seemed like an eternity."

"What happened?"

"Dad came in, caught it with a blanket, let it outside. He said it must have come in through the window. I didn't open my window again until I was eighteen."

They shared a small laugh, which felt even better than the smile.

"Well, now you're taking care of the biggest bat in the history of the world," Andy said.

"Gotta face your fears sometime. Besides, I think Bub's a wee bit too big to get tangled in my hair."

"You don't find him terrifying?"

"At first I did. Now I'm more intrigued than scared. Aren't you just a little bit curious about him?"

Andy rubbed his upper lip. "It's hard to be curious when breakfast is coming out of your nose."

"Just think about it for a second. Every person on earth, no matter what country or culture, has some kind of idea of the devil. But no one has ever seen him before. Don't you want to know more about him?"

"You think he's really Satan?"

"Actually, I find that pretty hard to believe."

"So what is he? An alien or something?" Andy asked.

"That's hard to believe too. But of the two, I'd buy the alien theory more than the biblical one. His physiology is just too strange."

"An alien, huh? So is he the kind that flies around with Elliott, or the kind that eats Sigourney Weaver?"

"I don't know yet. He seems friendly."

"Maybe that's because he's locked up. I wonder how friendly he'd be on the *other side* of the Plexiglas."

Race entered the mess hall with Dr. Harker. They were in midconversation and Sun caught the end of it.

". . . for what you've done with her. I still can't accept why you're here, but—"

"No thanks needed, General." A frowning Harker cut him off. "It's my job."

*Just visited Helen*, Sun guessed. Both looked grim. Harker retained the look; she probably scowled in her sleep as well.

Race, with the poise of any good leader, quickly hid

his feelings with a good-ole-boy smile. "Good, we're all here. Before we get started with the intros I'd like to announce that the Jacuzzi should be operational again by tomorrow. The same rules apply as with the pool, swimming suits are mandatory. You got that, Frank? We have ladies present."

Dr. Belgium gave Race a nod without turning his attention from the brewing coffee.

"Good. Now, I think all of you have met Andy Dennison by now, except for Julie. So let's start with you."

Harker had a long, hound-doggish face and a droning voice which left no doubt that she didn't kindly suffer fools. Sun learned after only a few meetings with her that Harker considered everyone a fool.

"I'm Dr. Julie Harker. I came on in 1980 to oversee the medical well-being of the Samhain team, including the dispensing of medication and monthly physicals. I've also been monitoring Bub's vitals since my arrival, and have been attending to the treatment of General Race's wife, Helen."

It didn't surprise Sun that it was the exact same speech she'd given to her a week prior, right down to the nasally inflection.

"Thank you, Julie," Race said, and Dr. Harker took a seat and removed a nail clipper from the chest pocket of her lab coat. She began to snip away at a hangnail. "How about you, Frank?"

"Hmm? Oh sure."

Dr. Frank Belgium touched the fresh cup of coffee to his lips and took a large slurp.

"Frank Belgium, molecular biologist. I'm the gene guy. I've been mapping Bub's genes. Hard, very hard.

As you may know, or, well, maybe you don't, it took ten years for the human genome to get sequenced, and we've only got twenty-three pairs of chromosomes, and less than twenty-five thousand genes. We've isolated forty-four pairs of chromosomes in Bub. Hard work. Hard hard hard." Belgium took another loud slurp of coffee.

"But he's from Earth. I'm sure. Bub has the same twenty amino acids as all life on this planet. Why is this important? Well there are about eighty different types of amino acids, and all can create proteins, but nothing on Earth uses those extra sixty. All life—plant, animal, bacteria—uses different combinations of those same twenty, and the reason is because we all evolved from one common ancestor. That's why all living organisms share genes. Everyone in this room, on this planet, shares ninety-nine-point-nine percent of the same DNA. We share ninety-eight-point-four with chimpanzees, ninety-eight-point-three with gorillas, all the way on down to blue-green algae."

Sun glanced at Andy. He was being drawn in by Frank's words, the same way Sun had been upon first hearing them.

"Now," Belgium continued, "if life started several times, rather than just once, we'd probably find different amino acids in different things on earth. But we don't, we all have the same genetic code, and Bub shares it as well.

"What I'm doing, is mapping sequences in Bub's genome to find out what on Earth he shares the most genes with. Very hit-or-miss when we're not sure where to look. It's kind of like searching for a single sentence in a single book in the Library of Congress."

Frank shrugged and drank more coffee.

"What do you believe Bub is, Doctor?" Race asked, glancing at Andy while he spoke.

"I think, well, I guess I think he's a little bit of everything. A mutation. Maybe he's a member of a prehistoric race that became extinct . . . since he's intelligent it would reason that we've never found fossils of his kind, perhaps they cremated their dead or buried them at sea. Or maybe he's a genetic experiment. Maybe our own government created him."

"In 1906?" snorted Harker.

"Dr. Harker, what proof do we have that he's actually been here since 1906? Were you here when he arrived? How do we know that we're not caught up in some crazy conspiracy to help test the latest in biological weapon technology?"

"At least that would stir things up a bit around here." Race gave a wide Southern grin.

"How about an extraterrestrial?" Andy asked. "Isn't there any possibility Bub is from another planet?"

Frank shook his head.

"Even if we discounted the problems associated with space travel from another galaxy, it would be a zillion to one, a gazillion to one, that life formed on another planet with the exact same genetic makeup as life on Earth. It would be easier for the same lottery number to come up every single night for a hundred years . . ."

"Unless it was intentional." Father Thrist cleared his throat and crossed his arms. "Unless God created Bub the same way He created man and all life on Earth.

That would explain Bub's genetic code without the need for evolution, molecular engineering, or space travel."

Frank raised an eyebrow. "I thought demons and angels had no physical presence. They're ethereal, only existing in heaven and hell."

Thrist laughed. It was the first time Sun had seen mirth from the terminally serious priest.

"All of my life, people have questioned my beliefs because there has been no physical evidence to substantiate them. Now here we have something that is clearly a demon, or even Satan himself. Something we can see and touch. And everyone is looking for a new answer, rather than the answer that Christianity has had for two thousand years."

"Judaism has had it for over three thousand," Rabbi Shotzen said, wagging a finger.

Thrist gave him a sideways glance. "All around is proof of God's creation. Me, you, trees, birds, the Earth, the universe—but since the beginning of this century mankind has worshipped the god of science, rather than our Lord Jesus Christ. Now here is something science cannot explain, yet you refuse to believe. Andrew"— Thrist gave the linguist his full attention—"what was your reaction when you first saw Bub?"

"Fear," Andy answered.

"But what did Bub represent to you? When you saw him?"

"A devil."

Thrist nodded. "Everyone who sees Bub recognizes a devil. They are concerning themselves with the how and the why, but the *what* has been answered. Bub is a devil. Where do devils come from, Andrew?"

"This one came from Panama."

Sun and the others laughed. Rabbi Shotzen had to be nudged by Thrist because his laughter went on longer than the others'.

"But before he was found in Panama, where did Bub come from?"

"Devils usually come from hell," Andy said.

"Or heaven," Shotzen added. "Depending on your interpretation of his creation. Lucifer, the Morning Star, had tried to shine brighter than Adonai and was cast out of heaven for his pride."

"Or, according to Enoch," Thrist said, "devils are angels who chose to fornicate with humans. Wasn't that the explanation Rabbi Eliezer gave in the eighth century? Something about fornicating with the daughters of Cain?"

Shotzen dismissed him. "Remember, Enoch wrote pseudepigrapha and apocrypha—nothing the scribe did went into the Torah."

"But," Thrist countered, "if we were to base our conceptions solely on the Bible, which encompasses the Torah, we'd have very little to go on."

"Devils and angels were created by ha-Shem as separate entities," Shotzen insisted. "Had Adonai created angels that became devils, it would contradict His perfection. Instead, ha-Shem created devils to punish sin. It can be interpreted that all evil, in fact, is Satanic rather than divine. The Book of Jubilees agrees."

"Either way," Thrist said, "we have a being here that is obviously supernatural and obviously created by God.

Shouldn't we be focusing our efforts on attempting to figure out why He allowed us to find Bub and what He expects us to do with this knowledge? Is this the beginning of the apocalypse? The first sign of Armageddon? Or should we take this as a message that God indeed exists, and use it to spread His word? And why, after almost a hundred years at this facility, and who knows how many more years buried in the ground, did Bub finally wake up?"

"That's why Andy is here," Race said. "To ask him. Right Andy?"

Sun glanced at Andy, who squirmed under the spotlight. She raised an eyebrow.

"Uh . . . are we sure he can't escape?" Andy asked.

Race grinned. "His enclosure is four-foot concrete with steel plates sandwiched in between each foot. The Plexiglas is bulletproof, shatterproof, fireproof, and has been tested up to sixteen thousand pounds per square inch. Even if he did escape the habitat, he's two hundred feet underground, and he'd have to go through those two titanium doors. Plus, there are safeguards."

"Such as?"

"In the '80s, the President decided that if Bub were to ever wake up, we'd need to have some control over him. Bub has two explosive charges surgically imbedded inside of him, one in the neck and one in the heart. Either one would render Bub out of commission, even with his rapid healing abilities. He's got enough boom in him to blow up a tank."

Andy's face scrunched up in thought. Sun watched

him. She wanted him to stay, she realized, and that surprised as much as scared her.

"I'll need some things: books, programs, access to the Internet. And that capsule that Bub was found in, are there pictures of the writing?"

"Son, we've got the whole damn capsule if you want to see it."

"I want to see it. It's as good a starting place as any. I also need the video recordings of Bub since he's been awake, anything that has him speaking. He's only said a few things to me so far."

"Could you understand him?" Race asked. The excitement was apparent in his voice.

"I'm not sure. But it sounded like an Indio language. I think he said *'How are things with you?'* and *'I am very hungry.'*"

"Doesn't sound hostile to me. Dr. Jones, would you mind taking Andy to Red 6 to see the capsule?"

Sun gave Race a look, knowing she was being used, and why. But it didn't bother her as much as she thought it should.

"I have some things to finish up in the records room, but I can free up some time."

"Great," Race said. He was one big smile, ready to shake hands with the world. "Now, who wants a microwave chili dog?"

Sun turned to Andy, who was staring at her with a lopsided grin on his face.

Part of her wanted to smile back, but she held that part in check.

"Need some help?" Andy asked. "In the records room?"

"You sure you want to help me again?"

Andy smiled. "After watching Bub eat, I think I could handle just about anything."

"How about chili dogs?"

The pain showed in his face. "I don't think I'm quite ready for chili dogs."

"Then, let's go."

As they left the mess hall, Sun noticed that Race winked at her. She restrained herself and didn't wink back.

# CHAPTER 4

Andy surprised Sun by being helpful in Red 3. For the first twenty minutes he was chatty and full of questions, but once he settled in with the actual organizing he proved himself a hard worker. They toiled for over two hours in companionable silence, Andy once going for Diet Cokes, and Sun once leaving for the bathroom (and to touch up her makeup, even though she didn't actually touch it up, just checked it).

While riffling through a large stack of invoices, Sun became absorbed in an inventory sheet listing some of the medical supplies and pharmaceuticals on-site.

It staggered her. Samhain was better stocked than a hospital pharmacy. Why the staff here would need seven gallons of morphine, or ten thousand tablets of aspirin, was beyond her scope of understanding. Total cost to the taxpayer: seven million dollars in drugs that would never be used. Not for the first time since her arrival, Sun felt underpaid.

"Look at this," Andy said. He handed her a piece of paper written in a language other than English.

"Spanish?" she asked.

"Italian. It's from Pope Pius the Tenth."

Sun briefly returned to the long, boring mornings of her youth, trapped in Sunday school memorizing prayers.

"Saint Pius," she corrected. "He was canonized in 1954."

"You're Catholic?"

"I was."

"When did you leave the church? Or is that too personal a question?"

"I don't think I really left the church. More like the church left me."

"How so?"

Sun hadn't ever talked about this with anyone. No one had ever asked.

"Five years ago . . . it was a bad time for me. I had a lot of problems. I met a man, Steven, he was a psychiatrist. I didn't meet him professionally—I met him in a bar, actually."

Sun turned away from Andy and busied herself moving papers around on the desk.

"He was a very sensitive man. Compassionate. We fell in love, got married. We wanted to start a family. I'm sure you know where this is going—woman gets a new shot at happiness, drunk driver kills her husband, woman loses faith in God. Cliché. Soon after that I lost my veterinary clinic."

Sun thought back to the creditors, one even calling her at Steven's wake. Steven had been kept alive for almost six months. Six months of wretched, useless hoping. Six months, at a cost of three thousand dollars a day. Insurance didn't even cover a third of the expense, and of course the asshole who ran headfirst into Steven was uninsured as well.

"So you blame God for taking him."

"What? No. At first, sure. It made no sense. When Steven died, I lost everything. But then it did make sense. I didn't blame God, because there was no God to blame. Shit just happens."

Sun finished fussing with the papers and turned back to Andy with a question of her own.

"You said to the holies that you were an atheist. Why?"

"It's kind of complicated. I never had any sort of organized religion in my life. God was something that other kids believed in."

"So you never learned about religion?"

"I had a friend, in grade school, his parents tried to take me to church once. I loved it."

"Why'd they only take you once?"

"Oh, I didn't love the Mass. I loved the language. The priest spoke in Latin, asking a question, I think it was something like *'Are you truly thankful?'* or something like that. Well, I thought he was asking us, so I answered."

"In Latin."

"Yeah. And it freaked him out. Everyone else too. So he asked me, in Latin, how I knew Latin. So I told him I knew about ten different languages. And he said that it's a miracle, that God has blessed me with the gift of tongues. I told him, in English, God didn't bless me, I studied my ass off!" Sun laughed.

"Needless to say, the family never took me with them

again. When I got into college, I read a lot of religious texts—for the language, not the content. But some of the content leaked through, obviously. And in every case, whether I was translating Hebrew, Latin, Greek, Arabic, Hindi, whatever, I found the same theme within the writing."

"Which was?"

"Scared men, looking for answers. I think that as a species, being self-aware means we have questions. Some of those questions are: What created the universe, where do we go when we die, and why do bad things happen? These questions don't have answers, but need to be answered. That's why men, all men, every people and tribe from Cro-Magnon on up, had to create gods. To answer these questions."

"So here we are, two atheists, trying to find the origin of a demon."

Andy grinned. "Almost seems as if God put us here, to show us the truth, doesn't it?"

Sun could tell Andy was joking, but she got a chill. That *was* what it seemed like. A second chance at faith.

"So what does Saint Pius say in the letter?"

"That the Vatican was sending over a bishop, and if President Roosevelt was wise he would not let Bub's existence be known because the panic could destroy the Western world. And that he was praying for everyone involved." Andy took the paper back and ran his finger over the Vatican seal.

"Funny, yesterday I was wondering how I was going to pay my electric bill, and now here I am holding a letter that is probably worth more than I make in a year. Sotheby's would kill for it."

"Sotheby's? You're thinking historical worth. Try the media. You could make a fortune, up until you were executed for treason."

Andy filed the paper away and Sun suggested they quit and go take a look at the capsule. She felt pretty good for someone who'd just recounted the biggest tragedy of her life. And for once, there was no guilt to accompany feeling good. Was there a statute of limitations on grieving?

Andy held the door for her and they took a short walk from Red 3 to Red 6. The room was small and brightly lit. It reminded Sun of an autopsy room. A small dehumidifier ran nonstop in the corner, humming quietly. In the center, sprawled out like a baby elephant corpse, was the capsule.

It was pale gray, so pale that it seemed to absorb the fluorescent light. Sun was again intrigued by the shape: it was a tube with rounded ends, almost like giant sausage, but the curves were perfect in their simplicity. It had been measured back in the '70s, and the scientist in charge found it was symmetrical to within ten-thousandths of an inch.

"It looks like a sarcophagus." Andy ran his hand over the carvings on top. "And it's so smooth! How can it feel so silky when it has all of these glyphs engraved into it? You can barely feel them. What's it made of?"

"A lot." Sun laughed. "Analysis came back with traces of everything: carbon, ferrite, silicon, lead, silver, iridium, petroleum, ivory . . ."

"Like elephant tusks?"

"Yeah. And here's the kicker. It's something like ten percent nylon."

"Nylon."

"Nylon was invented in 1938. So how did it get in something found in 1906, and buried for who knows how long before that?"

"Weird. So how does it open? I don't see any seams."

"Watch this." Sun ran her hand along the side of the capsule facing them. She found a small notch the size of a pinhead and pressed inward. The top came up on hinges, opening like the lid of a casket.

"Secret button. Found by accident around forty years ago, if you hear Race tell it. Before that they were using a crowbar to get it open. See the marks on the edge here?"

Andy didn't look when she pointed out the pry marks. He was totally absorbed in studying the inside of the capsule.

"This is odd," Andy said.

"No kidding."

"No, I mean, see these markings? Demotic Egyptian hieroglyphs. They were using these in 3000 BC. But on the cover, those are Maya glyphs. Used until about 1500 AD. Four and a half thousand years' difference."

"So it's old."

"Not just that. How the hell did it cross the Atlantic and get from Egypt to Central America?"

"Maybe the Spanish brought it. Conquistadors."

Andy nodded and ran his hands inside the capsule. "Different texture. Not smooth, but . . ."

"Soft," Sun said. "I found some old pictures. Bub fit

in here perfectly. I mean *perfectly*. Like it was made from a cast of his body. But it's kind of spongy and springy. Like foam. "Do you know what it says?"

"I have no idea," Andy said. Not too much call for translating hieroglyphs in today's market. Hasn't anyone tried before?"

"Race said yes. The inside, not the outside. The work is buried in Red 3 somewhere."

"Might be easier to start from scratch. I could translate the Dead Sea Scrolls quicker than it would take to find anything in that mess."

"What do you think Bub was speaking? Was that Maya?"

"Kind of. There are more than twenty different dialects that descended from the Maya language. I think Bub was speaking one of them. We're allowed to have Internet access, right?"

"Sure. It's monitored somehow, I'm guessing. For security. There are three computers you can use in the Octopus, the Cray in Red 14, and there's a room in the Green Arm, Green 4, with a link if you want privacy." Andy stared at the capsule, apparently lost in thought.

"Hungry?" Sun asked.

"Hmm? Oh. Yeah, I am actually."

"We all pretty much fend for ourselves around here, except when Race cooks up a batch of chili or stew. Want to grab an early dinner?"

Andy grinned. "Sure. But only if it's not mutton."

Sun led Andy to the mess hall and began to school him on the intricacies of microwave defrosting. From the massive walk-in freezer they selected some boneless chicken breast, cauliflower, pea pods, and green peppers. After thawing, Sun showed off her substantial wok skills.

Whenever Sun cooked, she thought of her mother and how embarrassed of her she was while growing up. Her friends' mothers baked cookies and went to the PTA and had college educations. Sun's mom spoke heavily accented, grammatically incorrect English, and wove baskets. The childhood taunts and teases were unrelenting.

Sun now realized what a graceful, introspective woman her mother had been. Hopefully she'd find that same inner peace someday. But even if she never did, her mother had passed a trickle of her wisdom on to her daughter:

Sun could wok like a fiend.

Dinner conversation with Andy was upbeat and impersonal. He knew an alarmingly large number of dumb blonde jokes, and rattled off two or three good ones that almost made Sun choke on her stir-fry. Dessert was a large can of fruit cocktail, dumped rather inelegantly into a mixing bowl.

They shared the bowl.

"So, I take it you've decided to stay."

"I don't think I'll be present at any more feedings, but yeah, I'm staying. I'm not captivated by Bub like some of the others are, but I can't pass up the challenge he represents."

Sun offered her hand. "Well then, welcome aboard, Andrew Dennison."

"Glad to be here, Sunshine Jones."

They shook, but Andy didn't drop her hand. The

moment stretched. Sun watched Andy's pupils widen, wondered if hers were doing the same thing.

They'd gone from zero to intimacy in less than five seconds.

Fast. Too fast.

Sun took her hand back.

"Andy . . ."

"Sorry . . ."

"It's just that . . ."

"I know."

An uncomfortable silence ensued.

"Are my ears red?" he asked.

They were the same shade as a fire hydrant.

"No. They're fine."

"I think I'm gonna call it a night. Low on sleep. Excuse me."

He stood up and walked to the door. Halfway there he touched his ear and stopped.

"They are red, aren't they?" he asked without turning around.

"You could stop traffic," Sun said.

Andy left without another word. There was some fruit cocktail left, but Sun was no longer hungry. She dumped it down the disposal and went back to her room.

Alone.

# CHAPTER 5

Sun woke up at half past nine in the morning. She'd always been an early riser, a fact that she recently discovered was dependent on sunlight. With no morning sun to wake her up, she'd been sleeping later than normal. One more thing to dislike about being two hundred feet underground.

After her exercises and a quick shower, she stopped by the mess hall, half hoping Andy was there. He wasn't. She made herself a bowl of shredded wheat with vacuum-packed milk and frozen strawberries, but only picked at it.

Sun wasn't exactly sure what she was feeling. Andy was attractive, and found her attractive, but this wasn't exactly the time or place to start a relationship. She felt flattered, and annoyed, and disappointed all at once.

*Romance sucks*, she decided. It was much simpler being a hermit.

She forced herself to finish breakfast and then put in some hard work at Red 3 with more enthusiasm than the mundane task warranted. Her current fixation—organizing the thousands of photographs—so absorbed her attention that when she checked the clock it was already a quarter after twelve. Bub's lunchtime.

Sun put some bounce in her step on the way to Orange 12, again hoping to bump into Andy. No such luck.

She was quick and thorough in selecting and examining the sheep, but it didn't hold the charm of the previous time with the linguist.

"I'm acting like a schoolgirl," Sun chided herself. Why didn't she just write him a love note and draw a heart on it and slip it in his locker?

Sun led the hooded animal down the Red Arm. Dr. Belgium, who practically lived in Red 14, wasn't around. She approached the habitat quietly, the only sound being the whirring fans of the Cray computer and the *tap-tap* of the sheep's footfalls on the tile floor.

Bub was squatting, his eyes closed and his arms on his haunches; a warped parody of the tai chi lotus. This was the position Bub slept in. She'd been recording his sleep patterns, and he took between ten and fifteen naps a day, never longer than twenty minutes each. All totaled, he slept about four hours daily. Far less than any animal she'd ever encountered.

Even squatting, Bub was taller than Sun. She watched his massive chest undulate in waves, his many lungs taking in air at slightly different rates. As usual, seeing Bub filled her with a mixture of awe and fear. Sun clearly recalled their first meeting. She'd walked up to the habitat, so cocksure, and when Bub came out from behind the trees her legs gave out on her and she squealed in fright, much to Race's amusement.

The fact that Bub looked demonic was only part of the shock. What most impressed Sun was the creature's size and obvious strength. It was like seeing a dinosaur up close. More than once Sun had wondered if that Plexiglas wall was truly strong enough to hold him.

Sun leaned closer to the partition, her forehead almost touching it.

"Sun is laaaaaate," Bub said, his voice remarkably clear coming from a mouth packed with so many teeth.

The sheep screamed and bucked, and Sun was so startled she let go of the harness. The sheep ran off toward Dr. Belgium's computers and barreled into a desk, upsetting papers and a coffee mug.

Sun took back control of her faculties and chased after the sheep, one arm locking around its large woolly neck and the other pulling tight on the harness. After a few seconds of struggling and talking, she managed to calm the sheep down enough to tether it to a door handle.

Bub watched the whole episode from his lotus position, his reptilian eyes keenly intelligent.

Sun chose her words carefully.

"I'm sorry. I was busy. Have you always known English?"

"Yooooou are Sun," Bub said. "That is luuunch." His voice was a throaty baritone, but soft and wet like a wheeze.

"Right. My name is Sun Jones."

"Joooooones."

"Yes."

"Yessssss," Bub hissed.

Sun approached the habitat slowly, unconsciously using the stalking approach that she'd used to get close to lions without spooking or threatening them.

Her mind whirred. With all the conversations she

and her cohorts had had in front of Bub, could he have picked up enough information to understand English?

"Can you understand me, or just repeat what I say?"

His hand raised up and a long claw uncurled from his fist, pointing at her.

"Suuuun Jooooones." He turned the talon on himself. "Buuuuub." Sun pointed at the sheep.

"Luuuuunch," Bub said.

She gestured over her shoulder, to the rear of the room.

"Compuuuuuuter," Bub said. "Craaaaaay. Four teraaaaabytes." Sun blew out some air. Bub startled her by repeating the gesture.

"Is Bub hungry?" Sun asked.

"Hungry Buuuuub. Eeeeeat." The demon looked beyond Sun.

"Fraaaaank."

"Good Lord," Dr. Frank Belgium whispered.

Sun hadn't even known he'd entered the room, so intense was her focus.

Bub sprang up on his legs and threw his hands in the air, just as Belgium had. The demon bellowed as loud as a thunder clap, "Goooooood Looooord!"

Both Sun and Frank Belgium jumped backward, and Frank kept backpedaling until he'd bumped into the sheep, which bleated a scream at the intrusion.

"Find Andy," Sun ordered. "And Race."

"Sure thing. Sure thing."

Dr. Belgium hit the door, repeating "sure thing" like a mantra.

"Buuuuub is huuuuungry," the demon said. He

lowered his head to her height, pressing his moist pig snout to the Plexiglas. It made a sticky wet spot.

"Lunch, noooooooow."

Sun, who had that jelly feeling back in her legs, fought the fear and stepped up to the glass.

"Where are you from?" Sun asked. "How do you know English? Did you just learn it?"

Bub's lips creased back, revealing a huge valley of yellow, jagged teeth.

*He could bite through a redwood with those teeth*, Sun thought.

"Lunch nooooooow. English laaaaaaater."

Sun, who hadn't taken an order from anyone since she was in grammar school, simply nodded. She went to the sheep, her gaze never leaving Bub. The sheep was rooted, shaking like a jackhammer. It refused to budge.

Sun located the box of Cap'n Crunch, dropped when she'd let go of the harness. There was still cereal left at the bottom, and she lifted the cowl and pushed the box over the sheep's snout like a feed bag. After a moment of struggle the animal began to munch, its muscles relaxing. Sun led it to the oversized door next to the habitat.

Bub watched intently, the terrible smile on his face never slipping. Sun took the sheep through the walkway alongside Bub's pen and stopped at the waist-level entrance hatch. The hatch was set inside a large hinged wall, kind of like a pet door. The wall was concrete, inlaid with the same titanium bars used in the Red Arm. It moved up and down like a garage door—industrial pneumatics—and it was the entrance Bub took when his vital signs indicated he was waking up from his coma.

Sun hadn't been present for that event. She'd arrived

shortly afterward. But Race spared no detail, telling her how he'd wheeled Bub into the habitat on a gigantic gurney, then used a crank to lift up one end until Bub slid off and onto the ground, twitching and blinking the whole time. Race had barely pushed the gurney back out the entrance and closed the door before Bub was on his feet.

The entrance remained locked, using yet another magnetic bolt operated by a keypad. The hatch in the middle was locked by a simple latch, reinforced with titanium. This was the entrance used for the sheep and the one Race took when he'd been in the habitat on those previous occasions. It was too small for Bub to fit through, but Sun still paused before opening it.

Now that Bub was talking, it made him more menacing to her, rather than less so.

She went a hard round with her fear, then pushed it away and opened the small hatch.

"Fooooooooood," Bub said.

He was squatting directly in front of the opening, and his breath, warm and fetid, blew against Sun like a sewer breeze. She felt an adrenaline jolt, like something had run in front of the car and she had to slam on the brakes. It was accompanied by instant sweating and a small cry that died in her throat.

The sheep tried to buck, but one of Bub's massive talons lashed out and gripped it by the head, dragging it through the hatchway.

Sun watched, transfixed, as Bub twisted the sheep in half only a few feet away from her, a tangle of intestines stretching out between the pieces like hot mozzarella on a pizza. Some blood spattered onto her pants. The sheep's legs were still kicking as Bub jammed them down his throat, not even bothering to chew. Then he uncurled the glistening entrails that hung around his shoulders like Mardi Gras beads and shoved them into his maw, smacking enthusiastically.

"Goooooooooood," Bub said to her.

He licked his talons and belched.

Sun kicked the hatch closed.

For a moment she stood there, her heart playing bongos inside of her ribs, trembling so violently her knees were knocking. She became aware that she was holding her breath, and tried to let it out slowly to regain some control.

*He's just an animal*, she said in her mind, over and over again.

Her mind wasn't buying it.

Sun forced composure to return, and then left the hallway and reentered the main room, willing herself to look at Bub through the Plexiglas.

The demon was almost done eating, his hairy chest matted dark with sheep's blood. He picked up the severed head and wedged it into the corner of his mouth. It cracked like a walnut. He chewed with a sound similar to a cement mixer, his eyes following Sun as she walked to the center of the room.

The door opened behind her, and Sun turned to see Race, Andy, and Frank rush in.

"He's talking?" Race asked Sun, his attention on the demon.

"Yes. He told me I was late for his lunch."

Andy came up beside Sun but didn't meet her gaze.

"Hello, Bub!" Race said, a wide grin on his face and a hand raised in greeting.

Bub glared at the general, and Sun noted it didn't seem friendly.

"Raaaaaace," Bub said.

Race scratched the back of his head. "I'll be damned. What else did he say?"

"He pointed to things and named them, like me, himself, his lunch."

"Son of a bitch."

Andy leaned closer to the Plexiglas. "Do you speak English?"

Bub closed one eye and the other locked on to Andy, as if scrutinizing him.

"*Hal tafham al arabiya?*" Andy asked.

"*Lam asma had min zaman,*" Bub answered.

"What?" Race asked. "What did you just say to him?"

"I asked him if he understood Arabic. He said he hasn't heard it in a long time. *Qui de Latinam es?*" Andy asked.

"*Latinam nosco. Multos sermones nosco. Mihi haec lingua patria quam dicis est nova.*"

"He says he also knows Latin. But you probably figured that out. He also knows many other languages, but English is new to him."

Sun checked the corner of the room where the video camera was, reflexively making sure it was still there. It was, red light blinking. This was all being digitally recorded.

"Okay," Race said, "there are questions. We've got a book in the Octopus for when this would happen, a hundred years of questions to ask. I've got to call the

President. And the holies, they'll want to be here." Race turned to leave, moving double time.

"*Ubi sum?*" Bub asked. *"Quis annus hic est?"*

"He wants to know where he is and what the year is," Andy translated.

"It looks like Race isn't the only one with questions." Sun frowned.

Bub glanced at Sun and squinted, his elliptical eyes narrowing in a way that she could only describe as *demonic*.

# Chapter 6

One-star general Regis Murdoch tried to keep his excitement in check as he walked briskly down the Red Arm. This had been an exciting week indeed. He could almost see the light at the end of the tunnel, the conclusion to over three decades of waiting.

Forty goddamn years, and he was almost out of this hole.

He reached the Octopus and sat down at the main terminal. The computer took forever to boot up. Once he was online, he accessed CONTACT, the President's portable Internet receiver. The President carried it on him at all times, and almost everyone thought it was a high-tech pager. Actually it was a mini computer, capable of receiving and storing more than forty gigabytes of information: pictures, spoken words, text, computer files and programs, even perfect digital copies of music and video.

Eight orbiting satellites controlled its transmissions, so the President could instantly receive information while anywhere in the world. It was waterproof, shockproof, and bulletproof. The President could even use it to launch a nuclear strike.

Deciding that the current situation didn't warrant

an interruption, Race contacted him with one beep. That would tell the President that he was receiving a message, but it wasn't of immediate urgency. The unit would either beep or vibrate once, depending on whether or not it was on silent mode. Two beeps and the President would check the message immediately. Three beeps and he'd plug a tiny earpiece into the CONTACT unit and speak into it like a portable phone.

When the connection was made, Race clicked on the microphone to speak.

His typing skills were considerably lacking.

"Mr. President, this is Race. Our subject is currently able to communicate. I'm going to begin the interrogation. I'll keep you updated, and remember what was promised to me."

Race hit the SEND icon. The spoken-word message would be translated into text, encrypted, and sent to the President's CONTACT unit within seconds. Even though the encryption code was the most complicated in the world and deemed unbreakable, Race still was leery of codes and always kept his messages somewhat vague. The Germans never thought Enigma would be cracked either.

The Roosevelt Book, as Race's predecessor called it, was in the table drawer next to the main terminal. It was one of Race's responsibilities at Samhain to maintain and update the information it held. Since Theodore Roosevelt began the project in 1906, a list of questions had been compiled to ask Bub should he ever awake and be judged sentient. There were many, some scientific, some historic, some theological.

Each successive President added his own questions

to the book, and questions were dropped when they became outdated—for example, they no longer needed to ask Bub the 1918 question: Is it possible to split the atom?

The book still had its original leather binding, though it had faded and cracked over the years. The first several dozen questions were typeset, but Roosevelt was wise enough to know that more questions would come up, so bound after the printed pages were two hundred blank ones.

Race had read through the book many times, and had even added several questions of his own. Now, after a century of sowing, it was time to reap.

With the book tucked firmly in his armpit, Race picked up the phone and hit the intercom line.

"Attention, this is Race. Our permanent guest is now talking, so it's showtime in Red 14. Will everyone please meet me there."

He hung up and took a microcassette recorder from a cabinet. Race checked the batteries and unwrapped a new tape and inserted it into the machine. Then he got up and headed down the Red Arm. His mind was a rubber ball bouncing around inside his skull. It was a familiar feeling; the long stretches of boredom, the careful preparation, and then *BOOM!*—everything happening at once.

*Just like combat*, Race thought.

He missed that so badly. Just like he missed everything about the army.

It was his family.

Race was born to command. First in his class at West Point, back in '50. He entered Korea in '51 as a "butter bar"—second lieutenant—and rose to the rank of captain in four years, most of his ascension due to battlefield victories.

Korea was where he came to be known as Race, as in *Race to the rescue*.

When the war ended, Race was a man to watch. He was stationed at Fort Sam Houston in 1959, headquarters for the Fifth U.S. Army. He paid his dues, did a tour in Vietnam, and generally worked his ass off, and on December 29, 1966, he had made brigadier general.

Then came the fall.

There was a second lieutenant named Harold Bright under Race's command. They'd graduated together, gone to Korea together, and were the best of friends. Harold was Race's best man when he married Helen. He was as close as a brother.

Which made the confession even worse.

On a drunken March night, two years after Race's promotion to one-star general, Harold disclosed the affair he'd had with Race's wife.

Race was slack-jawed at the betrayal. Harold went into detail about how lonely Helen was, how Race was never around, how it happened only a few times but now it was over.

The alcohol added to the rage. Race hit him. Harold defended himself. Race broke a bar stool over his best friend's head.

Harold suffered a concussion from the assault and later died from his injuries.

Helen blamed herself. She begged forgiveness. He forgave, and asked for hers in return. She was strong enough to stand by him during his trial, his discharge from his beloved army, and his inevitable imprisonment. To save her from the scandal Race offered no defense for his actions.

But somehow President Johnson found out the truth.

He admired Race's stoicism and manliness—LBJ's exact words. He didn't want to see Race go to jail, or get booted from the army. Not only had Race proven himself an excellent soldier, he'd also proven himself a man who had forsaken his own good to keep a secret. That, Johnson had said, was what patriotism was all about. So he gave Race an opportunity to redeem himself.

Samhain.

Race agreed, and quickly disappeared, along with all charges against him. Johnson also buried the civil case with Harold's family by giving them a modest cash settlement. All Race had to do, to keep up his end of the deal, was run the Samhain project until the time Bub awoke and the questions in the Roosevelt Book were answered. LBJ had given Race the impression that it would happen any day.

And now here it was, forty years later.

Race could have quit at any time. Many times he almost did, twice even going as far as telling the incumbent President he wanted out. But each time he was convinced to stay. Not through any slick blackmailing technique, or bland patriotic speeches about God and country. The carrot on the stick had always been his beloved army and the opportunity to someday command again.

So Race stuck it out, through years of boredom, through Helen's illness, through eleven different

Presidents. The current commander in chief even told Race that he had a space waiting for him on the Joint Chiefs of Staff when this was finally over.

It was all only a few hundred questions away.

Race arrived in Red 14 to find Andy sitting in a chair next to the Plexiglas.

Bub squatted on his haunches, his head at Andy's level. The image that came to Race's mind was two old women, sharing gossip.

"What have we learned so far?" he asked Andy, slapping a paternal hand on his shoulder.

"Well, not a lot. Bub apparently doesn't remember much about what happened to him before his coma. He doesn't even know how he came to be buried in Panama in the first place."

Race's eyes narrowed. This wouldn't do. Not at all. There were provisions for the possibility that Bub would be uncooperative. The main one involved a very large cattle prod.

But that was to be a last resort.

"Well, let's see what he does know, then, shall we?"

Race took a chair from the computer workstation and set it next to Andy, taking a seat. Bub glanced at Race and stretched out his mouth. He appeared to be attempting a smile, but Race found himself repulsed. It took him a moment to regain composure.

"This is called the Roosevelt Book; it's a list of questions to ask Bub going back to his discovery. I'll read the question, you interpret it and give me the answer."

Race took the cassette recorder from his pocket and hit the RECORD button. He rested it on his knee.

"What is your name?" Race asked the beast.

"Buuuuuub . . ." the demon answered, staring into Race's eyes before Andy had a chance to translate. He raised a claw and a talon snaked out, pointing at the general's chest.

"Raaaaace."

Race shivered. Had it gotten colder in the room? Must be the central-air unit, blowing down at them overhead. He folded his arms.

"Ask him for his previous name, before we started calling him that." Andy complied, and Bub whispered a reply.

"He says he's had many names."

"My God in heaven," Father Thrist exclaimed. He'd just entered the room, the thick Rabbi Shotzen in tow. "It speaks."

"Faaaaather," Bub said, his voice a cross between a whisper and a hiss.

"Raaaaaabbi."

"Oh my . . ." Rabbi Shotzen gasped.

"What has he said so far?" Father Thrist demanded. "Anything about God? Anything about heaven?"

"Heavaaaaaan," Bub said, raising a claw over his head and extending a finger upward. The way he said the word made it sound somehow unclean.

"What do you know about heaven?" Thrist approached the Plexiglas, his nose inches from Bub's. "Are you a fallen angel?"

Bub's mouth stretched open and he belched, a sound like a motorcycle starting. His breath fogged up the glass, and Race caught the stench of blood and wool.

"Father." Race stepped in, holding the aging priest by the shoulders. "All of those questions and more will be answered. They're all in my book. Let's all just sit down, relax, we're gonna be here for a while."

The holies went off in search of chairs, and Rabbi Shotzen dragged over an extra one for Dr. Belgium, who had just arrived.

"Can he talk?" Belgium asked.

"Heeeeee . . . taaaaaalks . . ." Bub answered.

Belgium made a sound like a hiccup, and Race watched him turn right around and leave the room.

"He's a quick study," Sun said. "He's already putting together nouns and verbs. I bet he could learn English quickly."

Race furrowed his brow. It would be much easier to interrogate Bub if he knew how to speak American. Save a helluva lot of time.

The disadvantage would be that Bub would understand everything they said, but indications showed that he was understanding a lot already. Besides, better to know what your enemy knows than to not know if he knows anything or not.

"Andy, you've taught several languages. Have you ever taught English?"

"To people."

"Can you do it?"

"I don't think . . . I mean . . . he's a . . ."

"Yes or no, Mr. Dennison?"

"I don't know. I'd need materials."

"Like what?"

"Well, some language programs. A chalkboard. Children's books."

"How about one of those phonics programs for kids?"

Sun suggested. "We could wheel in a big-screen TV and a DVD."

"That might work." Andy nodded.

"So when do you think he could know enough to answer questions in English?" Race asked.

"Well, I couldn't possibly predict when . . . I mean, there's no precedent for this."

"How long did it take you to learn Japanese?"

"I got a good grasp of the language in about a week, but it took a while before I was fluent."

"You have until tomorrow. Write down all of the supplies you'll need, I'll have them air-dropped here within the hour."

"Tomorrow? That's ridiculous. I wouldn't even know how to begin."

"With the ABCs," Race said, heading for the door. "I'll be in the Octopus. Let me know what you need."

*This was an interesting turn of events*, Race thought. Interesting indeed.

# Chapter 7

Why was she tied to this bed? Where was her husband? She called to him.

"Regis! Regis, help me!"

Then her legs began to tremble violently. She tried but couldn't control the shaking, which became more and more spastic. Her arms followed suit, flapping up and down on the short tethers as if she were being electrocuted.

Without the tethers she might have whacked herself in the face. Perhaps that's what they were for.

The tremors subsided, and a memory flickered in her mind, so quickly that it might have been simply a fleeting thought and not a memory at all. A memory of her mother, tethered to a bed like she was, cursing uncontrollably.

"Mother was sick," she said aloud, alone in her hospital bed.

This was a hospital, wasn't it? The walls were white. The bed had rails. There was medical equipment on a cart next to her. But when she listened, there were no other noises. Weren't hospitals noisy places, full of comings and goings and doctors and nurses and intercoms? If this wasn't a hospital, where was she?

"Regis!" she called out. "Regis, where am I? Help me, Regis!"

The door opened, and an old man walked in. He looked so familiar, but she couldn't place him. He was dressed in jeans and a flannel shirt. Not a doctor.

A visitor?

"I'm here, Helen. It's me."

"Do I know you?"

"It's Regis, Helen. Your husband."

"Bullshit," she spat. "My husband is a young man. You're an old fart!"

Rather than seem shocked, or even bothered by her outburst, the man simply picked up a hand mirror from one of the medical carts. He held it in front of her.

My God! She was old! How did she get so old?

"We're both old, Helen. You don't remember because you have Huntington's disease. You've had it for many years now."

"Oh my Lord."

The spike of realization pierced her heart. She remembered now—this awful disease that she inherited from her mother. It debilitated the nervous system, causing memory and motor function loss. The tethers were there to hold her arms down when the chorea hit—frenzied palsies that she couldn't control.

"Oh, I remember, Regis. Oh, dear Lord, I remember."

He held her close, running his hands over the back of her head.

"It will be okay soon, Helen. I promise. Things are happening. We'll leave here soon, get you better medical treatment. There's hope. They're making new advancements in gene therapy every day."

His words didn't cheer her. While they were admittedly hopeful, her husband's delivery was wrong. He was saying it like it was something he'd memorized and repeated a hundred times before.

And then it occurred to her . . . what if he had said it a hundred times before?

The chorea hit again, and he held her quivering body until it passed.

"I . . . love you . . . Regis."

"I love you too, Helen. Do you want to sleep for a while?"

She nodded. "And I'm thirsty."

He poured some water from a pitcher on a nearby table and held the glass while she drank. He also checked her diaper, which he found to be clean. She began to cry at the indignity of it.

"Oh, Regis . . ."

"Shh. I've got something that will help." Regis went to the medicine cabinet hanging on the far wall and removed a syringe and a bottle. He extracted some liquid like a pro.

"Regis, dear, where did you learn to do that?"

He put on a weak smile. "Just a little something to help you sleep and help with the seizures."

"Are you sure you can do this?"

He nodded and placed a hand on her face to stroke her cheek.

The shot didn't hurt at all. As she began to get drowsy, she concentrated on her husband's words.

"He has powers, Helen. Amazing powers. It'll all be okay soon. I promise."

"Who has powers, Regis?" she asked.

"Bub does, Helen. Everything will be okay soon."

She tried to focus on him and smiled. "I know it will, dear. I love you."

"I love you too, Helen. Sweet dreams."

She drifted off to sleep, thinking about her husband, wondering how he got so old.

# CHAPTER 8

Faith would be a thing of the past.

Electrified by the idea, Father Michael Thrist stared at Bub. The beast crouched in front of the Plexiglas while Andy, Sun, and Dr. Belgium pointed out the ABCs on a chalkboard. Could this demon be the thing Thrist had been searching for all these years?

Michael entered the priesthood thirty years ago. A double threat—severe acne and a facial tic than caused him to blink and twitch his upper lip at inopportune moments—made college hell, even at a prestigious school like Notre Dame.

Sophomore year he switched his major from biology to theology, partly because he believed he'd never get a date in his life, but mostly because he found science woefully inadequate to explain the many mysteries of the universe.

After completing his pretheologate, he served as a deacon for two years at a small church in Gary, Indiana. The area was poor, with one of the highest murder rates in the US. When he received the sixth sacrament and entered the priesthood, he requested a transfer from the archdiocese.

Then came his ascension, as he liked to call it.

Which led him to his current position at Samhain, and to watching a linguist and a vet try to teach a demon ABCs.

Shotzen leaned over and whispered to Thrist, "Soon they'll be roasting marshmallows and singing campfire songs."

Thrist ignored the comment. Couldn't Shotzen see what was before them? How could he remain skeptical? If anyone should be skeptical, it was Thrist.

He'd had the training.

After Indiana, Michael had been assigned to a low-income Hispanic neighborhood on Chicago's West Side. Though fluent in Spanish—a natural extension of the Latin he learned in school—his new flock never accepted an Anglo as one of their own, especially one who was always winking and twitching the left side of his face.

He'd been there for a year when the altar boy came to his room, jabbering about a miracle. A local woman had a painting of the Virgin Mary that was crying tears of blood. Thrist had gone to see for himself.

"You're not buying this, are you?" Shotzen whispered, interrupting his reverie.

"What do you mean?" Thrist replied. "And what's with the whispering?"

"Shh! Come here, in private."

The rabbi ushered the priest out of his chair and over to the corner of the room, between the data banks of the Cray computer.

"Don't you see what I see?" Shotzen urged, his cherubic eyes looking very serious.

"What do you see, Rabbi?"

"Bub, the demon. I think he already knows English. This is all deception."

"Ridiculous."

"If it were an angel in there, instead of a devil, wouldn't you think it already knew English? If this thing is from the pits of hell, surely they know English in hell? If hell exists, the English have been going there for a thousand years."

"But if he did know English already, why pretend otherwise?"

"Baalzebub is the Master of Lies, Father. It is his nature to deceive. You said so yourself. Perhaps he's buying some time."

"Buying time until what?"

The chubby holy man shrugged.

Thrist stopped short of rolling his eyes. "Look, Rabbi, the creature has only been awake for a week. He was discovered in Panama, which, the last time I checked, is not an English-speaking country. He'd been buried since the time of the Mayans. It's hardly likely he knows English."

Shotzen folded his arms. "I'm convinced he's deceiving us."

"Do you at least agree he's a demon?"

"I'm undecided. You're the debunking expert, yet you seem to be eating this up."

"If Bub's a fake, I can't spot it," Thrist said. "And I'm good at spotting deception."

The bleeding painting had been unremarkable in its execution, a typical pietà scene. But streaking down the

Virgin's face were trails of blood, and a puddle the size of a throw rug was pooling on the floor.

Thrist's first reaction to it was disbelief, but upon examination he couldn't find any holes or tubes behind the canvas, and the blood smelled, felt, and even tasted real. Could this truly be a miracle?

The gathering crowd seemed to think so. The old mestizo woman who owned the painting was charging people five dollars a head to come in and genuflect after dipping their fingers in the puddle of blood.

This incensed the priest. His parishioners were worshipping a false idol, rather than God. But he couldn't figure out the trick.

His epiphany would come the following day at lunch, when he was making himself a grilled cheese sandwich in the toaster oven. He'd left it in too long and the toast burned, all of the cheese melting and leaking out from between the bread.

That, of course, was the answer.

He had returned to the apartment, his Roman collar allowing him to bypass a line that stretched around the block, and again asked to examine the painting.

The several burly men standing over the growing pile of money almost refused, but the old woman relented. In one quick move Thrist seized the painting and dashed it to the floor.

There were several cries of horror. The cries turned to outrage when he held up the broken frame and showed the crowd the hollow middle where the blood had been stored. Then he tore the false canvas off the back of the painting, exposing the thin plastic tube that fed the blood from the reservoir in the frame to the Virgin's eyes. They had sandwiched the tube between two canvases, attempting to make them appear as one. Thrist guessed that there was a hole somewhere in the frame that they could use to refill it with chicken blood, or whatever blood they'd been using.

"Still searching for the fakery?" Shotzen mused. "It's there. You just aren't looking close enough."

"I've been looking for it for over thirty years," Thrist replied.

Shotzen sighed. "Michael, you've said it yourself. Adonai works in subtle ways. You've spoken to me about your acne and your facial tic, and how they went away during your early years as a priest. That's how ha-Shem works. He isn't a show-off like this."

Shortly after he'd proven the painting a fake, Thrist's childhood afflictions had gone away. But whether that had been a sign from God or simply a physical manifestation of his own growing self-confidence, Thrist had never decided.

"Rabbi, what other explanation is there? We've been discussing this since your arrival more than twenty years ago. We've done the research. We've posed the theories. Fallen angel, genetic experiment, biological weapon, man in a rubber suit—neither of us can find any evidence of fraud."

"So just because we can't see it, it isn't there? During your tour as Vatican examiner, did you ever authenticate a miracle?"

Thrist frowned. "No."

It had been a wonderful time for Thrist, serving the

Lord with a renewed vigor. His Eminence the cardinal removed him from the Chicago parish and Thrist traveled throughout the Americas, investigating miraculous phenomena. Sometimes the occurrence was amusing, such as the case in Texas where Christ's face had appeared simultaneously on several dozen cow patties—they turned out to be hoof marks. Sometimes it was appalling, such as the baby who was supposedly exhibiting signs of the stigmata, when actually it was his disturbed mother inflicting the wounds with a razor blade. But for all his travels, he never authenticated a miracle.

"Look at the mounting evidence," Thrist insisted. "Bub has mentioned both heaven and Jesus Christ. He can resurrect sheep. He speaks in ancient tongues . . ."

"What language is he speaking now?"

"I'm not sure. Sounds like Egyptian."

"I tell you, the beast is a liar. He can speak all languages, I'm convinced. Watch this."

Shotzen marched over to the Plexiglas and gave it a tap, drawing Bub's attention.

"*Anachnu holchim leshamen otcha ve'lehchol otcha*," he said to Bub.

Bub cocked his head to the side, doing a damn good imitation of confusion.

"What did he say?" Sun asked.

"He told Bub we're going to fatten him up and eat him." Andy turned to Shotzen. "Isn't the food here good enough for you, Rabbi?"

"Fah!" Shotzen said, pointing at the demon. "You understand me. I know you do. Admit it!"

Bub looked hard at Shotzen, and the holy man took a step back, dropping his arm.

"He understands me," Shotzen whispered. "Every word."

"Perhaps Yiddish?" Thrist offered a tight smile. Mirth was an emotion he rarely showed, but the whole idea of a demon speaking Hebrew amused him. Everyone knew demons spoke Latin.

*Epiphany.*

"Latin," Thrist said aloud.

He rushed the glass, pressing his palms against it.

*"Potense dicere Latinam?"* he asked Bub. *Can you speak Latin?*

The demon turned his attention to the priest. *"Ita, Latinam dico."* *Yes, I speak Latin.*

*"Ubi Latinam didicisti?"* Thrist asked. *Where did you learn Latin?*

*"Me abimperatore in loco appellato Roma ea docta est."* *It was taught to me by an emperor in a place called Rome.*

*"Quis rex erat? Quando regnabat?"* *Who was this king? When did he rule?*

*"Aliquem hac aetate eum noscere dubito. Misere cecidit. Membra senatus sui eum insidiis interfecerunt."* *I doubt anyone remembers him in this era. He died poorly. Members of his senate assassinated him.*

"Caesar!" Thrist cried, his voice cracking in an octave that was normally too high for him. "Julius Caesar!"

*"Illud erat nomen,"* Bub said. His voice was oddly sensual, almost a verbal caress. *"Quis nunc imperator tuus est?"* *That was his name. Who is your emperor in this age?*

"What just happened?" Sun asked.

"Apparently Julius Caesar taught Bub Latin," Andy replied.

Thrist's heart was threatening to burst from his rib cage. He was talking with a being who lived in the era of Christ. In the same part of the world. This was even more incredible than he'd imagined.

A demon by itself was ample evidence for the existence of God. But could this creature also prove without doubt that Jesus was God's son on earth?

This was the dawn of a new era. Religious differences, agnosticism, atheism, war, inhumanity; they'd all be things of the past. The world would embrace Bub's message and a collective effort would be made to worship the one true God. The Christian God.

Thrist's God.

*"Habesne cognitionem viri religiosi ex Galil qui in Bethlehem natus est? Iudaes qui multos disipulos habebat?"* Did you know of a religious man from Galilee, born in Bethlehem? A Jew with a large following?

"Jeeeesus Christ," Bub said the name in English. "I haaaaave seeeeen Jeeeeesus."

The breath caught in Thrist's throat and his lower jaw began to tremble. All the Bible study, all the research, all the prayers, none of it had brought Thrist as close to God as he was feeling right now.

*"Narro de eo, sis."* Please, tell me of him.

"Father," Rabbi Shotzen cut in, "we have time for this later."

*"Narro de eo,"* Thrist implored.

"Father," Shotzen sighed, "please let them get on with their work. This can wait."

"Bullshit!" the priest spat at Shotzen. The rabbi recoiled in surprise. "You don't want to hear of it because you don't want to hear the truth! For two thousand years you've been waiting for a Messiah that already came! You missed Him! Now's your chance to atone for your mistake!"

Thrist turned to Bub and begged, "Tell me of Jesus! Tell me what you know!"

The demon stretched his mouth wide in a grin. *"Serius, Pater. Tempus sine arbitrus mox habebimus."* *Later, Father. We'll have time alone soon.*

Bub was using the same soothing voice that he'd used with the sheep.

*"Sciendus sum! Eratne Deus? Estne natus ex virgine? Cognitionem eius habebas . . . erasne qui in desertis eum temptabas? Heu, sciendus sum!" I must know! Was he God? Was he born of a virgin? You knew him . . . were you the one that tempted him in the desert? I must know, dammit!*

"Soooooon," soothed the demon. He gave his attention back to Andy and Sun.

Thrist banged on the glass, but Bub paid him no mind.

Thrist stepped back and looked at the others. Andy looked embarrassed. Sun was frowning. Thrist turned to Rabbi Shotzen and was stunned to see the sadness on his friend's chubby face.

"I . . . I'm . . ."

Shotzen gave him his back.

"For a man of faith you're showing surprisingly little," the rabbi said.

Thrist opened his mouth, closed it again. His face became very hot. He didn't trust his voice. He reached for the crucifix hanging from his neck.

Christ felt cold in his hand.

Thrist hurried out the door, hurried down the Red Arm, fumbling the code for the first gate several times, fumbling several more times at the second, racing to his room, and falling on his knees next to his bed, his hands clasped in prayer but his mind unable to dismiss Shotzen's words and the possibility that they might be true.

# CHAPTER 9

Frank Belgium watched from the sanctuary of his computer terminal. He'd returned to Red 14 after spending half an hour in the bathroom, feeling the urge to vomit but unable to.

Belgium knew it was a physical response to fear. When the demon awoke last week, that was frightening enough. But his voice—soft, low, almost seductive—was the voice of a thousand nightmares.

Though he sat far enough away from the speech lesson to be unable to hear Bub, watching proved disconcerting all by itself. There was something upsetting and grotesque about a demon watching a children's television show. Bub's blank stare made Belgium wonder if he was indeed learning how to conjugate verbs, or if he was wondering how the child actors tasted.

The doctor shivered, nibbling on his lower lip.

*Get a grip*, he told himself. The demon seemed to be cooperating so far.

Maybe it wasn't his fault he was so frightening.

Andy stood, stretched, and said something to Sun. She stood as well, answered him and nodded, and they walked out of the room.

Bub watched them leave. His stare lingered on the door for almost ten seconds, then his eyes locked on Belgium.

Belgium tried to swallow, but couldn't.

"Fraaaaaank," Bub said, loud enough to be heard from across the room. "Fraaaaaank Beeeeeelgium . . ."

Belgium turned away, wondering if the demon would leave him alone if he pretended to be working. "Fraaaaaank . . ."

"I'm busy," he said, trying to make his voice sound unafraid. "Fraaaaaank . . . . . . what does Craaaaay computer dooooo?" That seemed like an innocent-enough question.

"Umm, the Cray? It stores and processes information."

"In Englissssssssh?"

"In computer language."

"Doooooooes it . . . taaaaaaalk?"

"Talk? No no no. Computers don't talk. But we can use them to talk to others who have computers with an Internet connection."

"Internet cooooooonnection?"

"The World Wide Web lets people with computers access all the information available in the world."

"Would the Woooorld Wide Web help me learn Engliiiiiiish?"

Belgium hunched down lower and ruffled some papers on his desk.

"Sure. The Internet has everything on it."

"I waaaaaant Internet cooooooonnection," Bub said.

Dr. Belgium turned around and ratcheted up his

spine. He didn't quite stare at Bub so much as stare in his general direction.

"You're too too too big. Sorry. You couldn't use the keyboard."

Bub didn't answer, and Belgium hoped the conversation had ended. Being alone in the room with the creature was freaking him out. He got up to leave.

"Come heeeeere," Bub said.

Belgium stopped, midstride, his mouth going dry.

"Coooooome heeeeeere, Fraaaaaank."

*Relax,* Belgium though. *He's behind the Plexiglas. He can't hurt me.*

He changed direction and approached Bub.

"Yes? What is it?"

Bub extended a claw and touched it to the Plexiglas. Then there was a shrill screeching sound and his finger became a blur, moving faster than any human being possibly could.

It was over in an instant, and Dr. Belgium was amazed to see that Bub had etched the entire English alphabet, both uppercase and lowercase letters, onto the glass in a space less than the size of a credit card. So impressed was the doctor, that it didn't occur to him that Bub had written it as a mirror image, which allowed Frank to see it the normal way.

"Well, I guess typing wouldn't be too difficult for you, then. Remarkable small muscle control. Yes yes yes."

"I waaaaant Internet cooooonnection," Bub said.

"I I I don't see how. We'd have to rig something up. Maybe we could use, um, a wireless router."

Bub moved closer to the Plexiglas, the corners of his

mouth turning up into a smile. He moved quite well for such a large creature, thought Belgium. Like a dancer, smooth and quick.

Or like a cobra.

"Let meeee ooooout," Bub said, "I caaaan use your compuuuuuuter."

Dr. Belgium blinked. "Uh, no, Bub. It's safer for you in there."

"Yoooou aaaare afraaaaaid."

"No no no. Not at all. I'm a scientist, Bub. I study things."

"You study meeeeee."

"Yes."

"With the Craaaaay compuuuuuuter."

"Yes. That's part of it."

"Hoooooow?"

"Well, Bub, I'm trying to sequence your DNA. Your karyotype shows you have eighty-eight chromosomes. This is over three hundred thousand genes, about six billion base pairs. I want to figure out what your genes are, so I can see what you're related to. All life on Earth is related to something, some things more than others." Bub stared, saying nothing. Belgium continued, fear making him ramble.

"What I'm doing is using the Sanger procedure, along with whole genome shotgun sequencing. First, I take some of your DNA—a blood sample—and make a template by subcloning into a YAC. I'm using restriction enzymes in gel electrophoresis to get a thousand sequence base read that the computer can interpret as a chromatogram. It's all very simple, really. Simple simple simple."

"Hoooow much of my DNA haaaaave you seeee-quenced?"

"Only about forty percent. The problem comes from not knowing enough about DNA. Only ten percent of an organism's chromosomes contain exon genes—those are the ones that protein code, which account for an organism's physiology. Intron genes are responsible for growing, aging, things we don't know yet . . . so sequencing is only half the battle. The Cray is also trying to sort out what is exon and what is intron, and trying to find matches with other life-forms."

Bub blinked. Belgium had never noticed him blink before. His eyelids closed sideways, like elevator doors. It was disconcerting.

"You analyze my bloooooood," Bub said. His voice had dropped an octave.

"What else do you anaaaaaaalyze?"

"We have tissue samples going back a hundred years." Bub appeared to think about this.

"Why do yooooou study meeee, Fraaaaaaank?"

"Hmm? Oh. To figure out what you are, my friend. Physiologically, you're more advanced than anything on Earth. Mentally too. You've been learning English for less than six hours and already you're conversant. You're an amazing specimen."

"Amaaaaaaazing."

"Very. For example, you clearly have the X and Y chromosomes, making you a male, but you have no genitalia . . . at least not that we've been able to find.

Nor do you have a belly button. How were you born? How does your kind reproduce? Or is there only one of you? Questions questions questions."

"Why are you heeeeere, Fraaaaank?"

"To study you, Bub. The opportunity you represent is limitless. I've been doing research for . . ."

Bub cut him off. "You have to beeee heeeeeeere."

Frank's words died in his mouth, leaving a foul taste. "What?" he managed.

"Did you do something wrong, Fraaaaaank?"

Dr. Belgium swallowed. His mind involuntarily returned to his prior life, graduating top of his class at Berkeley, already thrice published, a Nobel Prize almost a foregone conclusion . . .

He'd first taken speed in graduate school. The courses were highly demanding, and he had to postpone sleep in order to learn everything that needed to be learned. Simple caffeine pills at first. Then ephedrine, available over the counter in health stores as ma huang extract. These worked for a time, limiting his sleep to five hours a night, but when five hours became too long, he switched to harder stuff.

A friend was able to hook him up with a Benzedrine supply. Bennies got him through school, got him his job at BioloGen, the largest genetics lab in the world, got him his Porsche, his house, his trophy wife.

But the work was even more demanding than school had been. He switched from Benzedrine pills to injecting methedrine. To come down after a methedrine buzz he started taking Librium and later Nembutal. He was stoned on Nembutal when he blew up Labs 4, 5, and 6 at BioloGen.

The police report called it criminal negligence. He'd left the gas line live on a Bunsen burner after the flame had gone out. Not even a kid in high school would have made such a careless mistake. The irony was that the burner wasn't even being used in an experiment. Frank had been using it to heat his coffee.

The explosion caused almost two million dollars' worth of damage and lost research. Three people were killed. Frank had been in the bathroom and walked away without a mark.

He hid nothing. After admitting to the drugs, he demanded to be arrested.

A lawsuit was filed. So were manslaughter charges. Frank lost it all—career, money, wife—and he went to jail. That's where President Reagan found him.

Prison gave him a chance to kick the drugs, and it also gave him penance for his wrongs. Frank didn't want to leave. Reagan arranged for a trip to Samhain, to give Frank an idea of what his country needed him for.

Frank never left. He traded prison of one type for prison of another. This new one was quieter, more demanding, and gave him a chance to help the world while being punished at the same time. Frank hadn't seen a sunset in twenty years. He missed it every day, and that's why he stayed.

Even when the incumbent President pronounced his sentence over, Frank stayed. He would finish the job he started; sequencing Bub's DNA. Only then would his penance be complete.

"That was a long time ago," Frank whispered.

"I can help yoooou."

"How?"

"I knoooow of genetics. I can give you my whole seeeequence. But I need a compuuuuuter."

Frank thought it over. Twenty years without seeing the light of day. Was that long enough? Had he paid for his mistakes?

"I can get you a computer," Dr. Frank Belgium said.

The demon made a sound that Belgium swore was laughter.

# CHAPTER 10

"I like snow, but not a lot of it," Andy mumbled, taking a bite of his turkey sandwich.

"Yeah, not a lot," Sun agreed. "Too much snow and I hate it."

"Exactly. Too much snow isn't good."

Andy groaned inwardly. What the hell were they talking about? And why was Sun even bothering?

He stared at her across the cafeteria table and decided she must be patronizing him, hoping for an opportunity to escape. He couldn't really blame her. The only thing worse than their lame conversation was the food.

Andy looked down at his half-eaten sandwich. It needed fresh lettuce and tomato, neither of which were available. Canned tomatoes were a poor substitute. Even worse, the turkey was processed, and tasted it. Andy wondered how much was actually turkey, and what other chemicals, fillers, and by-products it contained.

"Good sandwich," Andy said.

Sun nodded and looked at her watch. Andy decided not to talk anymore. He'd die if his ears turned red like that again. Last night he had to soak his head in the sink to get them to stop burning.

"You're an attractive guy," Sun said, taking a bite of her sandwich.

Andy waited for the rest, the part where she told him that even though he was attractive, she wasn't interested and hoped they could just be friends.

That part never came.

Was she playing with him? What was he supposed to say back?

Andy opened his mouth to return the compliment, but closed it again when he considered his ears.

Their eyes locked. He realized he was going to say it anyway, but the phone saved him. He got up and answered.

"Who is this, Andy or Sun?"

"This is Andy, Dr. Belgium."

"Andy? This is Dr. Belgium."

"I know."

"I'm in Red 14 with Bub."

"I know. Sun and I are almost done. We'll be right by."

"No no no. Not necessary. Bub said, he said . . . all of this studying, he needed to rest for a bit. He took—he's taking—a nap. Rest rest rest, must have rest."

"Bub's sleeping," Andy repeated, for Sun's benefit.

"He doesn't sleep long," Sun said. "Maybe fifteen minutes at a time."

"Sun said he doesn't sleep long," Andy said into the receiver.

"I know, but Bub was clear that he wanted to take a break. Rest rest rest."

"Bub needs to rest rest rest," Andy told Sun. "How about an hour?"

"An hour. An hour an hour . . . make it two hours. I'll be here, when Bub is ready to resume I'll let you know."

"No problem." Andy hung up. "Frank said Bub needs two hours of rest."

"Interesting. Perhaps mental activities leave him more exhausted than physical ones."

"I've always heard sleep is for the mind, not the body."

"I've heard that too." *You're so damn beautiful*, Andy wanted to say.

Sun said, "So . . . have you had enough of this clever banter?"

"God, yes."

"Do you play racquetball?"

"I'm a racquetball king." Andy tried on a small smile, happy to have the conversation change. "If it ever becomes an Olympic event, I'm sure I'll be picked to represent my country."

"We have some time. Up for a game?"

"Yeah, okay."

"Are you sure? Most men have ego issues when it comes to losing, especially to a woman."

"Not a problem. I'm good at being a loser."

Sun smiled, and the realization of what he just said hit him. Open mouth, insert foot . . .

"I'll meet you in Purple 5. Say, twenty minutes?"

"Twenty minutes. Fine."

Sun finished her sandwich and stood up.

"It's a date." She spun on her toes and trotted off.

What did she mean by that? Did she mean *date* as in

a man and a woman having fun with a later possibility of sex? Or *date* as in a scheduled event on a calendar?

Fifteen minutes later he was dressed in some blue shorts and a sweatshirt, walking down the Purple Arm. The Secret Service had forwarded his gym shoes, but no gym socks, so he was forced to wear none. None were preferable to argyle, especially around pretty women.

Sun was waiting for him, squatting on the floor with her right leg extended in a stretch. She wore bike pants and a sports bra top, both black.

Did she have any idea of how good she looked? She must have.

So this was a real date.

Right?

On the floor next to her were two racquets. They resembled their tennis counterparts, except their handles were less than half the length. A blue rubber racquetball was in her hand, the manufacturer's label stamped on it in gold.

Mixed signals and potential embarrassment be damned, Andy willed himself to relax and have fun.

"I see you mean to distract me by playing on my weakness."

"What's that?"

"Spandex."

"Nice socks," Sun said. "You'll get blisters."

"I don't plan on doing much running."

"Maybe, since we both seem to be confident in our abilities, we should make a little bet on this game."

"Fine." Andy took a deep breath. "If I win, I get to kiss you." Sun's cheeks colored.

"I don't think so."

What little ego Andy had left shriveled up. But confidence isn't about how you feel. It's about what you project.

"Why not? Afraid you'll lose on purpose?"

Sun smiled, projecting quite a bit of confidence.

"I'm not going to lose."

"So you have nothing to worry about, then."

"Fine. So what do I get when I win?"

"You get to kiss me."

"How about a thousand bucks?"

"A thousand bucks? Can we afford it?"

"We're government employees." Sun bounced to her feet and handed him a racquet. "Of course we can afford it."

She gave him a heart-melting grin and trotted into Purple 5.

"You're not really serious, are you?" Andy called after her. "A thousand bucks?"

He walked into the room. It was a standard racquetball court, forty feet long by twenty feet wide. The walls were matte white, marred by several dozen chips and marks. Six fluorescent lights were set into the twenty-foot-high ceiling, making it as bright as an operating theater. The floor was wood, with red-painted markings for the service area and the fault line.

Andy closed the heavy door behind him. The door had no knob on the inside; there were no protrusions anywhere in the room. The handle was shaped like a half-moon and attached to a hinge, and when it wasn't in use it recessed into a depression. Andy likened the court to being inside of a large white box.

"Game is fifteen points, turn over the serve at fourteen, have to win by two. Do you want to stretch?"

"I'll be fine."

Andy grinned but Sun was all business.

"Zero serving zero, for one thousand dollars. Ready?"

Andy bent his knees and held his racquet up. The pose was familiar to him. He'd played racquetball a hundred times, and though the last time he'd played was several years ago, he'd been pretty good.

Sun was better.

Within two minutes she was four points up. Racquetball didn't have bizarre scoring like tennis. It was actually more like Ping-Pong. The goal was to return the ball to your opponent by bouncing it off the front wall, and you had to do this before it bounced on the floor twice.

By the time Sun was up six to zero, Andy realized she wasn't intending to lose on purpose. So much for wanting to be kissed.

But even though he was behind, he'd gotten a good feel for her game. She was faster than he was, and her ball control was better. On easy volleys she was able to hit the front wall only inches above the floor, making it impossible for him to return.

Andy, however, had the strength advantage, and could hit the ball harder than she could. It wasn't unusual for a racquetball to exceed speeds of ninety miles per hour, and when it was bouncing off four walls, that didn't make for an easy return. Andy was also several inches taller than Sun, so he hit the ball high whenever he had a chance, and often the bounce would sail over her head out of reach.

After twenty minutes Andy was able to cut Sun's lead down to one point. His sweatshirt was soaked enough to wring out, and it was becoming harder to catch his breath between volleys.

Sun didn't appear to be sweating at all.

"You can take a break if you need one," she told him. Her smirk was barely concealed.

He pursed his lips and didn't answer. She served and scored. "Twelve to ten. Are you sure you don't want to get some water?" Water did sound good.

"After the game. Serve."

It only took four more serves for Sun to win.

She shook his hand with vigor, her smile wide and genuine. Andy handled the loss easily. He just wanted something to drink.

A few minutes later they were in the mess hall, each with a large glass of water. Andy was on his third.

"You're better than I thought," Sun said. "You actually gave me a little trouble."

"You could play professionally."

"Well, I did, kind of. American Racquetball Association. Won a few tournaments. No big deal, really. Racquetball stars don't get too many product endorsements."

"You might have shared that info with me before we bet a thousand bucks."

"We've still got an hour before Bub is ready for his next lesson. Want to play again? Double or nothing?"

Andy could feel his muscles starting to cramp up. He

knew he wouldn't get through another game. But she was so earnest, so cute. Her eyes were wide and bright and her cheeks had a lovely flush to them. Such a change from the dour, strict woman he'd met yesterday.

"Race said something about a pool table. Do you play?"

"I haven't for a while."

"How about a game of nine ball, double or nothing?"

Sun grinned. "You're on. I need to shower and change first. See you in Purple 5 in twenty minutes?"

"It's a date," Andy said.

And as she trotted off, he sincerely hoped it was.

# Chapter 11

Rabbi Menachem Shotzen ended his nightly kaddish by asking G-d to help his friend, Father Thrist, with his crisis of faith.

He took off his braided *kippah*—a skull cap he received at bar mitzvah, and put it in his tallis bag on top of his tzitzit and his tefillin, both of which were worn only for morning prayer.

The rabbi glanced at his nightstand. He knew what it contained. And he knew that only minutes prior, he had pleaded with G-d to give him the strength to avoid it.

Shotzen turned away from the temptation and instead seated himself at a small desk to proofread the latest pages of his memoirs.

He hefted the manuscript, now over fifteen hundred handwritten pages, and its weight pleased him. Not too bad, especially considering one day and two nights of the week, Shabbes, he was forbidden by Jewish law to write. The first line still made him proud, and he said it softly to himself.

"Blessings and curses, I have had many of both."

He glanced at the nightstand again. One of the curses,

for sure. Bub may indeed be demonic, though Shotzen doubted it, but in that drawer was something even worse. Yetzer hara. A denial of G-d.

He approached it just the same.

The liquor was where he had left it, awaiting his return. Shotzen picked up the bottle—half-full of over-proof peppermint schnapps—then put it back down. It was a familiar ritual, with a familiar ending. Once the nightstand was opened, the bottle won.

This time the internal struggle lasted barely a minute. Shotzen poured himself a generous glass, cursing his weakness. On his second glass, his curse became a resignation. On his third, it became a toast.

He wasn't sure if he imagined the knock at the door or not. He stopped in midgulp and held his breath, listening. The second knock gave him a start.

"Yes?" he answered, almost choking on his schnapps. The bottle was on the desk, empty now, but Shotzen placed it back into the nightstand.

"Menachem? It's Michael."

Shotzen pursed his lips—this was his disapproving look—and he opened the door. Thrist was dressed for Mass, Roman collar pristine and starched and green cassock meticulously ironed.

"May I come in?" he asked.

His tone didn't match his dress; it was dull and lacking conviction.

"Of course."

Shotzen stepped aside and allowed him entrance. He closed the door quietly and found Thrist staring at his glass of schnapps. It still held a finger or so.

"Not on account of my reprehensible behavior, I hope," Thrist said.

"My disease needs no provocation," Shotzen answered. He and Thrist had talked many times about alcoholism. In fact, Thrist was the only one whom Shotzen discussed it with.

"I am sorry, Menachem."

"Passion is a refreshing emotion to see in you," Shotzen replied. "In our many dialogues throughout the years I don't recall you ever yelling like that before."

"It was inexcusable, both the tone and the content."

"Nothing is inexcusable, as long as there is remorse. Apology accepted, Father."

Shotzen offered his hand, which the priest clasped in both of his.

"You are a dear friend."

"As are you."

Thrist sat on the bed and nodded at the manuscript. "Working on the memoirs?"

"Pathetic, no? There sits my life, never to be read by anyone under penalty of government execution."

"Time passes, Rabbi, whether we want it to or not. At least you have something to show for it."

"True. My legacy. How preferable it is to a wife and child."

Thrist's long face became longer. "Have you ever heard from Reba?"

"Not once since I granted her the get, the divorce. And why should I? Ha-Shem told the Jews to be fruitful and multiply, and I . . . I have no lead in my pencil. Between the sterility and the alcohol, it is no wonder she grew to hate me."

"You could have adopted."

Shotzen smiled. "I could have stopped drinking as well. I'd still have it all—her, my synagogue, my congregation—perhaps even my father would still be alive. He died of shame, you know, when I showed up at temple and read from the Torah drunk as drunk can be."

"We all have our crosses to bear."

"I so dislike that expression." Shotzen frowned. "But what of you, Father? No desire for children? Women? Adonai made you a man, He cannot then deny you a man's needs."

"God can bless the beasts and the children, because I never cared much for either," Thrist said with the barest of smiles.

"And sex?"

"I was created to serve God. Perhaps that is why he denied me any charisma whatsoever."

Shotzen laughed. "I'm happy that you're able to find your sense of humor, after this afternoon. If I were the devil, I would have done the same thing to test your faith."

Thrist nodded. "So you agree it is a possibility that Bub is the devil?"

"No. No more than I agree that Jesus was the *moshiach*. But when something has the appearance of Satan it would make sense for it to also imitate the demeanor."

Thrist absorbed this. "And if Bub indeed knew Christ?"

"The beauty of faith, Michael, is that there is no need for proof. Belief in a feeling is more powerful than belief in a fact. Ha-Shem could surely appear to the world at any time and squelch all doubts. But Adonai prefers faith."

"But what if Bub is a sign from God? Think of it, Rabbi. Nothing happens by accident. The Lord pre-ordains all. Bub was sent here, by God, as proof of His existence. I agree with the power of faith, but Christ also taught us the power of proof."

"Familiar argument. Christ was not the son of Adonai. Ha-Shem cannot be man. None of the prophecies were fulfilled."

"They were all fulfilled."

Shotzen reached for his glass and finished the schnapps. He was halfway to the nightstand when he remembered the bottle was empty.

"Let's stick with the current argument," Shotzen said. He sat on his bed, facing Father Thrist. "What do we know of ha-Satan?"

"The Adversary. First mentioned in Job 1:6. Taken to mean the opponent of God."

Shotzen nodded, his double chin jiggling. "But before that was Mal'ak, the shadow side of ha-Shem, turned to humanity because Adonai was too bright to be seen by mortals. Later, in Jubilees, it had become a separate entity. Mastema, the Accusing Angel."

"Dualism," Thrist added, "probably taken from Zoroaster. Ahriman, the Lord of Darkness. Zarathustra's concept of good and evil as opposing forces."

"Zoroaster's era is highly debated; he could have lived anywhere from the eighteenth century BC up until the seventh . . . five hundred years after Moses. Giving him the benefit of the doubt, he may have taken his ideas of deities from the Egyptians, Set and Ra, and prior to them, the Mesopotamians with Ereshkigal, the Queen of the Underworld. The first recorded mention of hell."

Thrist nodded. "Mmm-hmm. Predating Judaism. But none of these would be an accurate description of our Bub, so let's move ahead."

"Agreed. In Enoch, Lucifer, the Bearer of Light, was cast out of heaven because of lust. Or pride, in Enoch's second chronicle, or free will, according to Origen of Alexandria, or disobedience, or a war in heaven . . ."

"He has many names and many incarnations. Satan-el. Abaddon. Astarot. Rahab. Rofocale. Moloch. Leviathan. Baal-Beryth. Metatron . . ."

"Metatron is an archangel."

"He is referred to in Exodus, interpreted as the lesser Yahweh, ordering atrocities upon his chosen people. He could indeed be the first devil, the shadow side of God."

"You are misguided, as usual, but let's go on. There's Beliel, the Prince of Sheol. Also Baalzebub. Azazel. Mastema. Mammon. Belphegor. Kakabel. Lahash. Sammael . . ."

"Tartaruchus," Thrist continued. "Zophiel. Xaphan. Baresches. Biqa. Salmael . . ."

"I said Salmael."

"You said Sammael, not Salmael."

"They aren't the same?"

"Sammael is the Angel of Poison, Sumerian in origin. Salmael is a duke of hell, who each year calls for the annihilation of the chosen tribes of Israel."

"Ah! How could I have forgotten that one? So which of these nasty beings do you believe Bub to be?"

Thrist touched his chin. "I'm not sure. He may not be any of them. He may be all of them. Our current conceptions of Satan and hell began after Rome fell. The hysterical visions of Pope Gregory the Great in the sixth century. Bede's *Ecclesiastical History of England* in the year 731. *The Vision of Tundale* in 1149 offers a detailed look at the tortures of hell."

Shotzen was familiar with them all. "Much more influential was Dante," the rabbi added. "He gave us the description of the circles of hell and its demons in 1321. William Blake, Bosch, Breughel, Giotto, Memling—all famous religious painters who gave modern man images of a bat-winged, cloven-hooved, horned angel from hell."

"Martin Luther, John Calvin, Milton's *Paradise Lost* . . . they also helped hone the modern image. And Marlowe and Goethe's versions of Faust."

"Yes." Shotzen nodded, his chins bouncing. "The devil as an intellectual. Gentleman Jack. Old Nick. Old Scratch. Mephistopheles. Old Horny. Black Bogey. And now, he's an icon of pop culture." Shotzen shrugged. "He's in cartoons, movies, television shows, commercials . . ."

"Worshipped by thousands of schoolchildren in the form of rock music. Did I ever tell you about the time the archdiocese sent me to a Black Sabbath concert in the early 1970s?"

Shotzen sighed. "Yes. You've shown me your souvenir T-shirt. I doubt there is anything about you I don't know."

"Which brings us back to topic. What do we have here?"

The rabbi felt good. His mind was clear, clearer than

it had been without the liquor. Shotzen once read that booze was proof that G-d loves us and wants us to be happy. The Talmud also stated that we would be held accountable in the world to come for every permitted food and drink we have had the opportunity to eat yet not eaten. Why should being drunk be considered a sin?

"Both of our religions believe in angels, correct?" Thrist asked.

"Yes."

"And angels can fall from grace, just as man can."

"Natch. But Jews don't believe in a fiery hell where souls are tortured for eternity by red devils with pitchforks. Sheol, the pit, is nothing more than the absence of God. And most believe it doesn't last any longer than eleven hours."

Thrist held up his hands as if stopping an oncoming car. "Let's hold off on hell for a second. Is it possible for a fallen angel to visit Earth?"

"Perhaps. But demons aren't prevalent in Jewish midrash. They're usually allegorical. For example, Kesef, the demon who attacked Moses at Horeb, is the Hebrew word for *silver*."

Thrist sighed. "Menachem, open your mind for a moment. When President Carter recruited you for Samhain, you were publishing that underground newsletter—"

"*The Wandering Jew*," Shotzen said with pride.

"You were America's foremost expert in Judaic mysticism."

Shotzen thought back to those years, living like a hermit in a one-bedroom apartment, studying and interpreting ancient texts. The Kabbalah and Zohar, a little-known Jewish tome which revealed how to obtain peace on earth. The fourth-century Haggadah, a collection of Jewish legends and exegetical treatises. The Apocrypha, the hidden scriptures of the Torah compiled during the period of exile in Babylonia.

"Michael, you've read the same texts. Seven heavens and seven earths, with twenty-one layers of reality hooked together by wires. Gehenna, a continent on Arqa that encompasses the seven layers of hell—this is all allegory."

"Take a good look at Bub, Rabbi, and tell me he is allegory. You agree fallen angels could visit the Earth?"

"Perhaps."

"Then perhaps this fallen angel, this devil, would take on a familiar appearance, even if it is the appearance that mankind gave him."

"Go on."

"If Bub was truly alive at the time of Christ . . ."

"Again with Christ?"

"Christ as Messiah isn't the point. Can you believe that there was once a living breathing person named Jesus Christ?"

"There is mention of him in Josephus, so yes. But every knee has not bowed, there is no universal peace, the lion has not lain down with the lamb, nor does every tongue swear loyalty to the one true God."

Thrist frowned. "You're missing the point. You have conceded that devils exist, and that Jesus existed. Now the gospels of Matthew, Mark, and Luke all make the claim that Beelzebub tempted Jesus while he fasted in the desert. Luke 4:5 *Then the Devil took him up . . .*"

"Please." Shotzen grimaced. "We don't want to play the scripture-quoting game again."

"Fine. The point is, if Julius Caesar indeed taught Bub how to speak Latin, and Caesar died in 44 BC, isn't it conceivable that it was Bub who tempted Christ in the desert?"

"That was eighty years later."

"Demons don't age. He's been here for a hundred years and looks exactly the same. Can't you at least admit it could be possible?"

"Possible, yes. Probable, no. Whether Bub is a demon or something pretending to be a demon, it makes sense for him to act like a demon. Lies, deceptions, flattery, bribery, bargaining, tempting, wheeling and dealing; these are Satan's tricks. I contend he heard the name *Christ* and played on your reaction to it."

Thrist's wrinkles deepened and he pursed his lips. "So he also heard the name *Julius Caesar*?" he countered.

"He was found in 1906. Say he was buried in the 1800s, or even the 1700s or 1600s. He could have known the names of both Christ and Caesar. He spoke Maya when he woke up, and the Mayans were conquered by the Spanish, who were Christians, if I remember my history. That was one of the ways they justified the genocide of the indigenous South American people. They claimed it was Adonai's will to slaughter the heathens."

"Bah!" Thrist threw his hands in the air and stood

up. "The problem with you, Rabbi, is your insistence on the past to explain the present. Until you find some kind of precedent for Bub in one of your ancient mystic texts, you'll continue to deny what you see with your own eyes."

"What is more important, Father—what I see with my eyes.or what I feel with my heart?"

"You were born and raised a Jew, and that's why you are a Jew. It was what you were taught. I'm Catholic because that's what I was taught. But faith is not a substitute for proof, no matter how much you insist. Anyone with a high school education can argue that the world is more than six thousand years old. Yet that is what our religions teach. Atheists have attacked the Bible from all angles, finding one discrepancy after another. How does the church refute these claims of no God? Faith! But that doesn't matter anymore!"

Thrist was shouting now, his finger pointing at Shotzen.

"I could show the entire world the Bible, and only some will believe. But if I showed the entire world our friend Bub, ALL WOULD BELIEVE!"

Thrist sprung to his feet, his face bright red, breathing as if he'd just run a marathon.

Shotzen chose his words carefully. "Bub is not a sign from ha-Shem, Father."

"Yes, he is."

"Perhaps you need some time off, to rest. Can't you confer with the archdiocese?"

Thrist stormed over to the door and opened it. He turned before leaving. "I need time off," Thrist said, "like you need another drink." Thrist left, closing the door behind him.

Shotzen mulled it over.

"I cannot argue with logic like that," he said.

Then he left his room to get another bottle of schnapps.

# Chapter 12

D r. Julie Harker walked by Rabbi Shotzen in the Purple Arm, avoiding eye contact.

"Good evening, Dr. Harker," Shotzen said as he passed.

Harker didn't bother replying.

She was on her way to Purple 8 to find a movie to watch. Something to kill the evening. Shotzen, the doctor surmised, was coming back from Purple 6. That's where the liquor was kept. The rabbi had been holding something at his side, trying to conceal it. Trying to hide his secret.

Harker knew about having secrets.

She entered Purple 8 and hit the light. The room was arranged like a library, which made sense because it was essentially just that. But unlike Red 3, which held documents about Project Samhain, this was put here for the entertainment needs of the staff. Harker walked past the shelving units filled with fiction, past the several large magazine racks (the compound had subscriptions to fifty-eight different magazines, and issues were dropped off every few months with supplies), and past the archaic film collection (actual 16 mm films in cans on reels).

The video collection was one aisle over from film. It included the obsolete reel-to-reel format, which replaced kinescope for recording television from the '60s, and the racks of three-quarter-inch tapes, which became standard in the '70s. None of these interested Harker. She continued down the aisle until she reached the first commercially produced tapes for home use. Betamax.

Samhain's Beta selection was among the largest in the world. It may have also been the only remaining one in the world as well, since the Sony format had become obsolete years prior. There were over twenty thousand titles, arranged alphabetically and according to genre.

Harker didn't give the Action/Adventure section a glance. She also passed up Drama, Westerns, and the Adult aisle. Samhain had an ample pornography section, both magazine and video, much of it vintage and also worth a lot of money. The armed forces have known for many years that a man's sex drive can put him off task, so the easiest thing to do was cater to it. Harker had no interest in that.

She came to a stop at Comedy and found the films she was looking for immediately. *Poor Little Rich Girl*. *Curly Top*. *Baby, Take a Bow*. Her eyes began to mist. These were three of her all-time favorites.

Harker loved Shirley Temple. Loved her so much that she named her daughter Shirley. It had been the realization of a lifelong dream.

Dr. Julie Harker was born to be a mother. In her earliest memories, she'd always had a doll. Something to feed, and change, and talk to. Something that loved her as much as she loved it. In Julie's childhood her dolls were real babies, and she was the perfect mama.

She knew the psychology behind it. She knew the reasons she had such a strong maternal urge. Both of Julie's parents had been unfit. Alcoholics. Abusers. They never should have had children. Kids were supposed to be a joy. But in Harker's house, she had been a burden.

*"You're so fat and ugly,"* she could remember her father saying over and over. *"We'll never be able to marry you off. We'll be stuck with you forever."*

Not if Julie could help it. She knew she wasn't attractive, even if her parents hadn't reminded her of the fact constantly. Besides her weight problem and somewhat masculine features, Julie was painfully shy. She went through four years of high school without a friend or a date. But there was more to life than looks.

Julie Harker graduated at the top of her class and had her pick of colleges. Medical school was tough, and her poor people skills were an obstacle, but Julie's saving grace was her way with children. She joined a pediatric practice after her internship, but that was only half of the equation. She still needed to have a child of her own.

With the tapes nestled safely under her arm, Harker left Purple 8 and returned to her room. She put *Curly Top* in the VCR and hit REWIND. Then she turned off the lights and undressed.

*Samhain wasn't so bad*, she decided. Compared to that month of sheer hell she spent in prison, this place was almost pleasant. True, it would never be like it was, raising Shirley and Shirley.

Harker frowned as the memory returned. The first Shirley had been hers. Julie had planned it carefully. She'd considered artificial insemination, but was leery about the honesty of the donors. Several times she went to bars, hoping to get picked up, but the men who hit on her didn't have the kind of genes she wanted passed on to her child.

She finally settled on her neighbor's son. He was seventeen, gawky, and inexperienced, but from good stock. Her first attempts at seduction were laughable, but she lucked out one night when his parents weren't home, and after sharing a bottle of wine they did the deed.

Nine months later, Shirley was born. There were complications—profuse bleeding that resulted in a full hysterectomy—but Shirley was perfect. Her daughter was beautiful, actually physically beautiful, and Julie Harker was happy beyond all expectations.

For seven wonderful months, Harker raised Shirley. It was the greatest time in her life. Shirley healed every scar Harker had retained from her upbringing.

She was a dream come true.

The autopsy report called it SIDS. Sudden infant death syndrome. Sometime during the night, Shirley had stopped breathing. When Harker found her in the morning, she was blue.

Dr. Julie Harker thought she handled the situation very well. Being a pediatrician, she easily gained admission to the hospital's nursery. She'd just lost a child and could never give birth to another, so why shouldn't she have a replacement? Julie was born to be a mother. It wasn't fair that she was denied her birthright.

The second Shirley was actually named Jennifer. She

was four days old when Harker smuggled her out of the hospital. That same day she fled the country, finding work as a nurse in Canada. She'd had this Shirley for almost a year, raising her and loving her as much as she had the first Shirley, before the authorities found her.

They came for her while she was nursing. She saw the police car outside.

She knew they'd try to take Shirley away from her.

Harker couldn't allow that.

She ran out the back door, Shirley wrapped in a blanket, ran into the woods with the police right behind her. She was hysterical, frantic, and never saw the branch she tripped over.

When Harker fell, she landed on top of Shirley.

After being extradited to the United States, she was tried and convicted of kidnapping and second-degree murder.

Prison almost destroyed Julie. She'd lost two kids in a ten-month period, and the grief consumed her. Prison was worse than school, with the teasing and harassment. Julie was attacked many times, and her mental state flip-flopped between constant grief and terror.

President Reagan's call was a blessing.

Harker had been in the prison infirmary, recovering from a botched suicide attempt. Reagan had made it very clear that he didn't like Harker, or the things she'd done, and didn't care one way or the other what happened to her. But he offered Harker a choice. She could either carry out her life sentence in prison, or at a fully equipped secret facility in New Mexico, looking after the daily health of a research team.

Harker made the obvious decision. The VCR stopped

and Harker pressed PLAY, then she curled up in bed to watch the video.

Yes, Samhain was a prison of sorts, and yes, she would probably die here, but life could be worse. And maybe, now that Bub was talking, the project would end. Maybe, after over twenty years of service, Harker would get a reprieve. There was always hope.

"Hello, Shirley," Harker said as the movie began, the tears starting to flow.

"Sing a song for Mama."

# CHAPTER 13

After her shower, Sun put on a pair of blue jeans and a snug black top with a V-neck. She spent ten minutes on her hair and makeup, and another two minutes searching for perfume before she remembered she didn't own any.

"It's just a game of pool," she said to her reflection.

Then she brushed her teeth.

Purple 5 had more to offer than just pool. It was a fully equipped game room, complete with darts, foosball, Ping-Pong, and an old Asteroids arcade game. Andy was at the table, rolling a cue across the slate to make sure it wasn't warped. He wore tan Dockers and a striped shirt, untucked with the sleeves rolled up. His hair was still wet from the shower.

Looking at him, Sun felt her stomach do little flip-flops. She silently cursed her hormones. This wasn't the time, or the place, to start a relationship.

*It doesn't have to be a relationship*, the little voice in her head told her. *It can just be sex.*

She told the little voice to shut up.

"What's your game?" Andy asked. "Eight ball or nine ball?"

"I prefer nine. Lag for the break?"

"Sure. Double or nothing, right?"

"Right. Two thousand dollars."

"Or two kisses."

Andy winked at her.

After selecting a stick from the rack and chalking the tip, Sun stood next to Andy and they both placed a cue ball on the table. Lagging was an art form. The trick was to bounce the cue ball off the far rail and have it return back. The one who got it closest to the near rail without touching won the break. Sun's parents had a pool table, and she grew up with the game. She hadn't played in a few years, but once she slid the stick onto the bridge of her fingers it all came back to her.

"Ready?"

Andy nodded.

Sun won the lag.

"You're a few inches short," she teased.

"I'm not sure how I should reply to that."

Sun used the triangle to rack the balls, leaving a perfect nine-ball diamond pattern on the table. She put her whole body into the break, getting good separation and sinking the four.

"Nice," Andy said. "Where did you learn to break like that?"

"I played the pro circuit for a while."

Sun lined up the one ball and flashed Andy a grin.

Andy said, "You're kidding, right?"

She banked the one into a corner pocket, leaving herself in position on the two.

"Most people think pool is a man's game. It's not. Football—running, throwing, hitting each other. That's a man's game."

Sun put away the two ball, setting up an easy shot on the three. She leaned over a bit farther than necessary, enjoying his eyes on her body.

"Pool," Sun continued. "Pool is all about angles and finesse and thinking ahead. Carefully plotting actions and executing them with precision." The three went in with a whisper, and the five was all lined up.

"Visualizing what you want, and getting it."

She pocketed the five and also put down the seven, crippled along the side pocket.

"It's like seduction," Sun said. "Something that a woman can do much better than a man."

"Is this a date?" Andy asked. "This is a date, right? I mean, not a going-out kind of date, because we're not out, but we've got this man-woman thing going on here, right?"

Sun smiled at him. "Why put labels on it? We're just two consenting adults, enjoying a two-thousand-dollar game of pool."

"We should really play foosball. Now, that's my game. I did that as a living, for a while. Hustling foosball."

"Good money?" Sun asked, eyeing the six.

"Yeah. I used to bring in four, five bucks a night."

"Sounds like a fun way to spend your childhood."

"Childhood? I did it until I turned thirty." Sun laughed, missing her shot.

"Okay, stand back," Andy said. "Now you'll see why they call me Fast Andy."

Andy took careful aim at the six ball, and with an easy, steady stroke, missed it completely and scratched the cue into the corner pocket.

"Because you lose so fast?" Sun asked.

Andy's eyes twinkled with the challenge. "I'd be winning if you weren't wearing that tight blouse."

"So if I took the blouse off, you'd be more focused?"

*I'm actually flirting*, Sun thought. It felt nice. Really nice.

She eyed the table. Andy was leaning against the rail, in the way of her shot.

"You wanna move, so I can win my two thousand dollars?"

"Not really, no."

Sun walked over to him and put her arms around his waist, still holding her cue.

"I knew this was a date," Andy said. "Right? Am I right?"

Sun placed the cue ball on the table and drew her stick back, shooting behind him. In one fluid movement she banked off the six and sunk the nine, winning the game.

"Nice shot." Andy looked down at her, putting his hands on her shoulders.

"Thanks." She let go of the cue, but her arms remained around his waist.

Their eyes locked. "I take cash and personal checks."

"I want to be honest with you. I only have four dollars to my name."

Andy's lips parted slightly. She could feel his heart through his ribs, and it seemed to beat a little louder. Though he had the barest hint of stubble on his face, Sun could smell aftershave. She moved her hand up his sides, feeling the muscles in his back, thinking that she hadn't touched a man like that in so long.

Sun stared at him, wondering if her pupils were as wide as his. She waited for him to move in for the kiss, unsure what she would do if he tried.

Neither of them moved.

The moment lingered, then passed. Sun dropped her hands and turned away.

"So foosball is your game?" she said, trying to sound upbeat.

"I'm supernatural at foosball. I'm ranked third in the world."

"Double or nothing?"

"You're on."

Sun beat him in four minutes.

"There's got to be something you can win at," she said after the final goal.

"Football," Andy said. "That was my game. All the running and the hitting. It's not a real sport unless you wear mouth protection. Would you like to see where I got kicked in the head with cleats?"

"How about Asteroids?" Sun said. "I stink at Asteroids."

Andy stunk worse. Sun played her last ship with her eyes closed, and still annihilated his score.

"What are we up to?" Andy asked. "Eight grand?"

"There's got to be something you can win at." Sun looked around the rec room, trying to find something she wasn't good at.

"How about arm wrestling?"

Sun declined. Andy looked strong, but if she beat him at arm wrestling she didn't think his ego would ever recover.

"How about Scrabble in Portuguese?" Andy suggested.

"Board games are in Purple 10."

As they walked out of the rec room, Sun noticed Andy's limp.

"Did you pull a muscle?"

"Blister." Andy made a face. "From not wearing socks."

"Let me see it."

"It's ugly."

"I'm a big girl."

Andy kicked off his shoe and peeled down his sock. It *was* ugly, covering much of his heel, red and inflamed.

"We need to dress that. Come on."

Sun took Andy's hand and led him into Yellow 6, the medical supply room.

She sat him on the padded examination table and removed his shoe and sock.

"Don't you need to muzzle me first?" Andy asked.

Sun grinned. "Have you had your shots?"

"I'm not sure. Let me check my tags."

Sun opened the closet and found some gauze, tape, hydrogen peroxide, and burn ointment on the well-stocked shelves.

"Are you sure you're qualified to do this?" Andy asked.

"I think I can manage."

"Remember, this is a blister. Not a neutering."

"I'll try to keep that in mind."

She dabbed peroxide on some gauze and cleaned the inflamed skin.

"So why did you become a vet?" Andy asked. "No desire to practice on people at all?"

Sun tried to think of something flippant, but nothing came to mind.

"Not that I'm knocking vets," Andy said quickly. "But it seems like you'd make a great MD."

She squirted on some ointment, but her good mood deflated like a leaky tire.

The memories came back. Memories she'd been trying for years to suppress.

"Sun? You okay?"

Could she tell him? Would that scare him away?

"Sun?"

"I . . . I used to be a doctor," she said. "A human doctor."

Sun taped on the bandage and waited for a response. None came. The silence stretched.

"If you want to talk about it," Andy said finally, "I want to know."

He reached down and took her hand. She gripped it, tight, and sat on the table next to him. The words, unspoken for so long, began to tumble out of her.

"I did my internship at Johns Hopkins, began my residency there. I was on the tail end of a twenty-hour shift; there was an apartment fire and we'd been working without a break for eight hours. A women came in with abdominal pain to the right iliac fossa. Her tongue was coated, she had foetor oris, high temp, vomiting; text book appendicitis. Hers was ready to rupture. We prepped her for a laparotomy, emptied her stomach with a nasogastric, and I scrubbed for surgery."

Sun could remember how tired she was, and how

determined that she wouldn't let fatigue get in the way of her job. The woman was Caucasian and overweight, but in a way she reminded Sun of her own mother. Even though her pain was severe she'd been stoic.

"I'd done a dozen appendectomies. It was a simple operation. I made a gridiron incision through McBurney's point, divided the mesoappendix, used a purse-string suture in the caecum. Then I closed her up and she was discharged a few days later."

Sun swallowed, held Andy's hand even tighter.

"She bounced back the next week. Temperature of a hundred and five. Peritonitis. Her peritoneal cavity was filled with pus and fecal matter." Sun took a deep breath. "My purse-string suture had opened. I hadn't tied it off. Her lower intestine emptied out into her abdominal cavity."

Sun turned away from Andy, stared at a spot on the wall.

"She didn't make it," she said softly.

Sun had been the one who opened her up the second time. The woman had come in and asked for Sun by name. Had trusted her to help.

"You lost your job," Andy said.

"The review committee was unanimous. Any first-year intern could have done that suture. I screwed up. The Maryland medical board revoked my license. The board had been taking some bad hits in the media, and they made an example out of me. I had over a hundred thousand dollars in student loans, and loss of my license meant I'd never pay them back. So I filed bankruptcy.

"I became a vet by studying at home. Not too big a leap, really. Animals and humans share a lot of the same medical problems. Then I met Steven, we got married, and he died, leaving me with another load of bills. I couldn't file bankruptcy again; you had to wait seven years. So I applied for a grant under a false name to study lions in Africa. Mainly to hide from my creditors."

Andy said, "Why did you leave Africa?"

"They found out I wasn't who I said I was and pulled my funding. I applied for citizenship in South Africa but was denied. When I was deported back to the US I had about ten different groups trying to sue me. That's when the President stepped in. I think he found me through the US embassy in South Africa. I made the headlines a few times while I was there, fighting for citizenship. He offered me a deal: Samhain for ten years or until the project ended, whichever came first. All of my debts would disappear if I agreed. Of course, I took it."

"And here you are."

"And here I am."

Andy put his hand on her cheek. "I'm glad you're here," he said.

She looked up at him, saw the warmth, and hugged him.

"Thanks for fixing up my foot."

Sun snorted. "Good thing you didn't need stitches."

"We all make mistakes, Sun. The hard part is forgiving ourselves."

Sun pursed her lips. "Her name was Madeline. She had a husband. A son. She was only sixty. I went to the funeral."

"That took guts."

"Her son spat in my face. It made me feel a little better."

Andy said, "I could spit on you now, if you want."

"Maybe later. Let's go feed the demon."

They left Sun's room and headed for the Octopus. Race was there, hunched over a computer. He looked up when he noticed Sun and Andy.

"How is the speech lesson coming?"

"Great," Andy answered. "Like teaching kindergarten, except snack time is messier."

"So he'll be ready to talk tomorrow morning?"

"I don't see why not."

Race beamed. "Excellent," he said.

The general turned back to his monitor. Race always wore his good-ole-boy attitude like cowboys wore hats, but Sun hadn't seen him so genuinely pleased before. The man looked ten years younger.

Sun and Andy took the Orange Arm to Orange 12. Andy was more help in procuring a sheep this time. He held the cereal, assisted in putting on the harness, and Sun taught him that the most effective way to startle sheep wasn't yelling "Boo!" It was clapping your hands.

"I can't get enough of this earthy smell," Andy said. "We should bottle it and sell it to urbanites."

"Where there's a wool, there's a way." Andy made a show of rolling his eyes.

"You never told me," Sun said, "about that problem you were having with the hieroglyphics on the capsule."

"I'm still stuck on it. You ready for a mini lecture?"

Sun nodded. She was happy to be talking about something other than her broken past.

"Okay. You see, it's known that glyphs are based on spoken language, but for a long time hieroglyphic Maya was thought to be logographic. Each picture was a word. But the current view is that it was a phonetic system; glyphs stand for sounds, like our own alphabet. So scholars have had to reevaluate everything. To make it even harder, current Maya language is filled with bits of Spanish, so to understand the ancient language, the language of the glyphs, you can't really use modern Maya."

"So how do you decipher it?" Sun asked.

"Lots of ways. I have a few computer programs, I check the work of other scholars, I find similar references in previously translated passages. A lot of it is basic logic. Once you understand the sentence structure of a language, it's like a cryptogram in a crossword puzzle book. You just look for the context clues."

Sun led the sheep over to the scale pen. "So what has the great translator perplexed?"

"There are several references to a *tuunich k'iinal*. *The hot rock*. I don't know what that means."

"Volcano?"

Andy shook his head. "That's a different word."

"Coals? For cooking?"

"No. A cooking pit is a *piib*. Different glyphs. There's also reference to Kukulcán. He's a flying warrior god who came from 'over the water.' Sort of the Mayan version of the Aztec Quetzalcoatl."

"Could that be Bub?"

"That's what I'm thinking. Quetzalcoatl means *feathered serpent*. Bub doesn't have feathers, but he does fly, and he could qualify as a serpent. The thought that ancient people were offering our Bub human sacrifices is a little unnerving. More than a hundred thousand were killed to satisfy Kukulcán's lust for blood."

"I should have paid more attention in history class," Sun said.

Sun finished jotting down the sheep's specs on the chart and they led it out of Orange 12 and down the hallway. Race was no longer in the Octopus.

"What's your impression of our General Race?" Andy asked, holding open the Red Arm door.

"He's good at manipulating people. I wonder why he's here though. The army only has so many generals. Why stick one underground for forty years?"

"Something to do with his wife?" Andy suggested. "Dr. Belgium told me about her disease."

"I don't think so. She didn't become symptomatic until a few years ago."

"Maybe we should ask him. He seems honest. Well, as honest as the military can get. What's Dr. Harker's problem?"

"You noticed it too?"

"Yeah. The lady seems to have a large assortment of bugs up her ass."

Sun punched in the code for the first gate. "She has problems relating to people, I think."

"And Dr. Belgium . . . don't get me wrong. I like the

guy. But he seems to be one slice short of a sandwich himself."

"Yeah," Sun agreed. "And the holies. Odd ducks, both of them. Father Thrist's little outburst didn't wear well with the Roman collar."

Andy said, "Maybe we're not all here because we're perfect for the job."

"Okay. Then, why?"

"Well, you didn't have a choice. I really didn't either. The President saw fit to mention a little problem that I would have with the IRS if I didn't cooperate. Maybe everyone here is stuck as well. Think about it. Not just everyone would give up their life, families, friends, possessions, to live down here, even though Bub is an interesting subject. Only those people with nothing to lose." Sun punched in the code for the second gate and thought it over.

"It's so American," she said.

"How so?"

"Here is the most top secret, and possibly the most important, project the world has ever known. And who's running it? Screwups and criminals."

Andy smiled, closing the gate behind them. "Well, it's been a hundred years, and no problems yet."

"Does that mean we should be encouraged?" Sun asked, "Or be worried that the problems are overdue?"

"What's the worst that can happen?"

"Bub kills us all, escapes, and destroys the world."

"That takes some of the pressure off," Andy said.

He opened the door to Red 14. Dr. Belgium was fiddling with the DVD, trying to shove a disc in.

"It helps if you turn it on," Sun suggested.

"Suuuuun," Bub said. "Aaaaaandy."

Sun almost backed up. It still freaked her out a little that something so big and ugly could talk.

Andy said, "Hello, Bub. How was your nap?"

"Huuuuungry. Need sheeeeep."

"Are sheep what you'd normally eat?" Sun asked. "Before you were able to talk, I could only guess."

"Sheeeeeep are goooood."

Sun had opened the small door and pushed the sheep through. Bub snatched it up in his claw and quickly snapped its neck.

"Bub, sometimes when you eat the sheep, you kill it and bring it back to life," Sun said. "How do you do this?"

Bub continued to twist the sheep's head until it came off like a bottle cap.

He sucked on the neck stump, tilting the body up as if it were a giant beer.

"Seeeeeeeecret," Bub said, gurgling from the liquid in his mouth. Some of the blood ran out of the corner and matted his chest hair.

"Can you do it now?" Sun asked.

"Yesssss."

Bub held the sheep's headless carcass tightly to his chest. A minute passed, and then the animal's legs began to twitch and buck. Bub dropped it to the ground, and the sheep took off in a sprint and rammed full speed into the Plexiglas barrier. It hit with a large crash, smearing the glass with blood.

The sheep righted itself, shook, then ran again, this time barreling into one of the artificial trees.

Bub croaked with baritone laughter. The sheep's head, still in his claw, opened and closed its mouth in silent protest, its eyes darting back and forth.

"Baa-aaa," Bub said, imitating the sheep's sound. He held the head in front of him like a hand puppet. "Baa-aaa."

Sun had to steel herself and hoped she hadn't lost composure. A glance at Dr. Belgium found him ashen, and Andy had a look on his face that predicted vomiting.

"Thank you, Bub," Sun said in metered tones. "That's enough." .

Bub tossed the sheep's head into his mouth like a piece of popcorn. It continued to squirm while being munched on. His other claw shot out and grazed the runaway sheep body. Its belly unzipped, intestines winding out like a fire hose. The demon grabbed a handful and shoveled them in.

"Goooood," Bub said.

"I've got to stop coming here during mealtime," Andy said, clutching his stomach.

The demon cocked his head to the side, appearing confused.

"Are you sick, Aaaaaandy?"

"No, Bub. It's just that your eating habits are a little . . . distressing."

"You wanted to seeeeee."

Andy was looking greener and greener, so Sun answered. "We want to learn from you, Bub, but we have a culture gap. Some things that you do aren't done in our culture, so we don't know how to react to them."

Bub jumped up to the Plexiglas, holding the sheep. Sun hadn't seen him jump before. The leap was over fifteen feet, and Bub landed hard enough to make the ground rumble. He yanked off one of the sheep's hind legs and held it to his chest. It began to twitch and then bend at the knee back and forth.

"Eeeeeach part is aliiiiive," Bub said.

"The little parts are called cells."

"Cells," Bub repeated. "When the body dieeeeees, the cells still live for some tiiiiiime. I can maaaaake them think the body is still aliiiiiiive."

"How?" Sun asked.

Bub held the twitching leg up for Sun to see. It was no longer bleeding—in fact, it looked as if it had healed.

"God," Bub said. "I have pooooowers from God."

Sun asked, "Can we have that leg so we can study it?"

Bub cocked his head to the side and appeared to think it over.

"Yessssssss." Bub walked over to the sheep door and squatted, waiting. Sun took a breath and forced herself to move. She unlatched the door and Bub thrust the leg through it, stump first. Sun held it with both hands. It was heavy, and she felt the muscle fibers in the thigh contract and expand, exactly as if the sheep were alive.

"Ressurrrrrrrrrrection," Bub said.

After he said it, the sheep's leg contracted and the hoof missed her head by inches. On reflex she dropped it, and it flopped around on the floor like a landed fish.

Bub laughed.

Sun fought the surrealism of the scene and bent over, this time grabbing the leg by the hoof. She walked it over to Dr. Belgium, who was watching the whole episode slack-jawed.

"Can you take some blood samples? Tissue and marrow too?"

Belgium seemed reluctant to touch the leg, but consented and held it by the hoof as Sun had. The leg jerked wildly, and Belgium dropped it. He and Sun bent down for it, and Belgium got a firmer, two-handed grip.

"I'll be in Red 5," Belgium said, indicating the lab. He walked off, holding the leg at arm's length of his body.

"Do you want moooore? I could maaake the organs moooove."

Andy's hand clamped over his face and he went from green to white.

"Thank you, Bub," Sun said. "There's no need for any more right now."

Bub nodded, then went back to eating.

"You okay?" Sun asked, rubbing Andy's back.

"I'm becoming a vegetarian," he replied.

Bub's munching sounds in the background made Andy gag again.

"Do we have any children's videos on table manners?" Sun asked.

Andy gave her a weak grin.

Behind the Plexiglas barrier, Bub grinned as well.

# CHAPTER 14

"I need more Internet tiiiiiiiiime," Bub told Dr. Belgium when he returned from Red 5. Sun and Andy had left.

"I don't think that's a good idea," Belgium answered. His Adam's apple wobbled up and down in his throat.

"I muuuuuust learn moooore."

Belgium laughed, high-pitched and near hysterical. "You're joking! You went through the entire website of the *Encyclopaedia Britannica* in an hour and a half. You can process information faster than it loads."

"Open the dooooor," Bub said. "Let meeeee ooooooout."

"I don't think . . ."

"I'll tell Raaaaace," Bub interrupted.

"What? Are you blackmailing me?"

"Fraaaaaank," Bub said softly, the trace of a purr in his voice. "I need more tiiiiiime to seeeeequence my geeeeenome." Belgium said nothing.

"Don't you want to leeeeave heeeere, Fraaaaank?"

Belgium pictured himself, in a boat on a lake, a rod in his hand, the sun in his eyes. He hadn't fished since he was in grade school, but right now it seemed like the most appealing thing in the world.

He hit the code to Bub's door. It rose pneumatically and the demon folded his wings and left his habitat for the second time that day. He squatted next to Dr. Belgium and gave him a pat on the head, which Frank recoiled from.

"Gooooood, Fraaaaaank."

Frank ducked down, away from the hand. The claws grazed his scalp. It was like a hairbrush made of needles.

"You maaaay goooooo," Bub said, lumbering over to the Cray computer.

Belgium squatted and stayed put, watching as Bub hunched over his workstation. The keyboard was like a pocket calculator to Bub, the monitor must have been like looking at a digital watch. Belgium laughed. It reminded him of an old cartoon, where an elephant moved into a mouse's house, dwarfing everything to comic proportions.

Using the tip of his pinky claw, Bub accessed the ISP and began to surf the World Wide Web. Samhain's Internet connection was fiber-optic. The load times were instantaneous. Bub's hand became a blur, as did the monitor. It seemed impossible that Bub could be absorbing all of that information that fast, but Belgium knew that he was.

He tried to think of all the reasons this was bad. Why shouldn't Bub be allowed to learn about the world he was in? Think of the things he could teach us, the bridges he could gap, the mysteries he could solve. Bub could be the key to solving all of the world's problems: disease, hunger, war, death. Bub could create a utopia.

Or he could destroy everything.

But what would be the point in that? Bub had shown

himself to be cooperative, and interested in humans. There would be no point in his using the world's knowledge for bad things.

Belgium laughed again, at the memory of the cartoon elephant drinking out of the mouse's tiny teacup.

"This is all insane," he said to himself.

Then he closed his eyes and imagined sitting on that boat, the sun warm on his face.

# CHAPTER 15

The alarm went off at 7:00 A.M., but Race was already up. He hadn't slept much; it seemed that every time he got comfortable his mind woke him up, offering images of combat and war games.

Soon. Very soon.

He hopped out of bed and did a quick round of calisthenics, working his muscles, feeling the sweat and increased respiration, enjoying it more than usual. Healthy body, healthy mind. He finished and hit the shower.

He was tempted to wake everyone up, get this show on the road, but restraint was as important a leadership quality as action. Race dressed in some chinos and a green crewneck and left his room for the mess hall. He made a large bowl of pancake batter and added two cans of blueberries to it while a pat of butter melted on the skillet. Helen had taught him how to make pancakes, years ago. He'd always hoped one day she would teach him other dishes. That was becoming more of a possibility with every passing day.

He made six cakes for himself and ate them with honey. Then he made twenty more with the rest of the batter for whoever wanted them. The thought amused him; a brigadier general making blueberry pancakes for his troops.

Even more amusing; the secretary of defense making blueberry pancakes.

Race chuckled to himself. He put two more pancakes on his plate and put the rest in the refrigerator. He then poured a glass of milk, and took that and the plate out of the mess hall, through the Octopus, and into Yellow 1.

"Who are you?" his wife asked. "What am I doing here? Why am I tied to this bed? Are you a doctor?"

"I'm your husband, dear."

He set the plate and glass on the nightstand and changed her diaper while fielding her usual questions. She had some diaper rash, and he applied ointment as she protested between sobs. Then he untethered her hands and helped her sit up.

"Oh, Race, how did we get so old?" she cried.

He checked her for bedsores and found none; Harker was good at her job in that respect.

"Can you get up, sit at the table for breakfast?"

She sniffled and nodded. Race put his arm around her waist and walked with her to the small breakfast bar on the other side of the room. Her legs were wobbly things, incapable of supporting her fragile body without his help.

"Remember how we used to cut the rug?" Race said, grinning.

Her teary eyes shone for a moment.

"You were quite the dancer," Helen said.

"You too. I was the envy of every CO on the base with a pretty thing like you at my side."

He sat her in a chair and fetched the pancakes and milk.

"Blueberry pancakes," Helen said. "Just like I make."

He helped her cut them up and she tried to feed herself until the chorea hit, her arm knocking the plate across the table. Race held her until it passed, then gave her some milk.

"Dr. Harker mentioned that Bub was speaking," Helen said.

This startled Race. Helen usually couldn't remember anything that happened within the last forty years.

"He is. I'm going to run the Roosevelt Book by him today."

"Then we can go home," Helen said.

Race's eyes welled up. He'd put up so many emotional defenses over the years it was rare when something slipped through.

"Yes, my love. Then we can go home."

Helen gave him a small kiss on the lips.

"Walk me back to bed, dear. I think I'll watch some television."

Race carried her back to bed and retied her arms. The television remote control was bolted to the frame under her right hand. He pressed the POWER button for her. Helen flipped channels until she found a game show, and Race kissed her forehead and left with the plate and glass. He found Father Thrist in the Octopus, typing away on a computer.

"Good morning, Father."

"Good morning, General. Today is the big day."

"It is. Hopefully I'll get all of it done. It depends how talkative he is."

"Yes. I would also like some time with Bub. When you've finished, of course. The President has granted me that."

"Of course, Father. You can sit in on my interrogation as well."

Thrist nodded and turned back to his terminal. Race returned to his room, Blue 1, and picked up his phone. He hit the intercom code and spoke into the receiver.

"Good morning. There are blueberry pancakes in the fridge in limited supply, first come, first serve. I would like everyone to meet in the mess hall by oh-nine-hundred hours. Today is the big day."

He hung up the phone and forced himself to concentrate. His focus should have been on the game, but his mind was already on the victory party. First would be a briefing with the President, of course. Before he accepted any appointments, Race wanted to take a vacation. See how much his country had changed over the last four decades. If things went according to his plan, Helen could accompany him. She always wanted to go to Hollywood. How could he say no?

The President would undoubtedly also want his input on the future of Samhain. Depending on the answers Race got from Bub, there were three possible avenues to take. Keep Bub a secret and let the project continue, end the project and go public, or end the project and terminate Bub. Samhain was home to Race, but it was a foster home, and he wouldn't miss it in the least. Race would help train his replacement, or he would talk with reporters, or he would push the buttons in Yellow 4 that would detonate Bub's implanted explosives. Whatever the President wanted, Race didn't care. It wasn't a soldier's job to care. But a forty-year tour was long enough. Race wanted out.

He picked up the Roosevelt Book from the dresser and tucked it in his armpit. When he arrived at the mess hall Andy and Sun were already there, digging into his pancakes.

"Good morning," Race beamed. "How's the grub?"

"Good, thanks," Andy said.

Sun nodded her approval; she was chewing. Race noted their close proximity to each other, one that implied intimacy, and thought of how times had changed. Race had dated Helen for six weeks before even getting a kiss. These two had known each other for two days and it was apparent they had something going on.

"How's our permanent resident?" Race asked. "Is he ready to be questioned?"

"He had breakfast earlier," Sun said. "He's talking up a storm."

Andy agreed. "His grasp of language is remarkable. It's as if he's been speaking it his whole life. By the time we were done with him last night, his English was better than mine."

"Great. We'll begin after everyone has breakfast. Good morning, Frank."

Dr. Belgium entered Green 2 wearing the rumpled lab coat he'd had on the night before. His face was stubbly and the bags under his eyes were large enough to pack.

"Morning," he mumbled.

"You look like hell, Doctor. Do you feel okay?"

"Headache. Didn't sleep well."

"Let Dr. Harker take a look at you later," Race said. "Good morning, Rabbi."

"Shalom," Rabbi Shotzen said. He sat down at the table. "So the demon is speaking English, yes?"

"Like a native," Andy said.

"And everyone thinks he learned an entire language overnight? No one is suspicious that he may have known English all along and has been feigning ignorance?"

"Have some pancakes, Rabbi." Race gave the holy man a pat on the back.

"Thank you, General, I will. You used the kashered cast iron skillet, yes? Good. Remember; we must take everything the demon says with two grains of salt. Bub may not be a fallen angel, but he's imitating one, and all of hell's angels lie. Now, if someone could pass me a plate maybe?"

Father Thrist came in next, and Race noted that he and Shotzen avoided each other. Thrist waved off on the pancakes and opted for black coffee instead. Dr. Harker was the last to arrive. Race wished her a good morning and suggested she examine Dr. Belgium after breakfast. Harker grunted acknowledgment and instead of pancakes she made herself some buttered toast.

*Quite a dysfunctional little family*, Race thought. It had always been like that, in its many incarnations dating back to 1968. Not like the army. On the battlefield, men were close-knit with strong bonds. It came from functioning as a unit, rather than as individuals.

The dozens of specialists that had lived at Samhain since its inception had never been like that. This motley bunch would last two minutes in combat. Good thing it would never have to be proven.

"If everyone is ready, I'd like to lay down some ground rules," Race said.

All eyes were on him. He stood up to project better.

"I'm sure we all have things to ask Bub, and everyone will get private time with him, I promise. But the first order of business is to get all of the questions in this book answered. If we go off on tangents, it'll take forever. We need to stay focused. I'm not going to ask you all to zip your lips, but I am asking for the extraneous questions to be kept to the barest minimum. I also ask that we remain united in our opinion. I've done interrogations before, and group numbers give us the psychological advantage. But if there's dissension, Bub could possibly play on that."

"What is our opinion, General?" Father Thrist asked.

"We haven't formed one yet. But we can't have any in-group bickering in front of Bub. Dr. Belgium, is the video operational?"

"Hmm? Oh, yes yes yes. I just put in a new DVD-R a little bit ago. It's good for six hours."

"Good. Remember, people, we're going into this treating Bub as a source of information. He's like a gold vein that we are trying to dig up. Personal opinions, preconceptions, whether you think he's the Antichrist or just a nice guy . . . file it all away. Our object is to get these questions answered."

"What if we figure out the demon is lying?" Rabbi Shotzen said.

"If Bub appears to be lying, or intentionally evasive, we'll have to regroup and approach the situation differently. But please let me be the judge of that. Any other questions?"

There were none. Race made eye contact with each member of the group, to make sure he was understood on all counts.

"Okay," he said, grinning broadly. "Let's go rattle the gates of hell."

# Chapter 16

"The gang's all heeeeeeere." Bub grinned his horrible grin.

No one laughed. Andy couldn't speak for the rest of the group, but he was very much awed by Bub. Not only by the demon's physical presence—which was substantial—or his apparent powers over the dead, but how quickly he learned. Bub mastered English in just a day, to the point where he was comfortable making jokes. That kind of genius, and all it implied, almost made the linguist speechless.

"We have questions, Bub," Race said. "Questions we've been waiting a very long time to have answered."

"You may aaaaaask," Bub said.

He squatted on his haunches in front of the Plexiglas, to the right of the large bloodstain the headless sheep had made the previous day. It had turned brown and begun to flake. Andy tried not to look at it.

Race sat in a chair facing Bub. The rest of the group formed a semicircle behind him. Andy sat next to Sun, the holies were on opposite ends, Dr. Harker sat way in the back, and Dr. Belgium stood, pacing back and forth like he was the one in the cage.

"Let's begin with your background," Race said. He

opened up the old book in his lap but didn't look at it. "You were found buried eighty feet in the ground in the Culebra Cut in Panama, one hundred years ago. How did you get there?" Bub tilted his head slightly and appeared to think about it, his elliptical eyes flicking left, then right.

"I was in a comaaaaaaa. My people thought I was deaaaaaad."

"Who were your people?"

"The Kanjobalán Mayaaaaaaa. We lived in a city called Coooooopán."

"Copán is in Honduras," Andy said, surprising himself by talking—he'd wanted to remain neutral and simply observe. "That's eight hundred miles away from Panama. Why were you buried eight hundred miles from Mayan boundaries?"

"I do not knooooow."

"How long were you with the Maya?" Race asked.

"Threeeeeee hundred years."

"And before that, you lived where?"

"Many plaaaaaces. Across the waaaaaater."

"How did you travel from place to place?" Race said.

Bub's wings unfurled behind him as if they were spring-loaded. They opened with the sound of a belt being snapped.

"I caaaaaan fly."

"Over the oceans?" Sun asked. "Carrying your capsule?"

"I'm strooooong." Bub's pectoral muscles twitched and bounced. It reminded Andy of a bodybuilder showing off.

"If you were in all of these places," Race asked, "why isn't there any record of you?"

Bub grinned his crooked grin and folded his wings behind his back. "There isssss," Bub said. "Look at hisssstory. Many deeeeemons."

"There are more of you?" Race asked.

"Yesssssss."

"What happened to them?"

"I don't knoooooow."

"Where did you come from," Race said, "originally?"

Bub's eyes took on a faraway cast.

"From liiiiiiiight," Bub said. "From light, to darknessssssss."

"What light?"

"Heavaaaaaaaaan. I was caaaaast out."

"Cast into hell?" Father Thrist asked, his voice quavering. "Incredible."

"Yeah, incredible," Sun repeated. But she didn't sound convinced. Andy wasn't sure if he was convinced either, but he forced himself to keep an open mind.

"Explain how the world began," Race said.

"God created everything. He created angels to be messengers between Hiiiiim and maaaaankiiiind."

"Why were you cast out?" Thrist asked.

"There was a . . . disagreeeeeeement."

Rabbi Shotzen made a snorting sound. Andy guessed him to be skeptical as well.

"What about evolution?" Race asked.

"Evolution is like planting seeeeeeeeds. When there was enough growth, God added maaaaaan."

"Like the Garden of Eden," Thrist said, looking up from his notes.

"What is your name?" Race asked, leaning closer to the Plexiglas. "Your true name?"

Bub seemed to grow. He stood up to his full height, stretched out his talons, swelled up his chest. When he spoke, it was deep and loud.

"I am the Prince of the Poooooower of Air. The Draaaagon of Dawn. Son of the Mooooorning and Bearer of Liiiiight. The naaame most know me by is Luuuuuuuuucifer."

He settled back down on his haunches. Andy realized he was clenching his fist so tightly his hand had fallen asleep. He shook it, wincing at the tingles of pain as the blood came back in.

"Were you the one who tempted Christ in the desert?" Thrist asked.

"I met him in the desert, Faaaaaather. But not to tempt. Only to warn him of his faaaaaate."

Thrist's voice became a whisper. "Was Christ the son of God?"

"Yesssssss. God had sent him down on Earth to dieeeeeee."

"Fa!" Rabbi Shotzen threw up his hands in disgust. "I've had enough of this nonsense."

Bub tilted his head at Shotzen. "Bad hangover, Raaaaaaabbi?"

The rabbi stood up and pointed at the demon. "I don't know what you are, but Satan you are not."

"Don't you beleeeeeeeive me?"

"Do not allow yourself to be misled," the rabbi told the group. "He shows only what he wants you to see. You are being manipulated."

"Foooooool," Bub said. "Jews are not the chosen peeeeeeeople."

Shotzen's face lost all color. He turned and left the room, closing the door quietly behind him.

"You warned Christ?" Thrist asked, apparently unaffected by Shotzen's outburst.

"Wanted to saaaaave him." Bub leaned back, assuming his lotus position.

"God wanted him deaaaaaaad."

Thrist shook his head. "Christ died for our sins. He wasn't being punished by God. He died so God would forgive us."

"God was jealoussssss," Bub said. "So he killed Hisssss son."

Thrist shook his head. "It was for our sins. God forgave us."

"God doesn't caaaaare about yooooou."

"What of the resurrection?" Thrist asked. "Christ rising from the dead?"

"Lieeeess."

"It had to happen," Thrist declared.

"His followers stole hissssss body from the toooooooomb."

The priest shook his head. "No."

"I saaaaaw them."

"That simply isn't true."

"It's truuuuuuuuuuue."

Thrist deflated in his chair. There was a silence that stretched on for over a minute. Andy wasn't sure if any of this was true, but he noticed that Father Thrist looked like he'd been beaten up.

"What of prayer?" Race asked finally. "Does God hear prayers?"

"God doesn't caaaare."

"I . . . I don't feel well," Thrist said quietly.

"When we die, do we go to heaven?" Race asked.

Bub brought a talon up to his beard and scratched it.

"I don't knoooooow."

Race furrowed his brow. "You don't know? Or you're not telling?" The demon's face got so ugly Andy had to turn away.

"I. Dooooooooooon't. Knoooooooooooooooooow."

"How about hell?" Sun asked.

Bub focused on Sun. The anger on his face vanished, replaced with a sly smile.

"Yooooooooou'll seeeeeeeee."

Andy looked at the others, wondering if they were as creeped out as he was.

They were, except for Race, who appeared more impatient than scared.

"Did God give you the ability to bring back the dead?" Race asked.

"Yesssssss."

"How about heal? Can you heal the sick?"

"Yessssss. I can cuuuuuuuuure your wiiiiiiife."

Race stood up suddenly, pressing his palms to the glass. "Helen?"

"Yesssssss." Bub touched the Plexiglas, placing his palm against Race's.

"Bring her to meeeeeeee."

Race paused for a nanosecond, then headed for the door.

"General," Sun warned, "that isn't a wise idea."

"We'll be right back."

Race practically yanked Dr. Harker out of her chair and they exited as fast as he could pull her. Andy saw Father Thrist take Race's place at the glass, both hands pressed against Bub's.

"Is there no way to win heaven?" Thrist asked. There were tears in his eyes.

"Such sadnessssss," Bub said. "God doesn't want you to be saaaaaaad. Maybe there is a waaaaaaaay."

Thrist nodded several times. "Yes. Of course there's a way. You just aren't aware of it. You've never read the Bible, have you?"

"Noooooooo."

"I'll bring you mine. You shall have mine. I'll be right back." Thrist also hurried out of the room.

Andy looked around. "The ranks are thinning."

"I have a few questions." Sun moved to Race's seat. "You said you were in a coma. How did that happen?"

"I don't knooooooow."

"Did you get sick? Injured somehow?"

"I don't knooooooow."

"I have studied your physiology. You are immune to all disease. We've tried practically every bug known to man. Nothing makes you sick."

Bub stared impassively at Sun. His black tongue snaked out of his mouth and licked the mucus from his right nostril.

Andy flinched. Sun asked, "Ever hear the name Kukulcán?" The demon's mouth twitched.

"Noooooo."

"You're lying," Sun said. "How about that hot rock thing. What's it called?"

"*Tuunich k'iinal*," Andy said.

"I don't knoooooow."

"But it's engraved in your capsule," Sun said.

"I don't knoooooow."

Sun folded her arms. "And taken eight hundred miles away from your city, buried seventy feet deep with hand tools. It sounds like they feared you. Feared you even when you were dead."

"Do you fear meeeeee? There's nothing to feaaaaaar but feaaaaaar itself."

*That and talking demons*, Andy thought.

But Sun stood her ground.

"Why did you wake up now?" she asked. Her voice was getting louder. "What's special about now? Why not ninety years ago? What took so goddamn long?"

"I was waaaaaaaaiting."

"For what?"

"The riiiiiiight time."

"Where did you really come from, Bub? Tell me the truth. None of this Bible-thumping bullshit."

The demon looked beyond them.

"Raaaaaace. Heeeeeeeeeelen."

Race pushed Helen forward in her wheelchair, stopping to give Sun a stern look.

"Don't let Helen go in there," Sun said. "You can't trust him."

"What happened to remaining united in our opinion?" Race asked brusquely.

"Bub has been lying. I bet everything he's said so far has been a lie." Race looked at Andy, a question in his eyes.

"She's overreacting," Andy said, shrugging.

Sun clenched her fist and Andy thought for a moment that she was going to deck him. Instead she spun on her heels and stormed out.

"Sun doesn't like meeeeeeeeee."

"I like you," Race said. "And I'll like you even more if you cure my wife." Andy tapped Race on the shoulder and whispered.

"Do you think making a deal with the devil is wise, General?"

Race offered a clipped grin. "I asked the other guy, and he wasn't listening. This is the only hope left."

"But don't you think . . ."

"There isn't a single thing you could say or do to stop me, son."

Andy watched Race and Harker wheel Helen over to the feeding door. As far as instincts went, Andy's weren't very good. Time and again he'd made the wrong decision, the bad call. But he couldn't help feeling that everything was about to go horribly, irrevocably wrong.

He got up and went after Sun.

# Chapter 17

Sun was punching in the code for the first gate when Andy caught up to her.

"Don't even," she warned. The affection she felt for the linguist was gone, replaced by a sense of betrayal.

"Shh," Andy put a finger in front of his lips. "Maybe he can still hear us." Sun swung the gate open, aiming for Andy's shoulder. She missed.

"Hey, hold on."

Sun lengthened her stride.

"I agree with you," he said, catching her arm.

"You what?"

He moved in front of Sun and faced her. "I agree with you!" Andy whispered. "Bub's lying."

"Well, why did . . ."

"Shh! Keep it down. Do you remember when Bub said the only thing to fear is fear itself?"

"Yeah. So?"

"So that's FDR. How has he heard that quote? I don't think it was on any of the phonics videos."

Some of Sun's anger evaporated. She pushed a strand of hair out of her face.

"Okay, we both know he's lying. So why didn't

you back me up? Race is going to put his wife in there with him."

"Race is going to do that no matter what we say. I think he made this decision a while ago. Calling Bub a liar isn't going to help the situation. We need to figure out why Bub is lying, and how can he know that quote."

Sun nodded. Her affection for Andy returned. He'd played it smart, and she'd reacted without thinking things through.

"Has he been awake since he was brought here and faking it?" Sun said, thinking out loud. "Maybe he's been biding his time, listening to everything going on around him, taking it all in. Even if he didn't know English, if he has an eidetic memory, he could remember everything that had been said since his arrival and then translate it after he learned English. Maybe that's how he knows so much. Or maybe, like Shotzen said, he's always known English."

"Possible, but I think that's reaching."

"What's another explanation?"

"Someone's been coaching him," Andy said.

"Who?"

"I don't know. But his habitat is always being video recorded, right?"

"Yeah. So we just need to watch the recordings and see who's been paying him visits."

"Right. And in the meantime, let's just play along with him. We know he's lying, but we don't know why. Better to let him believe we're on his side." It made sense to Sun.

"Okay. But I still think letting Bub near Helen is a bad idea."

"I'm beginning to think," Andy said, "that a lot about Samhain is a bad idea."

Andy punched in the code for the gate and they returned to Red 14. Race had wheeled Helen over to the pneumatic door on the side of Bub's habitat. The sheep's hatch was open, and he was talking to the demon through it. Sun and Andy got close enough to hear the exchange.

"I do have the authority, and the ability, to terminate you if I consider you a threat," Race said. "There are several safeguards, installed before we knew if you were hostile or not. I'm sure you understand."

"I want to heeeeeeelp yooooooou."

Race hesitated. Sun noticed that he had a large white object in his hand, the size of a baseball bat.

"It will be fine, Regis," Helen said.

Race touched his wife's neck. "Lower your head, dear."

Helen hunched down, and Race pushed her chair into the dwelling.

Bub waited, squatting down. Race moved slowly, the white object resting on the wheelchair's handles.

"Don't beeeee afraaaaaaid."

"This is called a cattle prod," Race said, holding out the white stick. "It's been modified, and has enough electricity to stop your heart."

Bub took a step toward them and reached for Helen, his movements slow and steady.

Helen sat stock-still, even when Bub touched her face.

"Relaaaaaaaaaax."

Bub picked Helen up, slowly and carefully, while

Race stood by holding the prod like a broadsword. Helen began to shake.

*This was bad*, Sun knew. Very bad. She took a step toward the habitat door, but Andy held her back.

"It's out of our control," Andy whispered.

Sun watched, helpless, as Helen's tremors became worse.

"It's the chorea," Race said.

"Waaaaaaaaaaaaait," Bub told him. The demon cradled Helen in his giant arms; close to his chest, like a child would hold a teddy bear. Her trembling gradually subsided.

Sun became aware she was biting her lower lip.

"I brought the Bible," Thrist said, bursting into the room. He stopped in midstep when he looked in the habitat. "Sweet Jesus," Thrist whispered.

Helen's head disappeared in Bub's massive claw as he appeared to anoint her. She yelped like a scared puppy. Race moved in with the cattle prod, but Bub set Helen down and quickly backed away.

"It's dooooooone."

Race looked at Bub, then at his wife, who was lying curled up on the ground.

"Helen?"

She held up her head. "Race?

And then she stood up.

"Helen . . . you're standing!"

Race dropped the cattle prod and ran to embrace her. "My dear, how do you feel? Are you okay?"

"I feel wonderful, Regis. Just wonderful." Race began to sob, and then Helen sobbed as well.

"We've witnessed a miracle," Father Thrist said.

He genuflected, kneeling down and making the sign of the cross. Sun sidled up to Dr. Belgium. She remained unimpressed.

"Did you run serum tests on that sheep leg yet?" Sun asked from the corner of her mouth.

"A few. It was still wiggling this morning when I checked. Some apoptosis—cell death, but it's still moving. Since there's no respiration or circulation, I think the leg is reabsorbing its own dead tissue for energy."

"Anything conclusive?"

"I'm running an amino acid detection to ID proteins and enzymes."

"Where are the recent video recordings of Bub's habitat?" Sun asked. "For the last week?"

"Uh . . . Red 4. I've been putting them there."

"Look, Regis! I can walk!"

Helen was strolling around the habitat, tentatively at first, and then prancing like a gazelle.

"Wonderful, Helen! It's wonderful!"

"We'll also need blood work on Helen," Sun said. "I don't trust Harker. Can you do it?"

Belgium nodded, several more times than necessary.

"What should we do now?" Andy asked Sun.

"First the recordings. I'd like a chance to examine Helen myself. I'd also like to spend some time in Red 3 and see what else I can find out about Bub's physiology. Frank, are you sequencing Bub's mitochondrial DNA?"

"Hmm? No. Nuclear."

"Mitochondrial?" Andy asked.

"The genome of an organism is found in the nucleus of a cell," Sun explained. "Mitochondria are organelles that produce energy for a cell. They also contain DNA, but fewer genes than nuclear DNA."

"I'll test for short tandem repeats," Belgium nodded. "I'm convinced Bub has a lot of the same genes that we do, and that other animals do, but so far I can't classify them. Maybe an STR of his mitochondria will turn up something."

"I'd like to get back to the capsule," Andy said. "See if I can make sense of that hot rock."

Race and Helen were slow dancing, wet cheek to wet cheek.

Father Thrist was on his knees, hands clasped in prayer.

Dr. Harker had her nail clippers out.

Bub was staring at Sun through the Plexiglas, the expression on his face unpleasant.

Sun shivered. "I liked him better before he could talk," she said. "Let's get started."

She left Red 14, feeling the demon's eyes on her the entire time.

# CHAPTER 18

*Pathetic*, Dr. Julie Harker thought.

Race had kissed so much demon ass his face was turning brown. The all-important Roosevelt Book had been left on his chair, forgotten. Race and Helen had danced out of Red 14 an hour ago, giggling like teenagers. Probably going to have sex, Harker guessed. The thought sickened her.

Just as sickening was Father Thrist, sucking up to Bub with sycophantic relish. He'd given Bub his precious Bible, preaching endlessly about the wonders of Jesus and the Holy Spirit. Harker had been a Christian, once. Her parish priest offered no explanation for her daughter's death, other than the lame *"The Lord works in mysterious ways."*

A child's death wasn't mysterious. It was reprehensible. Harker wanted no part of any religion that allowed such a thing to happen.

Harker sat patiently outside of the habitat, waiting. She had a question to ask Bub, but she wanted to be alone when she did. It was admittedly a long shot, but it kept Harker rooted to her chair, watching Father Thrist grovel and gesture. Harker passed the time by picking at her cuticles, a habit from her youth. A day didn't go by where she didn't draw some blood from one or two fingers, cutting down too deep.

After an interminable wait, the priest left. Running off to call the pope, Harker guessed. The only two remaining in Red 14 were herself and that flake Dr. Belgium. Belgium was busy at the computer, engrossed in some gene program. Harker decided to chance being overheard, and she approached the habitat slowly.

"Dr. Haaaaarker. Are you maaaaaaaad?"

"Mad? Why?"

"I heeeeeeealed Helen. You could noooooot."

"I haven't examined her yet, so I can't be sure the Huntington's is actually gone."

"You have dooooooubt."

"No. I just prefer facts to faith."

The demon nodded. Harker eyed him, hoof to horn. He was certainly formidable. But supernatural? Harker decided she didn't care, one way or the other.

"So you can raise the dead?" she asked.

"Yesssssssss."

"How long can they be dead before you can raise them? Minutes, hours . . . years?"

"Houuuuuurs."

Harker frowned. She'd been harboring a minor fantasy of digging up her beloved Shirley and bringing her to Bub. It was ridiculous, she knew. But better to ask than always wonder.

"Who diiiiiied?"

"Excuse me?"

"You want me to bring someone baaaaaaaack."

Harker's eyes began to glaze and her lower lip quivered. She couldn't help it. The pain never went away.

"I lost a child," Harker said.

Bub grinned. His grin was like opening a drawer full of steak knives.

"I can maaaaaaake a child." Harker blinked. "What?"

"A chiiiiild. I can maaaaaaaake one."

"A newborn?"

"Any aaaaaaaaage."

That would be perfect! All these years, without hope of ever holding a baby again . . .

"How?" Harker asked.

"A sheeeeeeeeeep." Harker frowned.

"You can make a baby out of a sheep?"

"I can change the geeeeeeeeenes. Make it huuuuuman."

"I'd like to see," Harker said.

"I neeeeed your help."

"How?"

The demon leaned closer to the Plexiglas and lowered his voice.

"We shouldn't beeeeeeeee here," Bub said.

Harker furrowed her brow. "What do you mean?"

"In Samhaaaaaaaain. You and I are trapped heeeeeeere."

*No kidding*, Harker thought.

"So what do you want?"

"To get ooooooooout."

Harker shook her head. "Impossible. I couldn't help you. The President would have me killed, plain and simple. He'd send me back to prison for even thinking about it. No way."

"Booooooy or giiiiiiirl?"

"There's too much security."

"Booooooy or giiiiiiirl?"

Harker could picture Shirley's face.

"A girl. A little girl."

"I can maaaaake a beautiful giiiiiirl."

"I can't. There's the door here, plus the two coded gates in the Red Arm.

There's also a camera right over my shoulder."

"Give meeee the coooooooodes."

Harker thought it over. That couldn't be traced back to her. And if Bub got out, so what? The demon had a right to be free. He didn't deserve to be locked up here any more than Harker did. In fact, if Bub escaped, Harker might even be allowed to leave. No more Bub, no more Project Samhain.

But even more important than that was the thought of having a child. If just for a few stolen hours. It had been so long. The feedings, the diapers, those little fingers and toes . . .

"I give you the door code, you make me a child," Harker confirmed.

Bub nodded.

"The child first," Harker said.

"I neeeeeeeed proof."

"How?"

"You'll think of sooooooomething."

Harker *would* think of something. Suddenly nothing else mattered to her. During her trial she'd been evaluated by a court-appointed shrink who did a thoroughly incompetent job, but who had managed to say something interesting. Harker had shown no remorse. And why should she have? She loved Shirley more than her birth parents ever could have. But because Harker never felt bad for her actions, the judge decided she could never be rehabilitated.

And never was a very long time.

"Everything you told the priest," Harker said, "that was all bullshit, wasn't it?"

"Whyyyyyyyyyy?"

"I need to know if I can trust you. Maybe if I let you escape you'll try to murder us all."

Bub laughed, a giant frog croaking.

"Truuuuuust meeeeee."

Harker decided that she didn't care what Bub's plans were. She was going to help him no matter what.

"Okay. I'll need some time to think of something. We'll also need some way to turn off the video camera. I don't want to get caught."

"I'll take caaaaare of that. Tell Sun I want two sheeeeeeeeep."

"Fine."

Harker checked her watch. She had about an hour. How could she somehow prove to Bub that she was giving him the real code, other than taking him out of his habitat and showing him?

*Showing him.*

"I'll see you at lunchtime," Harker said. She left Red 14, hoping she'd be able to make her plan work.


Dr. Frank Belgium was oblivious to the exchange. He was busy multitasking on the Cray. Switching focus from nuclear to mitochondrial DNA, Belgium used restriction enzymes to cut some specific sequences, then used a PCR—polymerase chain reaction—machine to amplify the sample for an STR test. The DNA molecules actually went through channels in a microchip and then passed through a laser beam, getting "fingerprinted" in the process. This would give him a tagged sequence that could be checked against samples from other life-forms in the database.

At the same time, he was using some proteomic tools to identify the amino acids in the serum sample he took from the reanimated sheep's leg. Genes were sort of like factories that could build themselves. DNA coded for protein. Some of the protein was used to make things like cells and antibodies, but some of it was used to make enzymes and hormones. These were chemicals that caused biochemical reactions within the body.

For instance, insulin was a hormone that lowered blood sugar, and a lack of it resulted in diabetes. HGH was responsible for human growth, and lack of it caused dwarfism, or too much of it caused NBA players. Enzymes speeded biochemical reactions—saliva contained enzymes that helped break down starches, aiding in digestion, and the restriction enzymes used so often in molecular science were chemicals that functioned like tiny pairs of scissors, cutting DNA molecules at specific sequences. These were essential to genetic research, because a single strand of DNA could have billions of base pairs, making it unwieldy indeed.

Belgium was convinced that Bub's power of resurrection was either hormonal or enzymic, and in order to prove it he had to identify the proteins. Since proteins were made of amino acids, that was what he searched for. Some of the tools he used were AACompIdent, PeptIdent, SWISS-PROT, and TrEMBL; all extremely sophisticated amino acid identifiers.

"Let meeee oooooout," Bub said, startling Belgium to the point that he almost fell out of his chair.

"What?"

"I want the Inteeeernet."

Belgium had already made the decision that he wouldn't let Bub out again. He knew Bub had lied during the interrogation. Bub had claimed to have never read the Bible, but Frank had checked the cookies in the temp file, and several of the websites Bub had been extensively surfing were biblical. That made everything the demon had said suspect.

Belgium wasn't sure why Bub would lie—he'd cured Race's wife and been friendly to everyone—but he decided he wasn't going to give Bub access to any more information.

The last twenty-four hours had been gut-wrenching for Belgium. He destroyed the video recordings of Bub leaving his habitat, but he was still worried the infraction would be discovered. He was even more worried once he realized Bub was lying. If Bub had done anything harmful, Belgium would consider himself to blame. After his screwup at BioloGen, Frank didn't want to be responsible for anyone getting hurt ever again. He would sequence Bub's genome without the demon's help, no matter how long it took.

"I'm sorry, Bub. The server is down. It happens all the time." Bub didn't answer right away.

"Are you lyyyyyyyying?" he finally asked. The tone in his voice seemed to bore into Frank's bones.

"Hmm? No no no, of course not, Bub. Our server is under construction. Maybe they're doing an upgrade."

"Use another server."

"We don't have a contract with another server. Besides, we couldn't access another server without using our current server."

"I wish to see."

"There's nothing to see, simple as that."

Belgium buried his face in his notes, pretending to be in deep concentration.

"I'll tellllllllll them," Bub said.

"Tell them what, Bub?"

"Tellllllllllll them that you let me oooooooout."

Belgium turned away from the monitor and faced Bub. He couldn't believe how scared he felt.

*Don't show fear*, he said to himself.

"I made a mistake letting you out. Twice. I won't do it again. If you want Internet time, you'll have to talk with Race. I'm sure he'll give you the world, after what you did with Helen."

Bub laughed. This confused Belgium, who wasn't aware he'd said anything funny.

He decided to finish up in Green 4. There was a computer there, and he could access the Cray without having to deal with Bub.

"Enjoy the time you haaaaaaaaaave," Bub said as Frank left.

Belgium didn't know what that meant, but he didn't like the sound of it. Not one bit.

# CHAPTER 19

"That was the last one," Sun said. "For a scientist, his organizational skills suck."

She and Andy had been in Red 4, fast-forwarding through the surveillance DVDs of Bub since he'd been put into the habitat.

They'd just zipped through Bub's first feeding, which was gory even at 32x speed. After the horrifying meal, Bub appeared to say something. Andy shuttled back and let it play at normal.

"Messy eater," Race said on the monitor.

"*Ba'ax u k'aat u ya'al le t'aano?*" Bub replied.

Andy translated the Mayan dialect in his head. "Bub was asking Race *What does that expression mean?*"

"So he didn't know English yet?"

"Apparently not."

They fast-forwarded through the two times Race went into the dwelling, changed discs, and sped through more eating and sleeping.

The discs were not labeled and they weren't in se-quential order. This was annoying, because Sun and Andy had to go through each disc to find the current one, and it turned out that one was missing.

An hour wasted. Andy picked up the phone and dialed Red 14.

"No answer," he said.

He tried Dr. Belgium's room, Blue 11. The doctor wasn't there either.

"Maybe he's the one that took the disc," Sun said. "He's in charge of them."

"Could be. But it could have been anyone. At least now we can be fairly certain that the disc is intentionally missing. Someone is trying to cover something up."

"So what does it prove?"

"More proof that Bub was lying, I guess. I don't know, I'm an interpreter, not a detective."

"Why would someone be helping Bub lie?"

Andy leaned back in his chair and laced his fingers behind his head. "Isn't it obvious? People make deals with the devil all the time."

Sun could see his point. She'd been here only a week, but she'd seen enough to accurately describe the Samhain staff as *dysfunctional*. She stood up and stretched.

"I'm going to Red 3, put some time in. I recall reading something in there that didn't make sense. I can't remember what the hell it was."

Andy said, "I'll be in Red 6 with the capsule. I want to check the Maya glyphs against the Egyptian ones, see if they say the same thing."

"I've got to feed Bub soon. Wanna meet me in Orange 12 in, say, forty minutes?"

"Sure. I'm hungry myself. We can grab a bite."

Andy held open the door for Sun, something that

Steven used to do for her all the time. She smiled. The memory no longer hurt.

"Hi, Dr. Harker," Andy said. The physician was standing in the hall, outside the door.

*Eavesdropping?* Sun wondered.

"Did you examine Helen yet?" Andy asked.

Dr. Harker looked briefly at Andy, surprise on her face. Then she looked at the floor.

"Not yet," Harker said.

"What's with the video camera?" Sun pointed at Harker's hand.

Harker was holding a palm-sized camcorder, one of the ultra-small models with the flip-out screen. She was trying unsuccessfully to put it into her lab coat pocket.

"I borrowed it from the AV room. I was going to take some footage of Bub and analyze it."

"Analyze it," Sun intoned. She made no attempt to keep the incredulity out of her voice.

Harker nodded.

"That blinking green light." Andy pointed to the camera. "That means it's taping."

Harker brought the camera up to eye level and stared at it as if it were an alien. Andy pressed the red button on the grip and the green light stopped blinking.

"Thanks," Harker mumbled. "When does Bub eat?"

"We're going to feed him at noon," Sun answered.

"Bub said . . . he told me . . . that he was very hungry and he wanted two sheep for lunch."

Harker wasn't speaking to Sun. She was speaking to a point over her right shoulder. How could anyone become a doctor with people skills that were this bad?

"Okay," Sun said. "We'll bring him two."

Andy briefly touched Sun's arm, and then walked across the hall and disappeared into Red 6. Harker avoided looking at Sun and made her way to the gate, fumbling with the code.

Sun watched her go. She disliked Harker, but now dislike had turned to outright suspicion. Harker did the barest minimum to get by at Samhain. She'd also taken a less than active interest in Bub, when everyone else had been buzzing like bees since the demon awoke. Why, all of a sudden, did she want to videotape him? Could this have something to do with the missing surveillance disc?

After almost a minute of fumbling, Harker made it through the gate. *Perhaps I should tell Race about Dr. Harker's new video fetish*, Sun thought. Whether Race would care or not was anyone's guess, but it was his show and he should be kept informed on what everyone was doing.

Unless Race was the one helping the demon out. After all, Bub just cured his wife. Or at least, he seemed to.

Sun tried to clear her mind and concentrate on the latest problem at hand: Red 3. Somewhere, in all of that paperwork, she'd seen something that was important. It tugged at her subconscious—perhaps one of the tests run on Bub.

There was something that she'd missed and she was determined to find it.

Sun passed Dr. Harker again, heading into the Octopus, and subconsciously noted that once again the green light was flashing on Harker's camcorder.

# Chapter 20

**B**ub had to die.

Rabbi Shotzen pondered and prayed and pondered and prayed, and that was the conclusion he came to. That was G-d's will. It was also a matter of survival.

Whether Bub was a demon or not didn't matter. If he was Lucifer, as he claimed, then Shotzen would be doing the world a favor by destroying him. If he was something else, at the very least Shotzen would be saving Judaism.

Father Thrist was proof.

Thrist was the most skeptical man Shotzen had ever met. If Bub had won him over that easily, he would have little difficulty convincing the rest of the world. All Bub had to do was go on television and talk about Jesus being the Messiah. The Jews, the chosen people of God, would again be persecuted in the name of Christ, this time to extinction.

The rabbi knew what would happen. There were two billion Christians in the world, three hundred million in North America alone. Muslims numbered over one billion. Jews? Fourteen million worldwide. The opposition outnumbered them two hundred to one. If Bub were to go public, spouting off about Jesus Christ, the repercussions would be enormous. The US might cease support of Israel, which could very well mean its destruction. In America, the vandalism of synagogues and the harassment of Jews would escalate and violence would no doubt erupt.

Shotzen couldn't let that happen. Christ was not *moschiach*. It was impossible. The Messiah was to be of Davidic lineage. If Christ was the son of G-d, how could he be descended from David? G-d was one being, not a trinity as the Catholics said. That was sacrilege.

So he had only one course of action. Bub had to be destroyed. Just as David had slain Goliath, Shotzen had to destroy a giant of his own. It was treason, he knew. The United States might very well execute him. But if he got out word to Jews worldwide, he believed the support would be total. He would truly be the savior of his people. They might even embrace him as a hero. And his memoirs, so long thought to be a pipe dream, might someday be studied at yeshivot around the globe, alongside with the work Rabbi Moses ben Maimon and Rabbi Akiba ben Joseph.

Normally, he would consult a beth din, a house of justice consisting of three rabbis, to discuss the legal points of killing Bub. The Talmud Tractate Sanhedrin discussed setting up a court to try crimes, but this only applied to humans, of which Bub was not. Jewish law did allow for *killing the pursuer* without a beth din. In fact, if there is an obvious threat, G-d commands Jews to respond with mortal judgment.

Bub was an obvious threat to fourteen million Jews, so Shotzen considered himself justified in destroying him.

Bub might kill him, of course. But he was willing to take the risk to save his people.

Shotzen outlined the plan in his memoirs; should he not survive there would at least be a record of his bravery and sacrifice. His first idea was to detonate the bombs that had been surgically implanted in Bub's head and chest. But the trigger for them was in Yellow 4, and it had a locked door with a keypad entrance. Only Race could get in there.

Shotzen decided the next best way to destroy Bub was with fire. The flames could possibly even set off the bombs. He could sneak into the habitat while Bub slept. But what to use?

The rabbi hearkened back to his youth and remembered a hate crime: a synagogue that had burned to the ground. Vandals had thrown a bottle filled with kerosene at the front door. That kind of incendiary weapon had a name, Shotzen recalled. A Molotov cocktail.

Samhain had a backup generator that ran on gasoline. Shotzen could fill an empty schnapps bottle with gas, stuff a sock down the bottle neck as a wick, and he'd have a fire bomb. One should be enough; after all, one destroyed an entire two-story synagogue. Shotzen decided to make two, just in case.

He had half a bottle of schnapps plus the empty from the night before. Shotzen indulged in a quick slug to calm his nerves, and then dumped the rest of the liquor down the sink. He placed both bottles in his pillowcase and left his room.

He walked quickly and with purpose. The Octopus was empty. Shotzen took the Yellow Arm to room 8, the generator room. He turned on the lights.

The generator sat silently in the corner, a large green appliance the size of several refrigerators. Off to the right was a gasoline pump, an older version of the modern-day gas station model. Shotzen set down the pillowcase and removed the bottles. The gasoline shot out of the nozzle like a garden hose, and the rabbi spilled as much as he bottled. Gas evaporated quickly, so Shotzen didn't worry himself over it.

He capped the bottles, put them back in the pillowcase, and headed for the Red Arm. He would check on Bub. If the demon was asleep, he would proceed. If not, he'd stick around until he had the chance.

Shotzen had trouble with the gates; his hands were shaking. When he approached Red 14, he opened the door just an inch and peeked inside. Dr. Harker was standing in front of the habitat, talking with the demon.

Rabbi Shotzen closed the door silently and contemplated his next move. He went through the first gate and decided to hold fort in Red 7. It was a small storage room. There were various cleaning supplies scattered around. Shotzen set the bottles down next to a collection of mop heads, then sat down and removed his socks. He unscrewed the bottle tops and stuffed one sock into each bottle neck. Then he tilted the bottles upside down, saturating the makeshift wicks with gas.

He had a several disposable lighters in his pocket. In his room was a collection of over thirty. His wife, Reba, had smoked, and Shotzen's method of discouraging her was to constantly take her lighters. She never did quit, but for some reason he'd never gotten rid of the lighters. Strangely, they were all he had left to remind him of

Reba. The get granted her possession of everything, down to the last photograph.

Shotzen said a quick blessing, wishing her the best wherever she was. He bore her no ill will. His sterility and his alcoholism were more than any woman should have had to bear.

He took out a lighter and flicked it once. Twice. No flame.

He tried a second one and it worked instantly. Shotzen adjusted the flame to its greatest height, almost two inches. Then he shook it to make sure there was plenty of fluid left.

There was.

He heard voices in the hallway. Sun and Andy. He could also make out the footfalls of sheep. They were bringing Bub his lunch. Good. Bub usually took a nap after eating. That would be the time to strike.

Shotzen checked his compass, something he'd gotten from Race and always carried around, and faced east. He took his siddur—his prayer book—from his pocket and read the afternoon service. Then, while still standing, he began to pray the Amidah. He prayed aloud and with kavvanah—intent—but he kept his voice a whisper.

When the prayer ended he began to shuckle, rocking back and forth, davening to Adonai for judgment, purpose, and strength.

He was going to need it.

# CHAPTER 21

**D**r. Julie Harker sat in the back of the room and watched impatiently as Sun led the two sheep into Bub's habitat. Andy Dennison, the interpreter, was helping her.

*She's screwing him*, Harker decided. Didn't waste much time either; the guy had only been here a few days. It reminded Harker of her mother. She used to sleep around too. Harker couldn't count all the times she was taken to different men's houses and left in front of the television while her mom hurried to the bedroom. One more horrible memory from a horrible childhood.

Harker turned on the camera and videotaped the hideous spectacle, giving further credence to her earlier lie. Bub got down to business quickly. As soon as the sheep entered his domain Bub had grabbed each by the head. With a quick twist of his giant talons he broke their necks in unison, and then began to feast.

As Bub gorged himself, Sun engaged him in some brief conversation, asking why his hunger had increased. Bub explained that a creature of his high metabolism needed a lot of calories to maintain itself. Bub had learned English only yesterday, Harker noted, and was already lying like a pro.

The demon ate quickly, stuffing the final bit of the first sheep into his gaping maw only minutes after beginning. Through the zoom of the camcorder lens Harker could see that Bub was able to unhinge his lower jaw like a snake to get the big pieces down.

He began to chow down on the second sheep, causing Harker to stop taping and shoot him a look. The extra sheep was to become Harker's little girl. Had she been tricked?

Sun and Andy neglected to stay for the second course, and when they left Bub stopped eating.

"That's supposed to be my child," Harker snapped as she approached the habitat. "You're eating my baby."

"Don't wooooooooorry," Bub cooed.

"I don't want a daughter with bite marks out of her."

"She'll be fiiiiiiiiiine."

"I want her perfect."

"She'll be fiiiiiiiiiine. Give me the coooooooodes."

Harker held the camcorder up to the Plexiglas. She pressed the STOP button and rewound the tape.

"I recorded myself punching in the code, so you know it works. See for yourself."

She faced the viewing screen at Bub and let the tape play. Bub kept perfectly still while he watched, like a cobra before it strikes.

"The second gaaaaaaate."

"The same code," Harker stated matter-of-factly. "I would have kept taping, but I was almost caught."

Bub eyed her closely. Julie wasn't quite sure why she lied. Perhaps it was because having a nine-foot demon

running around loose wasn't the smartest thing to allow.
Perhaps it was because she didn't entirely trust Bub to
make her a little girl. If all worked out, Harker might
give Bub the second code later on. Maybe in another
deal. Harker would enjoy having a little boy for her
daughter to play with.

"We have a deal, right?" Harker narrowed her eyes.
There was no way Bub could tell she was lying. Harker
was too good at deception.

"What color eeeeeeeeeyes?"

Harker blinked. She'd never considered it. "Blue
eyes. And blond hair. Curly blond hair." *Just like
Shirley*, Harker thought.

"Watch the dooooooooor," Bub instructed.

He dragged the carcass of the sheep farther back into
his habitat, coming to rest behind some bushes. Harker
stood in the doorway to Red 14, alternating her attention between the hall and the habitat.

"How about the surveillance camera?" she called
to Bub.

He didn't answer. Minutes passed. Harker could see
the legs of the sheep poking out from behind the brush.
At first they twitched, then the twitching became buck-
ing. When the blood started to spray, Harker left the
door to take a closer look.

Bub rested his palm on the sheep's chest. The sheep
was jerking wildly under his hold, almost as if an electric current were being passed through it. Slowly, it
began to expand. The wool, matted black with blood,
peeled away like strips of wet carpet. Then the skin
detached itself from the skeleton and puffed out until

the sheep was double its original size. It began to bleat, high-pitched and frantic.

*It's screaming*, Harker realized.

There was a large wet *POP* as the skin burst. A fine mist of blood sprayed Bub, covering him with droplets. With his free claw, Bub tore away the remaining skin. The muscles underneath were dark red and stringy and . . . *changing*.

All four legs shortened, seeming to shrink into themselves. As if its bones were made of rubber, bending and twisting until it no longer resembled a sheep, just a squirming mass of connective tissue.

The bleating became the choke of someone drowning.

Then the head imploded and promptly expanded into a human skull shape. "Watch the dooooooooooor," Bub commanded.

But Harker was rooted. The body convulsed, sending blood and stringy sinew in all directions like thrown spaghetti. It curled up into a position that was obviously fetal. Bub continued to keep his claw on its chest, in contact with the heart.

The musculature became a lighter and lighter red until it was pink. Harker realized it wasn't changing color; skin was forming. It kicked its legs, now ending in recognizable feet rather than hoofs. Harker watched as its hands, shaped like two mittens, began to divide and splay until they each had five fingers.

Bub's concentration was intense. He appeared to be almost in a trance.

The bleating was high-pitched now, almost the wail of a siren. It slowly died down, becoming rhythmic, more recognizable.

The cries of a child.

Harker tried to swallow, but the lump in her throat was too big.

The changes became more gradual. Harker came up to the habitat and pressed her forehead against the Plexiglas. She could make out fine hair, springing from the scalp wet with blood. As the girl cried, Harker could catch glimpses of the gums forming and the tongue taking shape.

"Incredible," Harker whispered.

The child blinked, revealing startling blue eyes. The details on her small body became sharper: nipples formed, fingernails grew, a belly button. Genitals, small and delicate. The many bends of the ear. Eyebrows and lashes. It was as if Harker were looking at her from far away through binoculars, slowly fine-tuning the focus.

"All dooooooooone."

The girl had stopped crying. She lay on her back, arms and legs twitching.

"She's done?" Harker asked.

"Yesssssssssss."

"Can she eat?"

"Sucking reeeeeeeflex."

"Bring her," Harker said.

Bub gently picked up the child with one claw and took her to the side door.

Harker hurried over to it.

"My daughter." Harker's voice broke.

She took the child in both arms, holding her close. It felt so natural. So good.

"Mama needs to clean you up, Shirley. You're all covered in blood."

The child gripped her blouse and Harker almost swooned from joy. She had to get her back to her room in the Blue Arm without being seen. How?

"Watch her for a moment," Harker said, handing the child back to Bub.

The girl closed her eyes and sucked her thumb.

Harker flew out of the room, through the gates, through the Octopus, into the Green Arm. Green 8 housed the two large food freezers. Harker went into the first, finding a large box filled with frozen loaves of bread. She emptied the bread onto the floor. The box seemed big enough.

She hurried back to Red 14 unseen. Shirley was sleeping in the palm of Bub's claw, curled up in a little ball. Perfect. Harker put the child into the box gently, so as not to wake her.

"Haaaaaaaave fun," Bub said, grinning.

Harker was too nervous, too excited to answer. The box was cumbersome, but she welcomed the burden. She held it tight to her chest, careful not to jostle and redistribute the precious weight inside. More valuable than gold. More valuable than even freedom.

*A box full of love*, Harker thought.

The tears came freely now. Joy so sharp it was painful. Once again, after years of fruitless fantasies and desperate dreams, Julie Harker was finally complete once again.

She was a mom.

# CHAPTER 22

Father Thrist had never felt so close to Jesus Christ. He felt Him in his heart. He felt Him running though his veins. He felt Him with every breath, every step, every pore.

He hurried down the Red Arm, anxious to perform his first baptism in over twenty years. Bub, having read the Bible Thrist had lent him, had decided to become Catholic.

Besides receiving the first sacrament, Bub was anxious for others as well; the second sacrament, penance, and the third sacrament, the Eucharist, receiving the body and blood of Christ in Holy Communion.

The world was soon going to change, Thrist knew for sure now. Bub would usher in a new era of religious awakening. His message of Christ's divinity would resonate to all corners of the earth. There would be no more doubters. Even the most stubborn contrary faiths would have to recant. Rabbi Shotzen's conviction that Jesus never met the criteria of the Messiah would soon be overturned. Every knee would bow. Every tongue would swear loyalty to the one true God. And when that happened, the lion would lay down with the lamb and there would be universal peace, praise be to Christ.

Thrist had dressed for the occasion. Over his green cassock and Roman collar, Thrist wore a white alb and amice, a stole, and a white floor-length chasuble. Pride was a sin, of course, but Thrist loved wearing full Christian liturgical garb. It made him feel holy.

He entered Red 14 with an uncharacteristic smile.

"Good afternoon, Bub."

"Faaaaaaaaaather."

The demon sat in the center of the habitat, his legs in an odd lotus position—odd because his knees bent forward rather than backward.

*He looks peaceful*, Thrist thought.

"Have you decided on a Christian name?" Thrist asked.

"Luuuuucifer Michaeeeeeeeeeel," Bub answered.

Father Thrist's chest swelled.

"I am honored. Lucifer Michael it is. I was named after the archangel Micha-el. Did you know him?"

"Nooooooooo."

"Tell me about God again," Thrist said.

He felt like a child who never tired of his favorite bedtime story.

"God is pure blisssssss. He's watching us right noooooow. He loves yoooooooou."

Thrist closed his eyes, trying to imagine being in the presence of God. Thrist had never known bliss. It sounded too wonderful to bear.

"Let us save your soul then," the priest said, "so you may once again be with God in heaven."

Father Thrist nodded and patted the satchel he carried. In it were two copies of the *Missale Romanum*—the Latin Mass. Bub would serve as the choir and read the responses. The bag also contained a vial of holy water, a goblet, an unleavened circle of bread with a cross imprinted upon it, and a small bottle of red wine.

"We shall celebrate Mass," Thrist said. "You shall be baptized, get penance, and finally receive the body and blood of Christ."

"Through the glassssssssss?" Bub asked.

The priest shook his head. "I shall be in the habitat with you."

The creature uncrossed his legs and stood. He approached the Plexiglas slowly.

Bub whispered, "Aren't you afraaaaaaaaaid?"

"Of course not, Bub. I have no reason to be."

Father Thrist marched over to the side hatch without fear. He opened the small door with the assurance of his faith.

Big mistake.

Bub was waiting for him when he entered. He grabbed the priest in his claw and held him up against the inner wall of the dwelling, five feet off the ground.

"What are you doing?" the priest asked, more surprised than afraid.

Bub grinned, a mouth of daggers.

"Open the dooooooooor," the demon said.

"This is not the way to be saved," Thrist said. "That door isn't the door you need to worry about. The door to heaven is . . ."

"Shhhhhhhhhhh," Bub held a talon over Thrist's mouth. "Enough talk of heaven and God and Jesussssss. I met Jesus, priest, but not in the dessssssssert. I met him in a whorehooooouse. He was fat and uuuuuugly."

"Lies." Thrist's voice was barely a whisper. He couldn't get his mind around what was happening. "Blasphemy."

"The whoooooooores didn't want to touch him. He had to pay extraaaaaa. But at least he didn't die a virrrrrgin . . . like yoooooooou."

The reality of the deceit now weighed fully on Thrist. His friend Rabbi Shotzen had been right all along. In his eagerness for proof, he had eschewed faith.

This time, the epiphany had come too late. He was a fool to think he could change the devil.

But he wasn't fool enough to listen to his lies.

"I . . . renounce you, Satan."

"Open the dooooooor."

Bub traced an upside-down cross on Thrist's left cheek, drawing blood.

Thrist was terrified, but the holy man refused to flinch.

"Let meeeee give you Holy Communion, Faaaaaaather." Bub barked a laugh. *"Hoc est enim corpus meum!" Take and eat this, for this is my body.*

Bub pinched himself in the pectoral muscle and removed several ounces of his own flesh. The wound knitted itself instantly.

Thrist tried to turn his head away, but Bub forced the raw meat into his mouth. It was warm and smelled of decay, and it seemed to wiggle and squirm as if still alive.

The priest vomited, staining his vestments.

It would be the first of many stains.

"Open the dooooooor."

"Never," Thrist spat. "I will not do the work of the devil."

"Christ died in paaaaaaaain," Bub said. "Your death can be woooooooorse."

Bub moved his face closer to the priest's. Thrist could smell his fetid breath and see ragged bits of sheep still clinging to his teeth.

"The Lord is my shepherd," Thrist said, "I shall not want."

"Heeeeere comes the paaaaaaaain."

Thrist felt Bub's claw sliding down his left leg. The demon grabbed it tight and slowly began to twist. There were cracking sounds, and then a loud pop when the knee gave out.

Thrist screamed, the first time he'd ever screamed in his life.

"Now waaaaatch."

The priest felt a pressure in his chest, akin to suffocation. Then his body was enveloped in a fold of warmth, a warmth so complete that Thrist thought the Holy Spirit had rescued him.

He was mistaken.

"I just healed yoooooour leg."

Thrist was astonished to find the agony completely gone. He moved his leg and it felt normal.

"Here it cooooomes."

Bub twisted the leg again, faster than before.

Again Thrist cried out, but this time Bub opened his toothy maw and a black tongue snaked out, slithering into Thrist's mouth and silencing the cry.

Tears streaked down the priest's face as Bub wiggled the broken leg this way and that way, his vile tongue raping Thrist's throat.

Father Thrist prayed for death.

It didn't come.

Just as he was close to passing out, Bub removed his tongue and allowed him to breathe again.

"Do you want me to heeeeeeeeeal you?" Bub whispered.

Thrist's face began to spasm, his left eye blinking uncontrollably. His facial tic had returned.

"Open the dooooooor."

The priest said nothing. The pain in his leg was overwhelming, but even worse was the left side of his face. Every twitch of his upper lip pierced his soul.

"What's wrong with your faaaaaaaaaaace?"

Thrist's entire world was reduced to despair. The facial tic was proof. His God had forsaken him.

"I can make it woooooooorse," Bub said.

He gave the leg a twist and Thrist blacked out.

When the holy man awoke, there was no pain.

"We can do this all daaaaaaay," Bub said.

He grabbed the same leg. Father Thrist gagged at the thought of the oncoming agony. He knew he couldn't handle it again. The very idea made his gorge rise.

". . . Please . . ."

"Where is your God noooooooow?"

Thrist's eyelid was blinking like crazy. ". . . No more . . ."

"Pray to me, Faaaaaather. Pray to me to not hurt yooooooooou."

"I . . . I . . ."

"Kneeeeeeeel, priest."

Thrist knew he was a dead man. The moment he'd stepped into the habitat, his fate had been sealed. But that was the fate of his body. The fate of his eternal soul remained unresolved.

Until now.

Father Michael Thrist silently asked God for the forgiveness of his sins, and thanked the Almighty for the privilege of his life and the opportunity presented to him. Thrist had come there today expecting a baptism, but it turned out he was the one about to be baptized.

The church called it the Baptism of Blood. Dying a violent death in the name of the Lord.

Thrist embraced martyrdom like a gift.

"No."

"Noooooooooooo?"

Thrist faced the demon. His facial tic had disappeared, and he stood proudly, without fear. Jesus died for mankind's sins, and Thrist was honored to die in His name.

"I shall not kneel."

Bub lifted the priest up and twisted each of his feet backward. Thrist began to cry, and Bub held him on the ground in a kneeling position. "Worship meeeeeeeee."

"No," the priest said through clenched teeth.

The demon took one of Thrist's arms and bent it back at the elbow. It snapped with the sound of a gunshot. Thrist screamed again.

"Proclaim your loyalty to meeeeeeee."

*There could be no worse death*, Thrist thought. *Or no greater death.*

"I proclaim . . . my loyalty . . ."

"Yesssssssssssss."

He looked up, past Bub, past the ceiling, past the two hundred feet of earth above them.

Thrist said it clear and strong, "To my Lord, Jesus Christ."

Bub went to work on the other arm, but Thrist had gone to another place in his mind. He knew Bub was twisting and breaking his body, but he no longer felt any pain. He could picture heaven, as Bub had described it. Eternal bliss.

His faith had been restored, and Thrist had no fear of death.

Not even when Bub pulled off his leg.

"Foooooooool," Bub hissed at him. "Open the fucking dooooooooor."

The priest looked up at Bub and smiled beatifically through his veil of tears and blood.

"I forgive you," Thrist whispered.

He didn't feel it when Bub bit off his head.

# CHAPTER 23

Rabbi Shotzen thought he heard a scream. He stopped his prayer and listened.

Silence.

He began again in earnest, intoning under his breath, "*Kadosh kadosh kadosh . . .*"

Another scream. This time he was sure he heard it. Moving cautiously, he approached the door and opened it a crack.

The Red Arm was empty.

He craned an ear to listen.

Nothing. Not a sound.

Perhaps it wasn't a scream. But he should check. He'd heard the gate open a few minutes ago. It had been Father Thrist, in full church regalia, visiting Bub. But that couldn't have been Thrist who screamed. Even he wasn't foolish enough to go into the habitat.

Then again . . .

Rabbi Shotzen was overcome by a sudden burst of urgency. He grabbed his bag of Molotov cocktails and held on to the lighter, and then he rushed out into the hall and saw . . .

Bub was crawling out of Red 14.

"Jesus Christ," Shotzen said.

The demon pulled himself through the tight fit of the door and cocked his head at Rabbi Shotzen.

"Shalom, Raaaaaaaabbi," Bub said.

Shotzen set down the bag and with shaking hands took out the first bottle.

Bub couldn't stand erect because the ceiling was too low. He crawled up to the first gate, and to Shotzen's amazement, punched in the code.

The bars swung open.

Shotzen flicked the lighter. Once. Twice. Three times. No flame. He looked at it and saw he had the wrong one.

"Your friend Faaaather Thrist," Bub said, crawling forward, "has something to saaaaaay."

The demon opened his mouth and coughed. A red ball flew out of his throat and bounced before him, sticky with goo.

Shotzen took a closer look and saw it wasn't a ball.

Bub picked it up and held it out to Shotzen.

Father Thrist's head, slicked in gore.

It blinked.

Then it blinked again, and opened its mouth as if to say something.

"What's thaaaaaat?" Bub asked, holding his other claw to his ear. "You'll have to speeeeeeak up." Shotzen gagged.

"He wants to talk to yoooooou."

The creature chucked Thrist's head at the rabbi. On reflex, Shotzen dropped the bottle and the lighter and caught it with both hands like a basketball. The fire-bomb fell to the ground and shattered.

Shotzen stared at the head in his hands.

"Kill me," the priest's lips clearly said.

Shotzen yelled out in shock.

Bub laughed so hard he vomited out Father Thrist's leg. It flopped onto the floor and wiggled like a fish.

Shotzen threw the head into the wall as hard as he could, hoping to end the priest's misery. He reached for the second Molotov cocktail and took another lighter from his pocket.

"Back to the pit with you," Shotzen declared, shaking with rage. He flicked the lighter and the two-inch flame jumped up to ignite the gasoline-soaked rag. The rabbi threw the bottle at the ground before the beast. It shattered, showering Bub with a wall of flames.

The demon screamed. The stench of burned hair and cooked meat invaded Shotzen's nostrils. Bub batted at the flames with its claws and rolled in the cramped hallway, trying to staunch the flames.

"What the hell?" Andy said. He'd come out into the hallway fifty yards farther down, on the other side of the second gate. Sun appeared a moment later.

"Stay back," Shotzen warned them.

Bub burned for almost a minute before the sprinklers came on.

The flames died down, and then smoldered out. Smoke began to clear. Shotzen stared in amazement as Bub's burned flesh seemed to wash away under the water stream. He shook like a wet dog and shed the scorched flesh.

Underneath his skin was new and unharmed.

"Now it's my turn," Bub said.

"Rabbi!" Andy yelled. "Come on!"

"Run!" Shotzen yelled back. "He knows the codes!"

Bub was on Shotzen in a single lunge, scooping up the holy man in a claw.

"Codes?" Bub asked. "There is moooooooore than one?" He dragged Shotzen to the second gate and punched in a code.

Nothing happened.

The demon roared. It was the most horrible sound Shotzen had ever heard.

Like the thunderclap of a terrible storm.

"What is the code for this dooooooooor?" Bub demanded.

The talons were digging deeply into Shotzen's body. If he'd been skinnier, it might have killed him. As it stood, the talons were imbedded only in fat, causing excruciating pain.

"Race!" Shotzen called to Andy. "The bombs!"

Andy nodded, grabbing Sun by the hand and disappearing into Red 3.

"The coooooooode," Bub said. He tightened his grip.

*It was like being prodded with hot pokers*, the rabbi thought. The pain was worse than anything he'd ever known.

"*Shema Yisraeil, Adonai Eloheinu, Adonai Echad*," Shotzen gasped.

"Ah, the Shemaaaaaa," Bub said. "Deuteronomy 6:4. Rabbi Akiba, riiiight?"

Shotzen thought of Rabbi Akiba ben Joseph, the man who compiled the Mishna in the first century. He suffered a horrible death, tortured by the Romans, but still proclaimed his love for God as he died. His last words were the Shema.

"How did Rabbi Akiba die?" Bub asked. "Remembeeeeer?"

Shotzen remembered. The thought of it had given him nightmares as a youth.

Bub said, "I want the doooooooor code."

Shotzen shut his eyes and prayed. *"Barukh shem k'vod malkhuto l'olam vaed." Blessed be the name of his glorious kingdom for ever and ever.*

"Rabbi Akiba was skinned aliiiiiiiive."

Shotzen quaked with fear. Bub pinned the rabbi to the ground and ripped away his clothing.

"Paaaaaaainful," the demon said. He sunk two claws into Shotzen's shoulder and began to pull.

"And you shall love the Lord your God with all your heart and with all your soul and with all your might!" Shotzen screamed.

He'd said the words a thousand times. Ten thousand. They were the words in his mezuzah on his doorway, the words in the tefillin he strapped to his arm and forehead for morning *Aleinu.*

"The cooooooode," Bub ordered.

Shotzen thought of his life. Of his parents. Of Reba. Of the congregation that didn't want him and the children he never had.

"Give me the code and I'll make yooooooooou better."

Bub had healed Race's wife. He had seen them together, in the Octopus, laughing like children. Shotzen had no doubt that Bub could heal him now. Perhaps even fix his sterility. Shotzen could live through this, maybe even start a family. He knew that if he gave Bub the code, he didn't have to die.

Bub began on his leg, pulling and ripping. Shotzen fought against the agony and continued to pray.

"And these words that I command you today shall be in your heart!"

Perhaps fifty thousand times he'd said the Shema in his life. He'd meant it every time. But he'd never truly understood what love was until that moment. Loving G-d with more than heart and soul and might. Loving Adonai with your life.

Shotzen's eyes were somehow forced open.

"Seeeeeee this?" Bub held up what looked like a bloody rag. "This is your faaaaaaaaaace."

Shotzen could no longer form words without lips, and an animal cry came from his throat. But his thoughts were focused.

*And you shall teach them diligently to your children, and you shall speak of them when you sit at home, and when you walk along the way, and when you lie down and when you rise up.*

"Fooooools," Bub spat. "Stupid religious foooooools."

The light was dimming, things became blurry. Shotzen was in incredible pain. Yet he was happy. He knew even though he hadn't killed Bub, his life was not in vain. Bub wouldn't get out. Race would set off the explosives implanted in Bub's body. Shotzen hoped to live long enough to hear the boom.

"You won't die until I get the coooooode. I'll keep resurrecting you, ooooover and ooooooover."

*You shall bind them as a sign on your hands, and they shall be frontlets between your eyes.*

Shotzen could no longer see. His own blood had pooled into his eye sockets.

Angry at the lack of response, Bub began to rip the rabbi in half.

*You shall write them on the doorposts of your house and on your gates* . . . Shotzen finished the prayer. His very last thought was his love for his Lord.

Bub cast aside the body of the holy man. Then he shook the titanium gate and howled.

# Chapter 24

"Where the hell is he?" Andy swore. He had the phone in his hand and had tried Race's room, the Octopus, the mess hall, the rec room, Helen's room, the library, and even the pool, all the while trying to remain in control while Shotzen screamed in the hallway.

"Use the intercom," Sun told him.

"How? What goddamn button? Was it star-something?"

"I forgot too, dammit!"

The floor shook and there was a tremendous clang. Sun and Andy exchanged glances and peeked out of Red 3 into the hall.

*CLANG!*

Bub had charged the gate and rammed it with his shoulder. His chest was soaked in blood, making the fine red hairs appear black. Behind him, Shotzen was lying on the floor in two large pieces, neither of which had any skin.

When Bub noticed Andy he smiled at him, stringy things sticking to his steak knife teeth.

"Aaaaaaaandy!"

"We are so out of here." Andy grabbed Sun's arm and they ran down the Red Arm, away from the demon.

"Let me ooooout!" Bub shouted after them.

They rushed into the Octopus. No Race.

"Okay, what were Race and Helen doing?" Andy said, thinking out loud.

"Dancing. They were dancing."

"Does this place have a disco?"

"No. But . . . the lounge! There's a stereo in the lounge."

"What room?"

"Purple something." Sun rubbed her forehead. "Um, the pool is two, the bar is eight, library is seven. Dammit, I don't know the lounge."

"We'll try them all."

Andy picked up the nearest phone and dialed Purple 1. No answer. Then he tried Purple 4.

"Howdy, you're interrupting a rumba lesson." *Thank God.*

"Jesus! General, Bub is out. He's killed Rabbi Shotzen and gotten through the first gate."

"I'll be right there."

"He's coming," Andy told Sun, hanging up the phone.

"What did he do to the rabbi?" Sun asked. "The screams . . ."

Andy put his arms around her. He tried to shake the image of Rabbi Shotzen being peeled by Bub, but it refused to go away.

The Purple door flew open, and Andy and Sun each jumped back.

"How did he get out?" Race demanded.

The general was in full-dress uniform. Helen was in a sequined evening gown. She looked worried.

"Shotzen said Bub knew the code."

"Sunshine, if you could wait with my wife. Andy . . ."

Race motioned for Andy to follow. Andy didn't want to. But Sun's eyes on him forced him to move. He trailed Race back into the Red Arm.

*CLANG!*

The gate was still holding. Bub rubbed his shoulder and squinted at the new arrival.

"Raaaaace. Let me ooooooooout."

Race approached slowly. Andy was even slower. He watched the general peer past Bub and down the hallway, which was charred black and drenched in gore.

It looked like a corridor of hell.

"Why did you kill Rabbi Shotzen?" Race asked.

"It was fuuuuuuun."

"Blow this bastard up," Andy told Race.

Bub leveled his eyes at Andy. "Open the dooooooor, Andy. You want to fuck Suuuuuun? I'll make her your whore if you let meeeeee ooooout." Andy had to clench hard to avoid wetting his pants.

"Here's the deal, Bub," Race said. "You go back into your habitat, lock yourself in, and I won't destroy you."

"Do you want power, Raaaaaace?" Bub hissed. "You can be a general in my army. I'll make you immooooooooortal."

Race took another step forward, still beyond grabbing range. He took his eyes off Bub to examine the gate.

"Hooooooow is Helen?" the demon cooed.

"She's fine." Race looked hard at the demon. "Why?"

Bub grinned slyly.

Race's voice was almost as scary as Bub's. "What did you do to her?"

"Let me ooooooooout. There's still time to fiiiiiiiix it."

"So help me, if anything happens to that woman . . ."

"She haaaaaaates you. She haaaaaaates you for bringing her heeeeeere. But I can fiiiiiiix that. Maaaaaaake her looooooove you again."

"You're bluffing. You're trapped, and you're bluffing." Bub barked, his laughter echoing down the hall.

"We'll seeeeeeeee."

Race turned around and walked briskly back down the Red Arm, Andy in tow.

"Let me ooooooooout!" Bub screeched.

*CLANG!* The ground shook as the demon rammed the gate again.

"What's going on, Race?" Andy asked. "Just detonate the bombs."

"I need to talk to the President."

"Then get his ass on the phone!"

They entered the Octopus, Race going to his wife. He held her face in his hands.

"Do you feel okay, dear? Anything wrong?"

"I feel fine, Regis."

"Sun, can you check her out?"

Sun nodded, and sat Helen down at one of the far tables.

Andy got up close to Race and thrust out his chest. "Why don't we kill him?" he demanded.

"He can't get through that gate. It's holding."

"What if—"

"I can only destroy Bub if he's a risk to any of the occupants of Samhain."

"Bullshit," Andy said. "We're expendable. The people involved in a top-secret project are always expendable."

Race jammed his finger into Andy's shoulder. "We are not expendable, understand? But I can't kill Bub unless he's a threat. Right now he's trapped. He cannot get out. And even if he does, we have backups."

Andy said, "The bombs implanted in his body."

"Yes. Plus we have something called *Lockdown*. See, above all the doors?"

Race pointed to every door in the Octopus. Above each of the frames was a large overhang with a slit in the bottom.

"More titanium gates—they completely seal off each arm and the Octopus. I just need to type in the code on the security screen, right here."

"What's the code?" Andy asked.

"*Lockdown*. One word, all caps."

"So what are you waiting for?"

"It can't be reset. Once we're in Lockdown, gates drop on all the arm entrances and in front of the exit at the end of the Yellow Arm. Plus three more titanium gates drop on the staircase leading to the outside. We'd be stuck here until someone cut us out, bar by bar, with a blowtorch. So that isn't necessary right now. You don't have to worry. We're safe."

Andy shook his head. "I've had it," he said. "I'm not a soldier. It's not my job to fight the devil. I know exactly what will happen. I saw *Jurassic Park*. Everything will go wrong. The systems will fail, Bub will get out, we'll all be dead by morning."

"Calm down, son."

"Bullshit! I want out. Me, Sun, the rest. Get us the hell out of here, Race." Andy met Race's gaze, trying to be just as impassive.

Race said, "Okay."

Andy stared at him, amazed. "Okay? That's it? We can go?"

"Of course you can go. I'll call the President right now, arrange for transport. We can have a chopper here within an hour."

Andy wasn't sure if he could believe him or not, but Race sat down at a terminal and accessed a program called CONTACT. He clicked the options bar on EMERGENCY.

"Direct link to the Prez," Race explained. "Unless he's having a press conference, he should be on line in a minute or so."

Within seconds another window appeared on screen. The message bar read AUDIO CONNECT.

"General?" came the President's voice from the monitor speaker.

"Mr. President, the occupant has breached the first two phases of security. He is extremely hostile, and we have civilian casualties. Request immediate evac."

"Is the occupant currently contained?"

"Yes. I'm going to stay with him. But I want the rest of the team picked up ASAP."

"Of course. I'll contact Fort Bliss."

"I'm going to need help to neutralize the subject. Maybe one of those big game hunters who captures elephants for zoos. With a tranquilizer gun and plenty of ammo."

"I'll find someone as soon as possible. A helicopter will be sent immediately to evacuate the team. I'll debrief them at Fort Bliss. How did this happen, General?"

"I'm not sure, sir. He got the codes for the gates somehow."

"I'll contact you soon. God be with you and your team, General."

The computer blinked MESSAGE ENDED.

"Well," Andy said, relief making him feel twenty pounds lighter, "he's an okay guy after all."

Race picked up the phone and hit *100. His voice boomed over the in-house speakers. *Dammit*, Andy thought. *That was the intercom code.*

"Attention, this is Race. Everyone meet in the Octopus for immediate evacuation. Repeat, everyone meet in the Octopus, we're all getting out of here. Move your asses, people."

"RAAAAAAAAAAAAAAACE!" Bub bellowed, his voice heard from all the way down the Red Arm.

"I guess he doesn't like the news," Andy said.

"Screw the son of a bitch. What the hell happened in there, Andy?"

"I don't know. I was in Red 6 translating the glyphs and I heard screams. It was Rabbi Shotzen, getting ripped apart."

"Shotzen let him out?"

"I don't think so. Bub . . . he skinned Shotzen to get the code for the second gate. The rabbi didn't give it up."

"Brave man. So how did Bub get the codes?"

"What's happening?" Dr. Belgium entered the Octopus through the Green door.

"Bub's out," Andy explained. "We're leaving."

"I'll get my things," Belgium turned for the Blue door.

"Pack light," Race said. "Have you seen Father Thrist or Dr. Harker?"

"Not lately. Do you think . . . ?"

"Race!" Sun said. "Your wife!"

The three of them hurried over to Helen, who was lying on the floor with Sun crouched over her.

"She was fine just a second ago," Sun said.

"Is it the Huntington's chorea?" Race asked. "Is it back?"

"No," Sun said, panic in her eyes. "This is something else."

# Chapter 25

Helen struggled in the throes of some kind of seizure. Her limbs flapped uncontrollably, and her back arched and twisted, but it didn't look like any convulsions Race had ever seen.

*Helen's legs and arms were bending backward.*

"Helen! Oh Lord!"

"Regis," she cried.

Race's eyes clouded over. He knelt next to his wife, holding her in an attempt to stop her body from snapping apart.

"Her feet." Dr. Belgium pointed.

Race stared as one of Helen's high heels split open. The shoe fell away, revealing toes that swelled and melded into a giant black mass that resembled . . .

"A hoof," Andy said.

Race could feel his wife expand in his arms, bulging and stretching.

*Changing.*

Helen howled, revealing several rows of long, sharp teeth.

"Oh my my my . . ." Dr. Belgium said.

"Race." Andy put a hand on the general's shoulder.

"I'm sorry, Helen. I'm so sorry."

"Race, we've got to take her out of here."

"Take her where?" Race accused. "This is my wife, dammit!"

"Race, your wife is growing hoofs and fangs. We've got to separate her from the group."

"I'm not leaving her!"

A deep growl came from Helen.

Andy put his arm around Race's neck and yanked him backward.

"Move her!" he yelled at Frank and Sun. They wasted no time, each grabbing a foot and dragging Helen out the nearest door, into the Yellow Arm.

"Helen!" Race choked. He held Andy's arm and twisted, flipping the younger man off him. Then he made a run for the Yellow door.

"Don't!" Sun stood in his way. "It's not Helen anymore! Stop and listen!"

Behind the Yellow door came a cacophony of screeches and yowls, sounds no human being could produce.

Race shoved Sun away and grabbed the doorknob. He paused, grief racking his face.

"Barricade it," he said through his teeth.

The next thirty seconds were a frenzy of chair throwing and table stacking, everyone waiting for the inevitable moment when the Helen-thing came crashing through the door.

The moment stretched, but never came.

"Maybe she left," Belgium said.

"The exit to the outside is down that hallway," Andy said. "Do you think she's trying to get out?"

"Do you want to open it and look?" Sun asked.

"Well, if she's in there, how are we supposed to get

out ourselves? The helicopter should be here within the hour. Race—"

One-star general Race Murdoch marched into the Red Arm, his heart a stone. He had never felt pain like this before. Helen's illness had been torture for Race, killing him a bit at a time in the same way it was killing her. But seeing Helen whole again, dancing with her after all of these years, and then watching helpless as she turned into that . . .

Bub was sitting behind the gate, a lopsided grin on his face.

"Hooooooooow's Helen?"

Race turned to the keypad on the wall and punched in the first two numbers of the code to open the gate.

"Goooooooood boooooooooy."

"You see that?" Race said, facing the demon. "You're four numbers away from being free—"

Bub's grin stretched.

"—and that's as close as you're ever going to get. It's over, Bub. It's not a question of you getting out. It's a question of you still being alive five minutes from now. You're about to go off like a Fourth of July firework." Bub darkened.

"Are you threatening meeeeeeee?"

"No, Bub. I'm killing you."

Race turned and headed back to the Octopus, getting intercepted halfway there by Sun, Andy, and Frank.

"I'm doing what I should have done forty years ago," Race told them.

He led the trio into the Octopus and began to take down the makeshift barricade in front of the Yellow Arm.

"General," Dr. Belgium said, "maybe you should

think this over. Helen—she might not be pleased to see you." Race smiled sadly.

"Hell, Frank, if a soldier can't handle the little woman, what good is he?" The last table was pushed away and Race took a deep breath.

"After I go in, put this back up, and don't open the door again until I give the all clear."

"I'm going with you," Andy said.

"They teach you hand-to-hand combat at Harvard, son?"

"Two have a better chance than one."

Race clasped his shoulder. "I respect your bravery, but this is my job, not yours. You stay here and keep an eye on your lady, let me tend to mine."

Andy stared hard into Race's eyes and offered his hand. "Good luck, General."

Race shook it and grinned. "I'll take training over luck any day." He winked and went through the Yellow door.

The hallway was empty. Race moved slowly at first, then broke into a jog. The years of daily exercise had paid off. He tried to push the emotional baggage aside and visualize his goal. Yellow 4.

That's where the bomb switch was.

He got within ten yards, and then Helen burst out of Yellow 3.

But it was no longer Helen.

She'd changed into a five-foot-tall version of Bub. Her chest was greenish, rather than red, and her wings didn't look large enough for flight. The legs had bent backward, like a goat's, ending in large cloven hoofs. Her arms ended in razor claws that resembled eagle talons. Hundreds of long, pointy teeth, thin as icicles, jutted from her mouth, so large that her lips were shredded and bleeding.

Race stared hard into her elliptical eyes, eyes the color of a furnace. He found no trace of his wife in their depths. A lump the size of a plum formed in his throat.

"Hello, dear," Race said.

It took two steps toward him, its piggish nostrils sniffing the air.

"Can you understand me, Helen?"

The creature growled, raising its talons. They ground together with the sound of knives being sharpened.

Race clenched his teeth and said, "I'm sorry."

Then he took a running start and dove at the thing that was once his wife.

It was like fighting a tiger, all claws and teeth and muscle. Race had the weight advantage, but the sheer ferocity of the demon's attack put him on the defensive. He was being torn apart in ten places at once.

She forced him to the ground and continued her assault, ripping at his clothes, snapping at his neck. The pain was electric. He felt as if he'd fallen into a meat grinder, and part of him wanted to just give up and die.

But Race was a soldier. A soldier with a debt to settle. For his country, that he loved so dearly. For his friend Harold, whose senseless death weighed upon Race every hour of every day. But most of all, for Helen.

Bub had to die. And so did this abomination that was once his wife.

Race went for the eyes, making his fingers stiff and jamming them in hard. The demon squealed, releasing its grip long enough for Race to crawl past and reach Yellow 4.

It was a keypad entrance. Race lifted his arm to punch in the code, but his arm wasn't working right. He took note of the puddle of blood forming around his feet.

He was hurt bad.

Race used his other hand, unable to stop it from shaking.

His first attempt at the code failed.

The thing that used to be Helen advanced on all fours, like a wolf.

The general ignored the threat and once more punched in the code. A talon wrapped around his leg and tugged, just as the door unlocked.

Race grabbed the doorframe and pulled himself into Yellow 4, breaking the beast's grip. He slammed the door shut with his feet, hoping it would hold.

"How do we know for sure the bombs will kill Bub?" Sun asked. "He heals so fast."

Andy was sitting with his arm around her, and he couldn't be sure if she was trembling, or he was.

"This could be interesting." Dr. Belgium got up and headed for the Red door. "I think I'll watch."

Andy said, "Be careful. Race said those charges were large enough to . . ." *Oh no.*

"Large enough to what?" Belgium asked.

"We have to stop him." Andy got to his feet. "Call Race, we have to stop him from setting off those bombs."

"Why why why would we do that?" Belgium asked.

"Do it!"

Andy knocked away a chair from the Yellow door barricade but Sun held him back.

"You can't go in there. That thing will tear you apart."

"Call Race!" Andy said. "He can't set off those bombs!"

Andy broke away from Sun, but rather than the Yellow door he went for the Red door. He half stumbled, half ran down the Red Arm.

Bub wasn't near the gate. And Andy saw why.

Race took a deep breath and choked on the blood. There wasn't an inch of him that didn't hurt. But that didn't matter. All that mattered was the detonation switch. Race was going to send Bub back to hell, where he belonged.

The phone rang. Race ignored it. He crawled to the side panel along the wall. There were several buttons and switches. Race turned on the power for the remote, then activated the radio transmitter and disengaged the safety.

"This is for you, Helen."

He hit the detonation switch.

Andy could see the gate, twenty yards ahead. Resting on the bars, near the lock, were two stainless steel pellets each about the size of a baseball. Even from that distance, Andy could see they were slick with blood.

Andy knew why the demon had taunted Race earlier.

Bub had dug the bombs out of his body and set them on the gate.

The linguist turned tail and ran back to the Octopus.

"Get down!" he said, slamming the Red door and pulling Sun to the floor.

The explosion rocked the complex, blowing the Red door off its hinges. Andy felt the floor vibrate like a mini earthquake, shaking so hard he bit his tongue. The *BOOM* was painful to his ears, and immediately followed by a wave of heat and smoke, which drifted through the Red Arm and into the Octopus.

Andy looked down the hallway, straining to see through the haze.

The titanium gate swung open.

"Reaaaaaaady or not," Bub said. "Heeeeeeeeere I coooooooooome." The demon crawled forward.

"What happened?" Sun said.

Andy ignored her and rushed to the computer terminal, grateful that it wasn't damaged. He booted up the main screen and searched for the SECURITY window. There were a dozen headings; COMMUNICATION, INVENTORY, HELP, PERSONAL, SECURITY . . .

"Aaaaaaaaaaaaandy!" Bub bellowed.

Sun said, "Jesus! He sounds close. Did he get through the gate?"

Andy glanced down the Red Arm and saw Bub making his way down the hall. He was about forty yards away, moving in a crouch.

"This is not good," Belgium whispered.

"Andy, what are you doing?" Sun shook him. "Can you stop him?"

Andy clicked on SECURITY and the password window came up. He typed in *lockdown*.

PASSWORD INCORRECT.

Andy retyped it, making sure he spelled it right.

PASSWORD INCORRECT.

"Goddammit, Race!" Andy smacked the desk with his fist. Race said "lockdown," one word no breaks. Andy tried *lock down*.

PASSWORD INCORRECT.

"Andy, whatever you're doing, do it fast."

Andy chanced a look over his shoulder. Bub was twenty yards away and closing.

"I'm not worried." Dr. Belgium put his hand to his chest. "I'll have a heart attack before he finally gets here." Andy typed *lock-down* with a hyphen.

PASSWORD INCORRECT.

Andy hit the HELP button. It read PASSWORDS ARE CASE SENSITIVE.

"Caps. It's all caps."

"We've got to run," Sun said. "He's almost at the door."

Andy typed in *LOCKDOWB*.

"Stand clear!" he yelled.

He hit ENTER.

PASSWORD INCORRECT.

"Oops. Typo."

"He's here!" Belgium screamed, high-pitched and frantic.

Andy pressed BACKSPACE, erasing the *B*. Then he hit *N* and ENTER.

LOCKDOWN ACTIVATED.

Six titanium gates dropped from the overhangs above all the doors in the Octopus, simultaneously sealing it off with a ground shaking *CLANG!*

Bub barely pulled his arm back in time, or he would have lost it. The demon stared at the new set of bars and scowled. He grabbed one and gave it a violent tug. It held.

The demon screamed, an unearthly wail that sounding like hundreds of souls being tortured.

Andy let out a deep breath. The adrenaline was wearing off and his whole body was shaking badly.

The phone rang, prompting Dr. Belgium to scream again.

Andy grabbed it.

"Did I get him?" Race asked on the other end. His voice was wet and sickly.

"No, General. He used the bombs to blow up the gate. I had to go into Lockdown."

"Dammit." Race's voice held none of the authority Andy had become used to. "I did just what the enemy wanted. Some soldier I am."

"He fooled us all, Race. Can we make it to the exit through, uh, Helen?"

"No," Race coughed and spat. "She turned into a demon like Bub, smaller but deadly. I'm bleeding to death. There's no way to get through. It doesn't matter anyway. When you activated Lockdown, a gate dropped over the only way to the surface, plus four more on the exit stairs." Despair hit Andy like a punch.

"When we aren't there to be picked up, won't the army come in?"

"This is a top secret base, son. They don't even know it exists."

"Can't the President—"

"The President's two top priorities are to keep Samhain secret, and to keep Bub contained. The safety of the staff is a long third."

Andy wanted to throw the phone across the room. He settled for swearing.

"Do we have any weapons? Guns? Explosives?"

"Nothing." Race's voice was solemn. "I don't even have my sidearm down here. No one ever thought we'd need anything."

"So what next?"

Race sighed, a bubbling sound. "I don't know. We wait for the President to call. Have you heard from Father Thrist or Dr. Harker?"

"We haven't seen Thrist or Harker."

Bub laughed, deep and cruel. His rage had vanished, and he sat in front of the gate, lotus style.

"Here's some of Faaaaaather Thrist." Bub spit a glob of something out between his teeth.

"So all we can do is wait," Andy said.

"I'm sorry, son. I am. I won't be able to make it back there, so let me know when the President calls. We'll think of something."

"Try to hold on," Andy told him.

"You too." Andy hung up.

Sun went to Andy and cradled his head in her arms. Andy put his hand on her cheek and closed his eyes.

"What now?" Sun asked.

"We have to wait for the President. There's no other way out of here."

"What about food?" Sun asked. "Or water? We can't get to the mess hall."

Belgium squinted. "Hey, where did Bub go?"

The demon was no longer by the titanium gate.

Sun stood up and walked over to the Red Arm. Andy didn't want to go with her—anywhere Bub went was better than him here, taunting them. But he went anyway. He wasn't sure the exact moment it happened, but he'd become extremely protective of the veterinarian.

"See him?" Sun asked.

Andy gripped her hand and tried to peer down the hallway. There was still some residual smoke, and some of the overhead lights had blown out when the bomb went off.

"Looking for meeeeeee?" Bub said in the distance. His vision was apparently better than Andy's.

Bub came into view, dragging something behind him.

"Oh, Jesus," Sun said, backing away.

"You all remember Raaaaaaaabbi Shotzen." Bub pulled the two halves up to the gate.

Andy didn't want to look at the ruined mess, but he couldn't help it. The body no longer looked human. It was just blood, guts, and bones.

"I'm ressurecting hiiiim. Would you like to seeeeeeee?"

Sun turned away. Andy glanced at Dr. Belgium and saw him taking his own pulse. He faced Bub.

"We're not afraid of you," Andy said.

Dr. Belgium cleared his throat. "Actually, um, I am."

"Shall I bring the rabbi back to life, Fraaaaaaank?"

"No no no, I wouldn't like that at all, Bub."

Bub stroked his chin with his talons, as if in thought. "How about this insteaaaaaaaad?"

The demon touched his claw to one of the larger parts, and a moment later, it began to shake.

# Chapter 26

The corpse's arms and legs rolled and squirmed as if they were boneless, like the tentacles of a squid. Organs inflated and split. The rabbi's skull expanded like a water balloon, undulating and jiggling.

Sun had witnessed death, up close. She remembered being a med student, visiting the morgue for the first time, and how creepy it felt even though she'd been prepared for it. Sun had encountered burn victims, and fatal car accidents, and once even operated on a man who'd gotten his hand caught in a meat grinder.

This was most horrible thing she'd ever seen.

And then it got worse.

The flesh began to blister and bubble, and when the bubbles reached the size of baseballs they separated from the body and shot into the air with a loud *PHLOP* sound. A few at first, and then all at once, like microwave popcorn.

Several of the chunks flew through the bars, landing at Sun's feet with wet thuds. She watched, holding her breath.

With frightening speed, the flesh took shape. Curled up at first, like an embryo, maturing in fast motion. The head formed, arms, legs, a tail. It stood up, about the size of a large vampire bat, with matching bat wings. Black and red, sporting tiny horns, and claws that looked like fish hooks. The thing opened its mouth, revealing rows of needle-sharp teeth.

"A little Bub," Belgium gasped.

Sun watched it waddle over to her and leap onto her shoe. Fear had paralyzed her, memories of her childhood and that horrible bat in her bedroom assaulting her mind.

The thing chirped like a bird and stretched open its jaws, ready to bite her leg.

Andy kicked it across the room.

More fist-sized chunks sailed through the bars. Dozens. A few took to the air and began to fly around the room in quick figure eights.

Sun still couldn't move. A demon landed on her shoulder, screeching like nails on a chalkboard. It was going to bite her, and she couldn't get her muscles to work.

"Ow!" Dr. Belgium yelped. He had a nasty gash across his cheek. "They're like flying razor blades!"

"Move it!" Andy smacked the demon off Sun's shoulder and yanked her away from the gate. The Octopus was full of them now, flapping and squealing, diving at the group with claws out and mouths wide. Fifty or more.

Andy pushed Sun under a desk and pulled another desk over, trying to seal her between them. The things, the batlings, circled around and around, diving in and taking bites out of Andy's hands and head. Sun could glimpse the blood through the swirling tornado of monsters.

Belgium picked up a chair and swatted at them,

knocking several out of the air. When they fell he picked up his knees and stomped, marching band–style, crushing them with his heels.

One managed to escape the stomping and hopped over to Sun's hiding place.

*Damn it, Sun, move!* her mind screamed.

But her body didn't listen.

The batling jumped up onto her shoulder. Its maw stretched open, bloody drool leaking down its chin.

*MOVE!*

But she didn't.

The demon bit into Sun's shoulder, hitting a nerve, doubling her over.

The pain galvanized her. Sun clenched the batling in her fist, feeling the pointy little bones snap under the pressure. She threw it aside and scrambled out from under the desk.

Fear be damned, she was ready to fight.

The demons saw a new victim and swarmed.

Sun grabbed a computer keyboard, yanked it free, and began to whack batlings left and right. But for each one she hit, ten hit her. The pain came from everywhere at once, pain like gigantic bee stings, sharp and burning. Nipping at her arms and back. Going for her eyes.

*They're eating me alive*, Sun thought.

Something bit into her ear and she smashed it against the side of her face. Another became tangled in her hair, clawing and gnawing at her head. She pulled it off, taking some hair with it.

Bub's giggling filled the room—a disturbing sound like a small child being tickled.

Sun could no longer see. Her torn scalp bled down into her eyes, burning like salt water. She wiped a sleeve across her face and saw a figure, covered with batlings, fall to his knees.

*Andy.*

In four steps she was at his side, rearing back the keyboard, smashing it against his chest. Eight batlings dropped off. She repeated the move with his back, putting all of her strength into the blow.

It probably hurt, but not as much as being eaten alive.

The demons she killed were quickly replaced by others, covering Andy like a fur coat.

*This is futile*, Sun realized. *We're all going to die.*

Which really pissed Sun off. She tried to block out some of the panic and think. They couldn't hide, or get away. Killing the batlings one at a time was too slow. What did she know about bats? They were nocturnal, they used radar to navigate, they were eaten by hawks, they hibernate when it gets cold . . . "Cold," Sun said aloud.

At the far end of the Octopus was a fire extinguisher. Sun beelined for it, tossing the keyboard aside. The extinguisher was a big one, at least sixty pounds, and the fire-engine red color meant it was filled with carbon dioxide.

She yanked it from the wall housing and pulled the pin.

In one hand, she grabbed the funnel cone and aimed at the cloud of batlings.

With the other, she pulled the trigger.

A spray of subzero $CO_2$ burst from the nozzle with an explosive *shhussh* sound, freezing batlings as they flew. They dropped from the air, covered in frost. When they hit the ground they twitched and flopped around in a stupor.

"Cover your eyes!" she yelled at Andy before giving him a healthy spritz of healing cold. She then zapped Dr. Belgium, who had curled up into a fetal position near the Purple door.

"Help me! Kill the ones on the floor!"

Frank and Andy began to step on the fallen batlings, while Sun tracked down the remaining few still circling the Octopus. She ran out of $CO_2$ with only one demon remaining, and she managed to swat that one out of the sky with a clipboard.

When the last batling had been crushed underfoot, the childhood giggling began again.

Bub.

The demon clapped his hands in glee, his lips peeling back and his tongue obscenely bathing his own face.

Sun ignored the demon and went to Andy, who looked like he'd dipped his head in a bucket of red paint.

"You're hurt," she said.

"So are you." He touched her cheek.

"Let me help you first."

She sat Andy down and saw most of the blood was coming from two major wounds: one on his nose and one on his scalp. She found a box of tissues in a desk drawer and gave him a handful to press against his face.

The head wound was worse—a four-inch gash that went down deep.

"You need stitches."

"Got a sewing kit handy?"

"No. But do you trust me?"

Andy offered a lame smile through the wad of bloody Kleenex. "Of course." Sun took a stapler off the desk.

"You're kidding," Andy said.

"Watch carefully. You'll have to do me next."

She opened up the stapler and pinched the edges of Andy's wound closed.

Then she lined it up and pushed down, hard.

*Chhhh-chhhhk.*

"Ow!"

"Only three or four more."

Dr. Belgium wandered over. He'd wrapped his lab coat around his head, like a giant red and white turban.

"Me next," he said.

Sun had to put six more staples into Andy's head and then three into Frank's.

"Thank you for stapling my head," Frank said.

"You're welcome."

When she finished, she handed the bloody stapler to Andy.

"Press down firm, to anchor them into bone."

"You and your sweet talk."

Sun sat and closed her eyes while Andy patched up the wound on her head.

She reached up a hand and gingerly felt his work.

"Not bad," she told him.

Andy looked like he'd been in a hockey fight, but he smiled shyly. Sun had a sudden urge to hug him, but didn't want to hurt him any more than he already was.

"The doors are all closed," Belgium said, looking around the room.

"What did you say, Frank?"

"All the doors in the Octopus. That means those bat things were contained. We wouldn't want any getting out and hurting anyone else."

"That wouldn't be good," Sun agreed.

"And speaking of anyone else—where where where is Dr. Harker?"

# Chapter 27

**D**r. Julie Harker had been bathing her new daughter in the sink when she heard the voice over the intercom.

"Attention, this is Race. Everyone meet in the Octopus for immediate evacuation. Repeat, everyone meet in the Octopus, we're all getting out of here. Move your asses, people."

Harker frowned at the news. Evacuation. Bub must have gotten out.

"No need to rush." Harker squeezed the sponge over Shirley's head, rinsing the shampoo from her hair. The water was pink with the blood from Shirley's creation.

*Birth*, Harker corrected herself. Shirley had been born today.

"Happy birthday to you," Harker sang.

She wrapped Shirley in a bath towel and carried her to the bed.

"Mama needs to find a diaper for her Shirley, yes, she does. Maybe an old sheet? What do you think, Shirley?"

Harker located a pillowcase and wrapped it expertly

around Shirley's bottom, securing the fabric with three paper clips.

"There you are. Your first diaper."

Harker smiled. There would be many more firsts. The first pee-pee and poo-poo. The first nap. The first steps. The first words. A whole lifetime of firsts to share together.

"How's my little girl?"

Shirley gurgled, and Harker's heart melted. Shirley was so beautiful. So perfect. Harker wanted to savor this moment, to make it last, but she knew she had to hurry. Shirley was just small enough that she could fit in Harker's suitcase. There was a good chance Harker could get her out of here without anyone knowing.

Julie set the baby down and searched the closet for her old luggage, coming out with a carry-on bag. Punch in a few airholes, and it should work fine.

"Perfect." She smiled. "Now, let's dry you off."

Harker put the towel over Shirley's head and rubbed.

Shirley snarled, low and hoarse, making Harker jump back.

Her daughter stared at her, deep blue eyes burning with hate.

Harker yelped.

Shirley no longer had a face. Harker looked at the towel in her hand and saw her daughter's scalp.

She'd torn it off.

"No. No no no. Oh my, oh my . . ."

Shirley hissed at her, a glistening red skull. She stretched her mouth wide to cry and Harker noticed she was growing teeth. They breached her gums with alarming speed, long and narrow and impossibly sharp.

"Oh my, Shirley . . ."

Shirley hissed at Julie. Her tiny body began to swell, tripling in size. Greasy fur sprouted all over her skin. Her shoulder blades jutted out in points, and her head inflated like a balloon, crackling as the skull bones separated, her eyes bulging out and changing from blue to milky white.

Harker felt faint. She turned to run for the door, but something wrapped around her ankle. Something sharp, that dug deep into the bone.

"MaaaaaaMaaaaaa," Shirley said.

The pain was unreal. Harker screamed. She continued to scream as Shirley pulled herself toward her mother, her giant mouth snapping like a bear trap, getting closer and closer until—

*Snap!*

The teeth closed on Harker's foot.

A symphony of agony thundered through Harker's nervous system.

Harker kicked with all of her might. She punched like a crazy woman. But Shirley hung on, continuing to chew.

Before Harker passed out, an ironic thought passed through her mind.

*This is Shirley's first meal.*

She woke up sometime later. There was no more pain in her foot. Harker quickly realized that was because most of her leg was gone.

Her daughter was perched on the bed, eyes closed.

She no longer resembled anything human. Shirley had six legs. She was pale white, with clawed feet and a body like a fat lizard. Her oversized head was crammed full of teeth, and they jutted from her closed mouth like fondue forks.

On the end of one, Harker spotted her skewered big toe.

Harker bit her lower lip to keep from screaming again. Shirley appeared to be asleep. Maybe she still had a chance to make it out of there alive.

She looked around the room. The phone was on the nearby dresser, but talking might wake the creature. Instead, she twisted toward the door, only a few feet away.

Harker pulled herself along the soggy carpet, using her arms and her remaining leg. She felt no fear. She was remote, detached from the situation.

And cold. So cold.

*I'm going into shock*, she thought, shivering. The edges of her world began to blur and slip away. She bit the inside of her cheek to stay awake.

Almost there. Just a little more.

*She made it!*

Julie reached up at the doorknob, turning . . . turning . . .

"MaaaaaMaaaaaa."

Harker screamed as Shirley sprung from the bed, scurrying over to her on many legs.

The demon climbed atop Harker and hissed.

"All I wanted was to love you," Harker moaned.

Shirley began to eat again. Harker closed her eyes, unable to put up a fight.

She gave in to shock, grateful that the cold was overtaking her.

At least she wouldn't feel any pain anymore.

As it turned out, Harker was able to feel more pain. For quite some time, in fact.

# Chapter 28

Andy leaned back in a chair, doing his best to fight exhaustion and one whopper of a headache. A search of the desk drawers had uncovered a bottle of Tylenol. They all took several. They hadn't found any water, and Andy felt like the tablets were still caught in his throat.

"How long can Bub go without food?" he asked Sun.

"I don't know."

"I'm immoooooortal," Bub answered through the bars of the titanium gate.

The demon giggled again, making all the hair on Andy's body stand on end.

"In his claws!" Dr. Belgium shouted, springing to his feet. He'd been scrutinizing one of the squashed little demons. "Yes yes yes. The sheep's leg had a puncture wound. I didn't know where it came from. But now I know."

"Know what, Frank?"

Andy and Sun came over and looked. Belgium spread the claw open, and a tiny needle came out of the center of the palm. When he released the pressure, the needle retracted.

"How Bub reproduces. No sex organs. When he

fixed Helen and brought the sheep back to life, he touched them with his talons."

Sun said, "Go on."

"Bub uses the syringe in his palm to inject organic matter with some kind of serum, something probably containing hormones and enzymes. This serum can restructure DNA; restriction enzymes cut the DNA up, then it's put back into any order Bub wants it to be in. Maybe he uses a virus, or a retrovirus, to take over the cells' operating machinery—that's how we splice genes—and then during mitosis the cells change into whatever Bub preprograms."

"That's how Helen changed into that monster," Sun said, nodding. "And how Rabbi Shotzen became those batlings."

"Right right right. Remember, humans are ninety percent intron genes—genes that don't code for protein. But they could be cut up with enzymes and patched back together so they *can* code for protein. There's a wealth of raw material in DNA, if it could only be activated by enzymes or hormones."

"That could also explain Bub's rapid healing abilities and why he doesn't age," Sun agreed.

"He can program his own DNA to heal itself."

"So why are the batlings so easy to kill?" Andy asked. "Why can't they heal themselves?"

Belgium shrugged. "Not mature enough yet. Their systems haven't fully developed. They're a generation removed from the host. I'm not sure. But there's a scientific explanation."

Andy stared at Bub and scowled. "Not a miracle at all."

Bub growled, his eyes becoming malevolent yellow slits.

"Did you get a workup of the proteins involved?" Sun asked Belgium.

"Not yet. Didn't have time."

"How about the mitochondrial DNA?"

"Hmm? Oh, that. Yes yes yes. The short tandem repeat got a hit on that."

"And . . . ?" Sun asked.

"His mitochondria encompassed seventy percent of the genome for *Methanococcus jannaschii*. An archaean."

Andy blinked. "I speak thirty languages, and I don't know what the hell you just said."

"It's a microscopic life-form," Sun answered. "It isn't quite a bacteria, isn't quite a plant or animal, and probably predates both, making it one of the oldest and maybe the first life-form on Earth."

"Archaea is an extremophile," Dr. Belgium added. "It's found in some of the harshest areas on the planet. It thrives in boiling water, in geysers, near black smokers at the bottom of the ocean, in extremely salty brines. We've also discovered archaea that live in rock, more than a mile deep in the Earth's crust. Think of it, bacteria living in solid stone."

The scientist began to pace around the room.

"Archaea can also withstand below-freezing temperatures. It doesn't need oxygen. Many archaeans are autotrophic; they get their energy from inorganic sources—iron, sulfur, hydrogen. It's suspected that there may be archaea on Mars, or on Callisto, a moon of Jupiter. Because it can survive in extreme environments, scientists expect archaea to be the first alien life-form found in the universe."

Belgium stopped pacing, and his eyes got very big.

"What is it, Frank?" Sun asked.

"Panspermia!" the biologist exclaimed. "Francis Crick!"

Belgium began to pace, eyes wide with excitement. "Crick won the Nobel Prize for discovering the structure of DNA. He had an idea called *directed panspermia*. What if an alien race shielded a microbe in some kind of spaceship and sent it to all corners of the galaxy, where it was likely to grow? Crick postulated it could be how life on Earth began. It was planted here."

Sun said, "If archaea was the first life-form on Earth, and it didn't need oxygen—"

"Which is exactly what Earth's early environment was like, no oxygen," Belgium interrupted.

"—it could have hitched a ride here in a meteorite made of iron, which would not only be a food source but also protect it from radiation. It could survive the deep cold of space—"

"Archaea have been found in five-million-year-old Siberian permafrost," Belgium exclaimed.

"—and it could also survive the tremendous heat when it entered the Earth's atmosphere. So if Bub has archaea in his genes . . ."

They all looked at the demon. Bub grinned wide and giggled.

"I created yooooooooou," the demon cooed. "I'm yoooooour god."

Andy was slack-jawed. He noticed similar expressions on his companions.

"This isn't happening." Andy shook his head. "Life on Earth isn't some garden planted by this bastard."

"It's truuuuuuuuue."

Sun said, "So where's your spaceship?"

"Einstein proved interstellar travel was impossible," Dr. Belgium concurred. "The nearest star is more than twenty-four trillion miles away. That's over four years' travel if you were moving at light speed, 186,000 miles a second, and light speed is impossible to attain. The faster an object moves, the heavier it becomes." Bub didn't answer.

"His capsule," Sun said, snapping her fingers. "It had iridium in it."

Belgium gasped. "Oh my goodness."

Andy asked, "Iridium? What's that?"

"It's not commonly found on Earth. But it's abundant in meteorites, or other objects that come from space."

"That gray thing is a spaceship?" Andy said, incredulous.

Sun put a hand on his arm. "Did you figure out the Egyptian glyphs?" Andy's shoulders slumped. He rubbed his eyes.

"Yeah. They told the story of a god who fell from the sky and helped them build the pyramids." The linguist shook his head. "I don't believe this."

"So all that talk of God," Sun said to Bub, "of heaven and Jesus and fallen angels. That was all bullshit?"

"Fraaaaaank gave me Inteeeeernet access."

Andy shot Belgium a look. The scientist seemed to shrink.

"Not my smartest move, in hindsight," Belgium said.

The computer beeped several times and the message

bar read INCOMING MESSAGE. Andy clicked on the video icon and the President's face came on the monitor.

"Mr. Dennison? I was just informed that none of you made it to the evacuation helicopter."

"We had to go into Lockdown, Mr. President. We're trapped in here."

"Is General Murdoch with you?" the President asked.

"He's stuck in another part of the compound. Hurt bad. His wife turned into a demon. Bub changed her somehow."

The commander in chief raised an eyebrow. "He can change people into demons?"

"You need to find a way to get us out of here, Mr. President. Can you get us any sort of weapons? Gas? Explosives? Something to cut through the bars?"

"Is it possible that I could speak to General Murdoch?"

"Just a second, I'll see if he's still alive."

Andy picked up the phone and dialed Yellow 4.

"Race, how are you doing?"

Race coughed. "Not dead yet." Though he didn't sound far from it.

"I've got the President on the monitor."

"Ask him," Race said, "if we can go ahead with Protocol 9."

"What's that?"

"Just ask him, Andy."

"Mr. President, Race wants to go ahead with Protocol 9. Is that an escape plan?"

"I grant acceptance for Protocol 9. Authorization

code . . ." The President looked at some papers on his desk. "Seven-six-five-eight-nine-nine-zero."

"He says to do it, Race, code number seven-six-five-eight-nine-nine-zero. What's Protocol 9?"

"God be with you folks," the President said.

The monitor went blank.

Andy's stomach did a slow roll. "What the hell just happened?" he demanded.

Sun reached out and gripped his arm. "I don't like this. Ask Race what's going on."

"It's the last safety measure," Race said, "in case all others fail. In 1967 I authorized a one-kiloton nuclear device to be buried under Samhain."

"What? A nuke?"

Sun closed her eyes. "A nuke."

"Race." Andy gripped the receiver, knuckles white, fighting to remain calm. "You can't blow us up."

"I'm sorry, son. If Bub gets out, he could destroy the world. I don't have a choice here."

"What about our choice?" Andy pleaded.

"It's in God's hands now."

"God?" Andy laughed. "Didn't you hear? Bub is God. He came from outer space and created all life on Earth."

Sun wrestled the phone from Andy.

"General, you have to give us a chance. Is the Yellow Arm the only way out?"

There was a pause. Andy put his ear next to the receiver and heard Race say, "Yes."

"You paused. Why did you pause? Is there another way out?"

"I'm sorry, Sunshine. It has to be this way."

"Don't do this, Race. Please."

"I'm setting the timer for an hour," Race said. "Give you time to make your peace, have one last fling, whatever you want to do."

"Race . . ."

"We're saving the world, Sun. Take some solace in that." The general hung up.

Andy stared at Sun, then at Dr. Belgium. They both looked devastated.

"We have to turn off that nuke," he said.

Sun met his eyes. "We don't even know if it can be turned off."

"We have to try."

Sun shook her head. "How do we get through the bars? And even if we manage that, how do we get past Helen?"

"We'll find a way. Race said we have an hour."

"An hour? We couldn't even do it with power tools."

"There's the central-air vent." Dr. Belgium pointed above to the left of the Blue door near the ceiling. "It's big enough to crawl in. Race had to go in there once, around ten years ago, to fix a weld."

Andy's heart leapt. "Where does it go?"

"The ducts go through the ceilings all over the compound."

"We still can't go into the Yellow Arm," Sun said. "Not without some kind of weapon."

"Race had that cattle prod. I'm betting it's in his room."

*CLANG-CLANG-CLANG-CLANG!*

They all turned to look at Bub, who'd gripped the titanium bars and shook them with ferocious power.

"Free meeeeeeee!" Bub hissed. "I'll help you turn off the bomb if you free meeeeeee. Fraaaaank . . ."

The demon focused his attention on the biologist.

"I know things about science that yoooooooou couldn't even comprehend. I could teeeeeach you. You'd surpass Crick. Surpass Einsteeeein." Frank looked away.

"Suuuuuuun," Bub implored. "I can take away your paaain, heal the wounds of the paaaaaaaast."

Sun gave Bub her back and folded her arms.

"Andy . . ."

Andy gave Bub the finger.

"Foooools. Then diiiiiiiiie!"

Bub roared, an unholy screech that made Andy's ears ring, then disappeared down the Red Arm.

"We have to defend ourselves somehow. Bub might making more of those things out of Father Thrist."

"How many can he make?" Andy asked.

Sun did a quick count. "There are about eighty dead ones here. So we should expect another eighty."

"Can we barricade the gate?" Belgium asked.

"He can fit his hands through the bars. He'll just push the barricade down."

"How about a net?"

"Made of what?"

Belgium scanned a desktop, then held up a pack of yellow Post-it notes.

"I don't think that will hold, Frank. But it can't hurt to start piling stuff up against the gate."

Andy set the timer on his watch for fifty-five minutes.

"Let's move like our lives depend on it," he said.

Belgium began to stack chairs against the Red Arm. Andy and Sun pushed a desk over to the air vent. Andy climbed on top. The grating was at waist level, held into place with four screws. Flatheads.

"See if you can find some kind of flat tool. A nail file. A ruler. Something to use as a screwdriver."

Sun rifled through the drawers, then handed him a staple remover. The metal edge fit into the groove on the screwhead. Andy twisted.

The screw didn't budge.

"Not enough leverage. Try to find something else."

Sun left to search for a better tool, while Andy struggled with the staple remover. He tried another screw, pushing down on it hard, his fingers turning white from the pressure.

It moved.

Andy leaned into it, his head pounding, the sweat starting to come.

An agonizing two minutes later, and the screw was out. A long son of a bitch too.

One down, three to go.

"Try this," Sun said. She handed him a piece of metal—one of the drawer tracks from a desk. Andy tried it in the screw.

"Too soft. It just bends."

"I'll keep looking."

Andy went back to work with the staple remover. His fingers were cramped and screaming, and the sweaty tool kept slipping off the screw, making him scrape his knuckles. But he managed to get another screw out.

Checking his watch, he saw they'd lost eight minutes.

"They're coming," Dr. Belgium said.

Andy looked over his shoulder. Belgium had piled a ceiling-high stack of chairs and desks against the Red Arm gate.

Sun ran up to him.

"Andy! You gotta hurry!"

Andy pried up an edge of the vent, stuck his fingers under it, and yanked. He was able to pull the vent to the side, revealing a very narrow opening.

"It's dark," he said, peering in. "And dusty. Does anyone have matches or a lighter?"

"Just get your ass in there," Sun said. "We should be able to see light through the vents when we're over them."

"Bats bats bats!" Belgium said, running up. "I hear them coming down the hall!"

Andy took off his shirt and wound it around his face to keep out the thick dust. Sun and Belgium did the same. Then Andy went in.

There wasn't much space, and Andy couldn't get on all fours to crawl. He moved forward by pulling himself with his fingers in a chin-up motion, using his tiptoes to assist. It was slow going, exhausting, claustrophobic, and it didn't help that Andy had wounds all over his body.

Before long his breathing was choked and labored, and his fingers and calves were cramping.

"Keep going," he heard Sun say behind him.

She touched his foot. It gave him a smidgeon of hope.

Then he heard the squeal of the batlings echo through the vent.

# Chapter 29

Sun didn't like enclosed spaces. With Andy in front of her and Dr. Belgium at her heels, she felt like a sardine. The dust coated the inside of her mouth and nose and made her eyes water.

Belgium tapped her ankle. "They're right behind me."

"Faster, Andy!"

"There's a light ahead. Just a few feet."

Sun scurried forward, trying to push Andy's feet to move him quicker.

"There's a vent. I'm over a hallway."

A clanging sound; Andy banging on the vent, trying to force it open.

Behind Sun, Dr. Belgium screamed.

"Biting me! They're biting!"

Two more clangs, and then Andy disappeared.

Sun saw the light ahead. Andy had knocked out the grating and gone face-first through the opening on the bottom of the vent.

"Keep moving, Frank!" she yelled. "Just a few more feet!"

Sun got her head over the opening and blanched at the ten-foot drop. Andy knelt on the floor, moaning softly. His staples had come loose, and his head gushed blood.

"Andy!"

He glanced up at Sun, his face bathed in confusion. He must have hit the floor hard.

Sun couldn't wait for him to get his bearings.

"Andy! Catch me!"

She wiggled through the opening and fell into his arms. He caught her and hugged her tight to his chest, and they tumbled over onto their sides.

Andy blinked, then grinned at her.

"We've got to stop meeting like this," he said. "People will talk."

"Coming down!"

Dr. Belgium dropped through the grate like a stone, landing on top of the couple. He hit Sun with such force that she saw stars and had the air knocked out of her chest.

Belgium was followed by a dark wave of batlings, which quickly filled the hall with swirling fury.

Sun sucked in a breath and looked around. They were in the Blue Arm, only a few yards away from her room. She had a can of Mace in there. Along with something that might be even more helpful.

Sun managed to get to her feet and scrambled for her door, batlings swooping on her at all angles. She tugged the knob, dove onto the bed, and wrapped her fists around the two racquetball racquets she'd left there since her earlier game with Andy.

Sun rushed back into the fray in time to see Dr. Belgium run screaming down the hall.

"Andy!" she yelled, tossing him a racquet.

The batlings went straight for blood, biting at Sun's

wounds. She pulled off the ones that had begun to chew and adopted her game stance.

The demons flew fast, but not as fast as a racquetball bounced. On Sun's first swing she smacked one down the hall, splattering it against a door.

It felt good.

Another dove straight at her face, screeching, and she backhanded it to the left.

*Whack!*

She forearmed another into the ceiling.

*Whack!*

Two flew at her head-on, and with an overhand smash she catapulted both into the floor. Sun hit another so hard its claws got stuck in her racquet string.

She yanked it out and tossed it aside.

The former American Racquetball Association women's champion swung again and again, her racquet slicing through the air in all directions, knocking away batlings as fast as they could fly at her.

She chanced a look at Andy, who was displacing so many demons he seemed to be waving around a large net.

The batlings smartened up. They stayed out of Sun's swinging range and tried to attack her from the side and from behind. Sun dodged left, jumped, and hammered two more.

Less than twenty remained, and Sun kicked it into overdrive, bringing the fight to her attackers. She set her jaw and sprang into the thick of them, staying on the balls of her feet, moving the racquet as fast as she could. Blood hung in the air like a mist, coating her face, making the racquet handle slippery. The constant flapping and screeching became intermittent, and then almost nonexistent.

Just a handful remained, and the veterinarian hunted them down, one at a time.

A final demon, screaming like a smoke alarm, bee-lined for Sun's face in a suicidal attempt to get at her throat.

Sun whacked it so hard it bounced off two walls.

The veterinarian turned completely around, searching for another flying attacker.

There were none. The floor was littered with the dead and dying; almost a hundred of them. Several were still twitching or trying to flap their broken wings. The once-pristine hallway now resembled a slaughterhouse.

Something touched her shoulder, and Sun whirled around, ready to swing.

*Andy.*

"I'm checking Race's room for the cattle prod." She touched his head. He flinched.

"I've got some superglue in my room."

"For what?" Andy's eyes looked up, as if he could see his own scalp.

"You're kidding, right?"

"It's better than staples. Surgeons use it. What time do you have?"

Andy checked his watch. "Thirty-six minutes until we're fried."

"I'll meet you back out here in two minutes." Sun turned to go, but Andy caught her arm.

"Wait a sec."

She turned. "What is it?"

Sun searched his face, saw tenderness.

"Watching you, since all of this began, you're so brave."

"We're both brave."

"No. I'm just trying to stay alive. You told me about your fear of bats, how they freaked you out. You faced that fear, and won. I want to be like that."

Injured as he was, she never had a man look at her with so much longing.

"It's easy to be brave," she breathed. "Don't think about it. Just do it."

Andy put his arm around the small of her back, pulled her close, and kissed her.

Sun hurt in a hundred places. Andy tasted like blood and sweat and dust, and he smelled even worse, and his hand was pressed right up against an open batling bite on her side, and this was the worst possible timing in the history of male-female relations.

It was also the best kiss of Sun's life.

She kissed him back, enjoying the spark of electricity that ran helter-skelter over her nerve endings. She may have even moaned a little.

When they finally broke the kiss, Andy said, "Wow."

No one had ever given Sun a "Wow" before.

"Meet me back here in two minutes," she said. "And be careful. We don't know what else is running around here."

Sun hurried to her room, and only after closing the door did she wonder what happened to Dr. Belgium.

# CHAPTER 30

When the hallway filled with batlings, Dr. Belgium looked to Sun and Andy to tell him what to do. He watched Sun tear down the hall and run into her room.

*Good idea*, Belgium thought.

He took off after Sun, a swarm of demons striking him from all directions. He almost panicked. The batlings instilled the same primordial fear as a swarm of bees or a nest of vipers. Even worse, they were intelligent, aiming for Belgium's eyes, biting at his legs and back and other places he couldn't swat with his hands.

The high-pitched squealing sound they made, the electric pain appearing all over his body like bullet hits, the blood blinding his eyes—part of him wanted to just give up and die.

He quickly realized he wasn't going to reach his room alive. The creatures were in his face, and he couldn't see. Every time he knocked one off, another took its place.

So Belgium did what he was taught in grammar school.

Stop, drop, and roll.

The batlings that clung to him were crushed under

his weight. The others couldn't land on him. Dizziness be damned, this was the perfect protection.

Until he hit the wall.

Disoriented, he reached up, his fingers finding purchase on a doorknob. He got to his knees and entered the room, slamming the door closed behind him.

He checked his clothes, to see if any batlings still clung to him. One was gnawing on his left calf, and he tore it off and tossed it at the bed.

It was then that he noticed what was left of Dr. Harker.

". . . oh dear oh dear oh dear."

Something had gotten to her. Something big and hungry. Her dead eyes were wide open, and her mouth frozen in a scream of raw agony. Glancing at her lower body, Belgium could guess she'd been alive for much of the meal.

The batling on the bed squeaked, shook itself off, and took flight. It came straight at Belgium, and he moved up his forearm to shield his face from the attack.

But before the demon reached him, a long pink whip snatched it out of the air with a *thwack!* The batling, and the tongue that held it, vanished behind the bed.

Then came munching sounds.

Belgium held his breath, reaching his hand behind him, seeking the doorknob.

In the hallway he could hear the squealing of the brood. Going back out there wasn't a viable option.

Maybe if he kept very still, the thing behind the bed wouldn't come out.

As soon as the thought left his head, the thing behind the bed came out.

It looked like an albino alligator, with a grossly inflated and misshapen human head. Bulging, cloudy white eyes without pupils darted left, then right, eventually resting on Belgium. The creature blinked and stretched open its mouth.

It had more teeth than Bub did.

"Oh shit shit shit."

Its six legs bent, and it hopped onto the bed. Belgium watched its nostrils flare as it sniffed the air.

The hallway was looking better and better.

"Um, hello there," Belgium said, his mouth so dry he felt as if he'd gargled with sand.

The creature cocked its head to the side. The milky eyes regarded him.

"Hello," it said. Its voice was that of a child.

Frank came very close to wetting his pants. "I'm, um, Dr. Belgium. What's your name?" It moved closer.

"Do you have a name?" Belgium asked again.

"Shirley," said the monster.

Belgium glanced to the left. The bathroom. If he could get in there and lock the door . . .

Shirley's tongue fired from its mouth as if spring-loaded, wrapping around Belgium's ankle.

He screamed, then threw his whole body toward the bathroom, barely getting out of the way as Shirley leapt at him.

Frank moved faster than he'd ever moved in his life, diving for the tile floor, kicking the bathroom door shut—it wouldn't close.

Shirley's tongue was still around his leg.

Belgium placed both feet on the door and pushed until the veins stood out on his forehead.

Shirley let out a heart-wrenching cry, and then the tongue severed, becoming slack.

Belgium pressed the lock button on the door knob, kicked away the slimy tongue, and almost wept with relief.

The relief was interrupted by an odd sound—a mixture of scratching and gurgling—coming from the door.

Belgium crab-walked away from the sound and watched in horrific fascination as a small hole appeared.

Shirley, like an organic chainsaw, was chewing her way through the wood at an alarming rate.

Frank looked around for a weapon. He picked up a toothbrush from the sink, then put it back down. In the medicine cabinet were various pill bottles, some tweezers, and a comb.

He checked the door again, and Shirley had widened the hole to a ten-inch circumference. She'd be crawling through any second.

Belgium reached up for the shower curtain rod, but it was bolted to the walls. The curtain itself was thin, useless. He spun and faced the toilet. Maybe the toilet seat? No time to unscrew it. But atop the tank was a heavy, porcelain cover. Belgium hefted it, whirling around just as Shirley stuck her head through the hole in the door.

He gave the swing everything he had, cracking her skull so hard that the lid split in two. The creature was knocked backward, out of the hole.

Belgium craned an ear, listening. He could hear only his own beating heart.

Did he kill it? Was the thing dead?

He slowly reached for the doorknob, but then thought better of it. Instead he took a step away from the door, then cautiously bent over to look through the hole.

*Almost there . . . can almost see . . .*

The tongue slapped against his face like a garden hose and wrapped around his neck, pulling Belgium to his knees. He gasped in horror as Shirley stuck her head through the opening, mouth open wide.

She began to reel her tongue in.

At first, Belgium's mind couldn't grasp the situation. Inch by inch, he was being drawn into her gaping jaws.

Then reality hit, and once again he screamed.

Unwilling to submit to the impending facectomy, Belgium planted both feet against the door and pulled hard.

Shirley answered by pulling even harder, tightening the tongue noose around his neck.

Belgium's oxygen got cut off, and he began to lose the tug-of-war. Though he loathed to touch the beast, he made a V with his fingers and poked them right into Shirley's bulging white eyes.

She cried out, the tongue loosening its hold. Belgium yanked on it with both hands, stretched it upward, and tied it in a quick granny knot around the doorknob.

Then he shoved the door open and crawled past the thrashing, screaming Shirley.

Batlings be damned, he had to get the hell out of there.

Belgium threw open the door and rushed out into the Blue Arm, slamming the door shut behind him.

There were no batlings left.

He just about wept with relief.

Then he heard the familiar scratching-gurgling sound.

Shirley was free, and biting through the door. Soon she'd be in the hallway.

Andy stuck his head out of Blue 1, and Belgium ran in and slammed the door behind him.

"Frank? Are you okay?"

"We need need need to get out of here."

"What's going on?"

Belgium's eyes scanned the room, frantic.

"Weapon. We need a weapon."

Something hit the door with a tremendous thump.

"What the hell is that?" Andy said.

"That's Shirley," Belgium said, gasping. "She ate Harker, and she's still hungry."

Andy picked up the phone and dialed a number.

"Sun, there's something in the hallway. Don't leave your room."

The biting sound came from behind the door. Belgium watched the sawdust begin to fly, and the blur of gnashing teeth.

"Did you find the cattle prod?" Belgium asked.

"Not yet. Maybe it's not even here."

"He's military, he'd keep his only weapon nearby."

Belgium looked under the bed and came up with a white stick. "It doesn't look big enough," Belgium said.

"Figure out how it works."

Andy went into the general's closet and began taking clothes off hangers.

"What are you going to do, dress it?" Belgium said.

Andy knocked away hangers and pulled out the closet rod. It was four feet long and two and a half inches wide, solid wood.

"Can you use that prod?" Andy asked.

"I think so."

Andy raised the rod above the hole.

But, as quickly as it had begun, the chewing stopped.

Andy bent down to look through the hole. Belgium stopped him.

"Don't. It knows that trick."

They waited for almost a full minute.

"It's going after Sun," Andy said. "We have to go get her."

Frank couldn't think of anything he wanted to do less, but the thought of that nice veterinarian alone with that horrible thing forced him to move.

Andy motioned with his chin for Belgium to open the door.

Dr. Belgium fought every ounce of common sense he had and reached for the knob, slowly turning it.

Andy gave him a nod.

*Here goes nothing.*

Belgium flung the door open and Andy gripped the rod and brought it back like a baseball bat.

The demon wasn't there.

Belgium crept into the hallway, looking right, looking left.

"Where the hell did it go?" Andy asked.

"Maybe it went back to Harker's room. Or maybe . . ."

Belgium looked at the floor, making out the faint bloody footprints the thing had left while chasing him. The prints stopped at Race's room, then went over to the opposite wall, and . . .

"Up the wall," Belgium said.

Andy and Frank raised their heads, slowly, to the

ceiling. The demon was hanging upside down like a giant gecko, staring at them with its milky eyes.

It pounced. Andy swung, but it landed inside the arc of the rod and hit him squarely in the chest, knocking him back into Race's room.

Belgium watched as the creature dug in its claws and snapped at Andy's neck. Andy shoved the closet rod into the hinge of its jaws, forcing its head back.

Frank rushed to help the linguist.

"Take that that that!" Dr. Belgium yelled.

Frank hit the thing in the side with the cattle prod.

Nothing happened.

Belgium looked at the prod and flipped the switch in the other direction and tried again.

Nothing.

"Dammit, Frank!" Andy yelped, struggling with the beast. "You're a goddamn molecular biologist! Figure the damn thing out!"

Belgium flipped the switch twice more, then noticed the handle could turn.

He twisted it, heard a click, and touched the prod to the hellspawn.

There was a loud crack and a spark at the contact point. The thing squealed and rolled off Andy. Belgium thrust the prod at the creature again and nothing happened.

"Reset it!" Andy yelled, getting to his feet.

The demon lunged at Belgium, toppling him over and sending the cattle prod skittering across the floor.

*Snap snap snap* went the beast's jaws. Belgium gripped its neck and tried to force it away, a battle he was quickly losing as the teeth inched closer. Its breath was hot and sour, and the injured tongue shot out and once more got Frank in a stranglehold.

As his vision blurred, Frank saw Andy step behind the demon and swing the rod like a home run champion. The contact was solid, and Belgium could feel the shock of the blow vibrating through the monster's tongue.

The thing rolled from Dr. Belgium's chest, and Andy followed up with another vicious swing to its head. The wet *whap* was accompanied by a cracking sound, and Shirley slumped over.

Belgium reached for the dropped cattle prod. He turned the handle and shoved it at the demon's body, causing a burn where it made contact.

Belgium did it again, and then once more.

Shirley didn't move.

"I think we got it," Andy said.

Belgium zapped it twice more.

Sun appeared, clutching a towel and a tiny cylinder of pepper spray.

"What was it?" she asked.

"One more reason to avoid working for the government," Andy said. "We need to find the vent that'll lead to the Yellow Arm. Frank!" Belgium was still zapping the dead creature.

"Frank! It's dead! Save the battery!"

"Better safe than sorry."

"The Yellow Arm is to the right of the Blue Arm," Sun said. "Down the hall here there's another ceiling vent. I bet it goes both ways, left to the Purple arm and right to the Yellow."

"We'll drag a dresser out here to stand on. Frank! Enough with the cattle prod!"

Belgium zapped the demon once more, for good measure, and then joined them.

With a little difficulty, they pushed a dresser out into the hall under the ceiling grill, up onto its end. Andy took out the drawers, which allowed him to climb the piece of furniture like a ladder. He pulled off the vent and peered inside. "The duct ends in a T, going off in both left and right directions."

"How much time left?" Sun asked.

Andy checked his watch.

"Twenty-six minutes."

"Hold still."

Sun used the towel to wipe away the blood on Andy's scalp, and then went to work on his wound with a tube of superglue.

"Is this going to . . . ow! Jesus!"

"Hold still. I'll be done in a second."

Belgium took a deep, calming breath, which was no help at all. Everything hurt. He felt miserable. Not just for himself, but for this cute young couple, who'd done nothing to bring this shitstorm down on themselves.

"Sun, Andy," he said. "I'm really sorry. This is all my fault."

"Were you the one who gave him the code for the gate?" Sun asked.

"What? No no no. Of course not. I let him use the Internet because I thought it would help teach him to read. Now I see—"

"Don't worry about it." Sun pocketed the superglue and patted his shoulder.

"But—"

"No buts. Bub has been planning this all along. He got to all of us, in one way or another. Don't beat yourself up over it. This isn't your fault."

Belgium felt a lump grow in his throat. Sun had no way of knowing it, but she'd given him the nicest gift he'd ever received.

"Thank you, Sun."

"Now let's go stop a nuclear explosion."

# Chapter 31

Since Bub first walked the Earth there had been over five hundred attempts on his life. Sometimes it was just a single assassin armed with an ineffectual club or a useless dagger. Other times it was a conspiracy of many, or a carefully prepared trap.

He'd eluded death in all situations. Besides the fact that he was extremely hard to kill, Bub had developed a knack for thinking like humans. They rarely surprised him. The closest he'd ever been to actual death was at the hands of the Maya, and only then because they'd been extremely lucky.

But this time, Bub was worried. A one-kiloton weapon, the equivalent of two million pounds of TNT, was more than enough to blow him into oblivion.

And even if the nuke didn't explode, it still posed a threat.

Something had to be done. Something quick.

The demon went to the end of the hallway and stared at the air-conditioning vent. He put his ear to it, listening to the faint sounds of the humans inching their way through. Bub was much too big to fit inside the small duct, but that could be fixed.

With one talon he yanked off the grating.

The demon closed his eyes and focused on his own DNA structure. He hadn't lied to Belgium about that. Bub knew his genome like a man knows his name. He'd memorized every base pair, every gene, every chromosome, and knew what every one of them did.

He did some quick equations in his head, decided what needed to be done, and placed his right claw on his chest, injecting himself with his own essence.

Genetic manipulation had limits. Bub couldn't make the drastic changes to himself as he did with other life-forms. If he altered his own genome too much, he'd become something entirely different and wouldn't be able to change back.

He also had a set mass to work with, and it was impossible to make himself larger or smaller. Bub could not have turned into a rat in order to fit through the bars of the gate. But he could change his genome enough to fit into the air-conditioning duct. He'd done it earlier today, when he escaped his habitat through the sheep's door, after that zealot Father Thrist refused to help.

All it took was a little time and effort.

Without pain, his shoulders dislocated and moved up alongside his neck. His skull elongated and his mouth shrank, his ram's horns flattening against his face and curved inward. With a crackling sound, Bub's ribs stretched out and compacted, making his torso longer and thinner. Both hips popped audibly from their sockets and slid closer together. His organs shifted around in his body cavity, adjusting to their new spaces.

Bub was now twice as long and half as thick. He resembled a fun house mirror reflection of himself.

He stuck his head into the vent and glared in the

direction of the humans. They could wait. For the moment, they were allies, no more wanting to explode in a nuclear fireball than he did.

Bub looked to the left, sniffing the air. That was where the sheep were.

The demon wormed his way into the vent and slithered snakelike to the Orange Arm. He knocked out the ceiling grate with a flick of his wrist and poured himself out of the duct and into the Orange Arm hallway.

His nose took him to Orange 12, and he went in. Inside were over a dozen sheep. But Bub wasn't hungry.

In order to escape Samhain, Bub had to be able to bypass these titanium gates. They'd been built to withstand a creature of his size and strength. But how would they hold up to a much larger creature?

Bub looked at the thousands of pounds of raw material around him and got started.

# CHAPTER 32

Andy looked down into the Yellow Arm from the ceiling vent.

No Helen.

He carefully bent the grating down and eased himself over the opening, going through legs-first rather than face-first like he had in the Blue Arm.

His landing was louder than he would have liked. His eyes nervously scanned both directions to see if the creature was coming.

So far, so good.

Sun handed him the clothes rod, and he helped her exit the duct. They both assisted Dr. Belgium.

"Where do you think she is?" Frank whispered.

They moved down the hall slowly, Andy paying special attention to the ceiling—he wasn't going to let anything drop on him again.

"Do you hear that?" Sun said.

Andy held his breath and listened.

"It sounds like laughter."

"A laugh track," Sun said. "It's a television."

"She's watching TV?"

"Not beyond the scope of possibility," Belgium said.

"Helen watched a lot of TV. Maybe when Bub changed her genome, some of her memory remained intact."

There was faint applause, then a recognizable soda jingle. Dr. Belgium hummed along with it.

Down the hall, at Helen's old room, the door opened.

"Uh-oh," Frank said.

The Helen demon stepped out into the hallway, hoofs clicking on the tile floor. Andy noted that it was three times as big as that alligator monster they'd just killed. The curtain rod suddenly felt ineffectual.

"We should go back up the vent," Andy said softly.

"Come on." Sun tugged him. "In here."

They slipped silently into Yellow 9, an empty closet.

"It's too big," Andy whispered. "We won't be able to kill it."

"Maybe we can sneak past it."

The three of them cautiously peeked out the doorway. The demon had moved down the hall and stopped in front of Yellow 4. It sniffed at the keypad, then squatted down next to the door.

"That's where Race is," Dr. Belgium said. "The bomb room." They waited. Minutes passed. The demon stayed put.

Andy checked his watch. They had thirteen minutes left.

"We're running out of time," Dr. Belgium said. "We have to distract it, yes yes yes."

"Sure. I'll throw a stick, see if it'll fetch."

"We should attack," Sun said.

Andy stared at her, incredulous. "It practically killed Race, and he's a lot tougher than we are."

"Hold on." Belgium rubbed his chin. "If it watches

TV, maybe part of Helen is still in there somewhere. Let me try to talk to her." The demon yawned, showing more teeth than a dog kennel.

"Maybe that's not too smart of an idea," Sun said.

"I have to try. Helen?" Belgium stepped out of the closet, his hands raised in supplication. "It's me, Frank. Remember?"

The demon leapt to its feet and, red eyes narrowing, turned to face Belgium.

Belgium took a slow step toward it.

"Hello, Helen. Remember how I used to come to your room and we'd play checkers?"

A guttural sound came from the Helen-thing's mouth.

"See see see?" Frank said. "She remembers." He took another step forward.

"This is going to end badly," Andy whispered to Sun. "We should do something."

"Frank . . ." Sun warned.

"It's okay." Belgium shooed them back. "Helen, we could play checkers again someday. Would you like that?"

The demon's wings suddenly opened, and it stretched out its arms the width of the hallway, scraping at the plaster with its talons.

"Frank," Andy said slowly, "I don't think the hell-spawn wants to play checkers with you."

"I know part of you is still human," Belgium went on. "Maybe we could somehow change you back. If not, well . . . I understand there are some very nice zoos."

The creature howled and launched itself down the hall.

"Run, Frank!"

Belgium backpedaled, then turned around and passed by Andy and Sun.

The demon sprang, knocking Sun aside and latching its claws onto Andy's shoulder. Its grip was agonizing. Andy swung at its face and the beast snapped down on his hand, razor teeth slicing into his wrist. Andy screamed and tried frantically to yank it free.

Sun Maced the creature in the face. The creature didn't seem to be bothered much, but when the pepper spray hit Andy's chewed hand, he reached a whole new level of pain.

From the corner of his eye, he watched the demon swat Sun away.

"Andy!" Dr. Belgium yelled.

He rushed up to Helen and rammed the cattle prod into the demon's mouth, past the sharp teeth, and bent the prod upward.

Andy pulled out his hand, giving Belgium more room to jam the prod in farther, down the thing's throat.

The effect was immediate. The demon dropped Andy and grabbed the biologist, drawing him close in a bear hug. It shook its head back and forth, trying to dislodge the obstruction.

Frank kept his grip on the prod and shoved once more, grunting with effort. It went down the demon's throat almost to the hilt. Then he turned the handle and gave the beast some juice.

Helen's whole body went rigid, smoke curling out the corners of her mouth. She released Frank and collapsed onto the floor, her red eyes rolling up in her head.

Sun jumped on her with the curtain rod, swinging it

over and over, until the demon's head cracked open like a dropped watermelon.

Helen twitched twice, then ceased all movement.

"Well," Belgium said. "That was horrible." He nudged the creature with his foot. "Dead dead dead."

Andy clutched his wrist. Blood spurted through his fingers with his heartbeat, a good amount of it pooling on the floor.

He dropped to his knees.


*An artery*, Sun thought, looking at Andy.

She knelt next to him. He was pale, his face clammy and cold, his breathing shallow. A quick inspection of the wound found it to be ugly; the creature had bitten him almost to the bone. She took Andy's pulse. Weak. She unbuckled his belt and pulled it off his waist, cinching it tight about the wound.

"Hold here," she told Belgium, taking his hand and putting it on Andy's wrist below the tourniquet. "Don't let him close his eyes."

Sun ran down the hall into the med supply room, Yellow 6. She grabbed everything in a whirlwind; a 100-cc bag of saline solution with an IV drip, a surgical needle, a bottle of rubbing alcohol, a pack of cotton swabs, a scalpel, a gallon jug of sterile water. She searched quickly for clamps, but couldn't find any.

The hell with it; there was no time. If she didn't stop the bleeding now, Sun knew Andy was going to die.

"Pour this on your hands," she said to Belgium, tossing him the alcohol. When he finished, she repeated the procedure with her own hands and then poured the remaining alcohol onto Andy's wound.

He moaned weakly.

"Open the scalpel package," Sun told Belgium. "Pour some water on him, clear away the blood."

Keeping pressure on his wrist, Sun spread open the gash with her fingers to peer inside. The blood flow had stopped, so she loosened the belt to see its source.

When the blood came, it came fast.

"Now."

Belgium poured, washing blood away. The ulnar artery was completely severed, as was the median antebrachial vein. The radial artery had a gash in it. Sun cinched the belt tight.

"Scalpel," Sun ordered, "and open the needle pack."

Belgium complied. Sun cut into Andy's flesh, lengthening the width of the wound so she could fit her fingers in. Andy yelped and tried to pull away.

"Hold his arm steady. You can't let him squirm."

"Okay okay okay."

"You see, here? I need you to put your fingers on that artery and squeeze."

Belgium kept one hand on Andy's forearm and stuck the other into the gash, doing what he was told.

Sun poured more water on the wound, then took hold of the prethreaded half-moon needle.

"Don't worry," she told Andy. "I'm gonna do this right. Just hold real still."

Sun tied off the artery, greatly reducing the blood flow. She didn't have a clamp to hold the needle, so she did it freehand, her fingers slick with blood. Belgium had to let go of Andy's twitching forearm to dump more water on the wound.

Quickly, expertly, Sun sutured the ulnar artery back together. Her next job was the gash in the radial. It was on the underside and tough to see. "Hold him," Sun said. She tied the artery off and then tugged on it lightly to get a better look.

"Jesus!" Andy cried.

"You're not getting religious on me, are you?" Sun said.

Sun sewed up the radial artery, then got to work on the severed antebrachial vein. Her concentration was pinpoint. She was tired, hurt all over, and emotionally frazzled, but she wouldn't allow it to get in the way of her job.

Not this time.

She finished, and then cut the thread she'd used to tie off the arteries. They filled with pumping blood. Sun poured on more water and looked for leaks.

None.

She smiled to herself.

"Get something to put under his feet," Sun told Belgium.

Andy's blood pressure was still weak. She ripped open the IV pack and dug the needle into a vein on his good hand. Belgium came back with a chair and raised Andy's feet up onto the seat.

"I have to close him up. What's our time?" Belgium glanced at Andy's watch.

"Four minutes."

"Find Race, shut off the bomb." Belgium nodded, hurrying off.

Sun hung the saline bag on the end of the chair and began to stitch Andy's wrist closed.

"You'll make it," she told him. "But I don't know if we will."

# CHAPTER 33

Race was dying.

It suited him just fine. Losing Helen was devastating. He'd spent years trying to become emotionally detached, and then for one brief, magic moment, she was his again, body and soul.

He realized, after more than four decades of marriage, that he'd made the wrong choice. Helen was more important than Samhain, more important than even his beloved army. Race should have cherished his years with her, rather than wasted them here.

And now she was gone.

Bub's words had hit home. Helen surely must have hated him for keeping her here all that time. When she developed Huntington's, Race considered her his burden. But all along, he was her burden.

Race welcomed death. The thought of it warmed him. Never a religious man, the one-in-a-million chance that there was an afterlife, and that Helen might be there waiting for him, far outweighed his desire for this world.

"Race?" A knock. "It's Frank Belgium. The door is locked. Are you in there?"

"Yeah, I'm here."

The words took great effort. Race figured he'd lost more than two pints of blood.

"Can you let me in?"

"Code is one-seven-one-nine-five-nine."

His wedding anniversary.

The lock disengaged and Dr. Belgium came into the room. He was just as bloody as Race, his lab coat more red than white.

"How did you get through Lockdown?"

"Air ducts."

"Helen?" Race asked.

"She's at peace now. I'm sorry. Dr. Harker is dead too. Andy's badly hurt."

"Bub?"

"Still locked in the Red Arm."

Race sighed painfully. "For a hundred years of planning and safeguards, it all went to hell pretty fast."

"The best-laid plans often go astray," the biologist said. "It's not your fault."

"Of course it's my fault. Armies don't lose wars. Leaders lose wars."

"Race . . ." Belgium put a hand on his shoulder. "We want you to shut off the nuke."

The general said nothing.

"We've known each other what, twenty years? You know why I came to Samhain, right?" Race nodded.

"General, I let Bub out of the habitat. He went on the Internet. All of those questions he answered . . . it was all garbage garbage garbage. Stuff he picked up off the Web."

"Stupid thing to do."

"I know. You think I would have learned after twenty years." Belgium eased himself into a sitting position, next to Race.

"Did you know I was married?"

Race gave his head a slight shake.

"I thought I loved her, but in reality I suppose I didn't. All I ever loved was my work. Such a beautiful thing, genetics. So beautiful and perfect. Perfect perfect perfect."

Belgium stared deeply into Race's eyes. "That's what life is all about, General. Loving something. Maybe a person, or a thing, but something. Like you loved Helen."

The general's eyes became glassy.

"You've seen Andy and Sun together . . . Race, we're older, you and I. We've lived our lives. And we've had to live with our mistakes. Please. I can't let them die. Not because of me."

"Doesn't matter," Race said. "I switch off the nuke, the President will still destroy Samhain. It's a hardened target, two hundred feet underground, but he could get it done within two hours."

"At least that gives us two more hours. You, above all people, should know how precious a few hours can be." Race knew.

*"How about that?"* Helen had said, zipping up her evening gown only hours before. *"Still fits."*

*"You know you're even more beautiful than the day I met you,"* Race told her.

*She smiled. It lit up the room. Race would have given her the world, right then, if she'd only asked.*

*"Oh, Regis. This is so perfect, being with you right now. I love you, my dear."*

*"I love you too, Helen. Now let's cut up that rug, shall we?"*

He could still smell her perfume on him, beneath all the blood.

"The panel," Race told Belgium. "Turn the switch to the left, then punch in these numbers. Six, three, six, zero, niner."

Belgium stood up and punched in the code. There was a beep, and the timer stopped with two minutes to spare.

"Is there another way out of Samhain?" Belgium asked.

Race coughed. A thin line of blood dripped down his chin.

"Maybe. Most of Samhain is made of natural caverns—this area is full of them. When they were building this compound, they came in through the underground from a few miles away. Then they sealed off the connecting tunnel when they were done."

"Where is it?"

"Somewhere in the Green Arm. You need to bust through a wall, I don't know which one. You'll have to find the old blueprints. They should be in Red 3."

"How about tools? Shovels, picks, axes?"

"In one of the Green rooms there's a bunch of old excavating equipment. And I mean old. Left here from when they built the compound. Maybe you can dig your way into the original access tunnel, if you can find it, and escape through the caverns before the President nukes the whole area."

"Can you come with us?"

Race shook his head.

Dr. Belgium took Race's hand and grasped it firmly. "Thank you, General. It was an honor serving under you."

"Promise me something." Race stared hard at Frank.

"Yes?"

"Whatever happens, see to it Bub doesn't live for another day."

Dr. Belgium smiled warmly. "Consider it done done done."

The general watched the biologist leave. He'd always liked Dr. Belgium.

He liked Sun and Andy too, even though he barely knew them.

It was too bad. Even if they did break through to the caverns, it wasn't likely they could get far enough away in time. When the Samhain nuke didn't go off, the President wouldn't take any chances. He'd drop something substantially bigger than a single kiloton to guarantee zero chance of survival. There were strategic bomber bases in both Roswell and Amarillo. Race guessed he'd send an F-111E equipped with a B83 bomb, capped by a nuclear warhead of at least twenty kilotons.

Slightly larger than the payload of Little Boy in the Hiroshima blast.

A surface impact would disintegrate Samhain, and pretty much everything else for a mile in all directions. Even if they managed to navigate the caves and get two miles away, they'd still have to deal with second-to-third-degree burns, hundred-mile-per-hour winds from the overpressure, and the radiation exposure, depending on the fissile material used.

*A shame*, the general thought.

But better to go down swinging than lie there like a lump, as he was doing.

One-star general Regis Murdoch sighed. Then he closed his eyes and waited quietly for death.

# Chapter 34

Andy opened his eyes to the concerned face of Dr. Sunshine Jones. She had blood and dust smeared over both cheeks, and her hair was matted and tangled.

"You're beautiful," Andy said.

"You're delirious. How do you feel?"

He lifted his hand and wiggled the fingers. The wrist was expertly taped up.

"It's numb."

"Lidocaine. You won't be able to use it for a while." Sun ran her fingers over Andy's forehead.

Andy said, "Thanks. You know, for saving my life."

"That's what we doctors do."

"How about the bomb?"

"Race switched it off. But there's still a problem. He said the President would nuke Samhain anyway."

"Our tax dollars at work."

"Can you move?"

Andy sat up. His vision began to swirl and he instantly felt sick.

"Dizzy," he said. "How long do we have?"

"An hour, maybe two. Dr. Belgium went to the Octopus to contact the President. But if that doesn't work, we may still have a chance." Sun outlined the plan as Belgium had relayed it to her.

"The blueprints are in Red 3?" Andy asked.

"Yes. I remember filing them."

"Bub's in the Red Arm."

"I know."

"Are we supposed to tiptoe in while he's sleeping?"

"Maybe we won't have to," Sun said. "In the med supply room there are over a thousand different pharmaceuticals. How about I make Bub a little cocktail?"

Andy smiled. "Make it a big one."


Sun left Andy in the hall and went into Yellow 6. She found a reusable enema on a shelf: a large rubber squeeze bulb with a thin plastic nozzle. To the end of the nozzle she attached a short length of plastic tubing and an IV needle. She now had a very big syringe.

Recalling Bub's medical test history, Sun couldn't remember which drugs had been tested on him. He'd been given many diseases, all of which caused no effect. So what would be good to try?

She began by looking at some sedatives.


Frank Belgium crawled through the air-conditioning duct and into the Octopus, heaving with effort. His muscles were screaming at him. Even during the years at school and at BioloGen, he'd never been so exhausted. He sat down in the nearest chair and rubbed his neck and shoulders. After a few seconds he became aware of something wrong.

Bub was gone.

Belgium walked to the Red Arm and pulled down the stacked chairs, searching for the demon.

There was nothing, as far back as he could see.

Perhaps Bub had given up and locked himself back in the habitat. A pleasant thought, but Belgium didn't think that was the case.

Moving quickly, Belgium reached through the bars in the gates and opened up the doors for all the arms, searching for the demon.

He didn't find a trace of him.

"Andy! Sun!" Belgium called down the Yellow Arm.

"Yeah?" Andy yelled back. He was sitting next to the doorway to Yellow 6.

"Bub's gone!" Belgium said. "He's not in the Red Arm. I checked the others and he's not there either."

"Keep your eyes open," Andy replied. "I don't see how he could have gotten through that gate, but he's a sneaky bastard."

*He sure is*, the biologist thought, paranoia creeping up. He could feel the demon's eyes on the back of his neck.

Belgium walked around the Octopus again, to make sure Bub wasn't in the room with him. Satisfied he was alone, he sat down at the computer terminal and accessed CONTACT, clicking on EMERGENCY.

Then he waited nervously for the President to answer.


Andy wiggled his fingers and tried to make a fist. He could close his hand only halfway. That wouldn't be good enough; if they were to dig their way out of there he had to be able to hold a pick.

He tried again, straining with effort, and managed a little better. So intent was Andy on his injury that he didn't notice the movement to his right until it was within ten yards.

When he turned to look, his breath caught in his throat.

Bub was snaking silently out of the ceiling vent twenty yards to his right. The demon had somehow stretched its body to over eighteen feet in length. He moved like an inchworm, his middle section rising up in a hump as his rear section met his front claws.

"Aaaaaaaandy."

Bub's elastic face split into a toothy grin. Andy opened his mouth to scream, but Bub was on him before he had the chance.


Dr. Belgium tapped his fingers on the desk, waiting for the President to get on the damn video phone. He heard movement far behind him and felt the hair on the back of his neck spring to attention.

Belgium swiveled around and stared down the Yellow Arm.

Bub had Andy.


Andy had never felt so helpless. Bub had him clutched tightly in one claw. The other was pressed over his mouth, the talons tickling the back of his head.

The demon looked surprisingly different; like a sea serpent or a long, thin Chinese dragon. His face was elongated, reminding Andy of the times as a child he'd pressed Silly Putty onto a comic book and then stretched and distorted the figures. But the bloodshot eyes and the evil grin were pure Bub.

"Has the bomb been deeeeeeeactivated?" Bub whispered, bathing Andy's face with decay.

He removed his claw so Andy could answer.

"No," Andy stammered.

"Liaaaaaaaaaaar."

Andy felt the talons dig into his sides. He was being crushed and couldn't draw a breath. Tears were squeezed from his eyes.

"It was shut off," Andy whimpered.

Bub released his grip slightly and Andy gulped in some air.

"How do I get out of heeeeeere?"

Andy thought about the Green Arm, digging into the original tunnel. If Bub found out about it, it could very well mean the end of the human race.

"The Yellow Arm," Andy said with as much emotion as he could muster.

"There are four gates blocking the exit."

"That's the only waaaaaaaay?"

"Yes."

"Liaaaaaaaaaaaar."

Bub moved his claw down Andy's body. "Here comes the paaaaaaaaain."

* * *

The phone rang in Yellow 6, giving Sun a major startle. She picked it up with more than a little trepidation.

"Bub's in the Yellow Arm," Belgium's voice said in a whisper. "He's got Andy."

Sun thought fast. Already in the enema was enough liquid sodium secobarbital to kill an elephant. She filled the remaining space with the potassium cyanide she'd been looking at and snapped on the nozzle.

Before opening the door she put her ear to it.

Andy was right outside, whimpering.

Sun took a lungful of air and swung open the door.


Bub had heard the phone ring and was ready for Sun. When the door flung open he had a long spindly claw outstretched to wrap around her.

What he hadn't anticipated was her weapon.

As the giant talons encircled Sun's body, she jabbed him in the wrist with some kind of small spear.

This amused Bub, but his demeanor quickly changed to shock when he felt the foreign liquid pulsing into his body, burning as it went.

*What had she done?*

He shoved Sun away, pushing her back into the med supply room, and then tossed Andy aside to yank the weapon out of his palm.

Bub stared at his hand, watching as the hole healed, but his expression was pure bewilderment. The nictitating membranes over his eyes fluttered once, twice. His head swayed back and forth, and then his chin hit the ground with a *SLAP*.

\* \* \*

"Run!" Dr. Belgium yelled at them from the Octopus, looking at them through the gate. But they didn't need to.

Bub was sprawled out on his face.

Sun limped out of Yellow 6, staring at the demon.

"Is he dead?" yelled Dr. Belgium.

"I'm not sure."

She moved closer, reaching out her hand to take Bub's pulse.

"Bad idea." Andy grabbed her shoulder.

"We have to make sure he's dead. If not, I can get more drugs and . . ." Bub's eyelids flicked open and his claw shot out at Sun.

Andy yanked her out of the way and they stumbled down the hall to the air-conditioning vent. Sun went first, up the bookcase Belgium had pushed into the hallway for his ascension. Andy followed quickly.

Bub flopped over onto his belly and moaned, but he didn't chase them.

*Maybe the bastard was going to die after all*, Belgium hoped.

The computer monitor beeped. Dr. Belgium dragged his attention away from the Yellow Arm and went to the desk. The message bar read VIDEO INTERFACE ACTIVE and the President came on the screen. He looked as he always did: rosy cheeked and rested.

"I see Protocol 9 has failed," he said.

Belgium frowned.

"We turned off the nuclear device. I'm sorry to disappoint you, but we're all still alive."

"I didn't like the decision, Dr. Belgium, but I don't regret it. The needs of the many outweigh the needs of the few. You can understand that."

"Yes I can, Mr. President. I can also understand what it's like to live with innocent blood on my hands. It isn't pleasant. Though perhaps your political bearing makes you more tolerant of it than I."

"You do realize the area still has to be neutralized."

"Neutralized. That's a nice way to put it. Like spraying a smoky room with disinfectant. Five people have already been neutralized by this ill-conceived little project. I don't want the rest of us to follow suit."

"I'm sorry, Dr. Belgium. My hands are tied."

"Look, we've managed to knock out Bub. He may even be dead. And we got rid of the thing Helen turned into."

"This is the way it has to be, Frank. We cannot allow for the slightest possibility that the occupant may escape. You knew this when you signed on at Samhain. You voluntarily accepted the risks."

"Yes yes yes. But if there's a chance of saving us and still destroying Bub, shouldn't it be considered?"

"I am sorry, Frank. I truly am."

He didn't look sorry. Not a bit. He might have been talking about the economy or the budget.

"How long do we have?"

"Operation Slim Bob has already begun. It will reach completion in eighty-seven minutes."

"Can we have more time?"

"That's impossible."

"No chance of a rescue?"

"Your country recognizes the sacrifice you're making, Frank. May God be with you."

Belgium rubbed his eyes and let out a deep breath.

"There is another favor, a personal one, that I would like to ask."

"If it is within my power, consider it done."

"It is within your power, Mr. President. And you could even do it right now."

"Yes, Frank?"

"Go fuck fuck fuck yourself."

Belgium hit the DISCONNECT button.

"Eighty-seven minutes," he said softly. "That isn't enough—"

*CLANG!*

Belgium jumped six inches out of his chair and spun in the direction of the noise.

Crouching in the Orange Arm was another creature. Bigger than a hippopotamus, covered head to toe with coal black scales. The thing cocked its head and stared at Frank with a bloodshot eye the size of a dinner plate.

It was on all fours, and its back nearly touched the hallway ceiling.

The animal moved backward, much quicker than Belgium would have anticipated for something so large, and then reared on its hind legs and charged the gate again.

*CLANG!*

The ground shook and Belgium watched in amazement as the titanium gate bent slightly inward.

"What the hell is that sound?" Andy asked.

The biologist turned and saw Andy and Sun were

now in the Red Arm. The Orange Arm was to their right, so they hadn't noticed the latest complication.

*CLANG!*

"It's, um, proof that things can always get worse. We'd better hurry."

"Get out of there, Frank," Sun said. "Meet us in the Green Arm. What's Bub doing?"

Belgium tore his eyes away from the ramming demon and looked down the Yellow Arm.

"He's still there. But he's . . . changing."

"How?"

"I think he's turning back to his regular size."

"Good, then he can't get through the vents."

*CLANG!*

"I talked to the President. We only have about eighty-five minutes," Belgium said.

"Find the digging equipment. We need to get the blueprints." Belgium nodded. He stole a glance at the Orange Arm gate.

*CLANG!*

The lower half was bending away from the doorway.

Belgium hurried into the duct, not daring to look back again.

# CHAPTER 35

"Check that cabinet," Sun told Andy. "They're in a brown folder, legal sized, about an inch thick."

Sun was pretty sure she'd filed them away rather than left them in one of her growing piles, but she wanted to double-check. She quickly sorted through the large SAMHAIN pile on the desk, then for caution's sake went through the BUB pile.

Something caught her eye.

Not the blueprints, but an old report on Bub's stool samples. She picked it up, trying to figure out what her subconscious was trying to tell her.

Since Bub had been brought here, he'd had several bowel movements while in the coma. Back in 1921 the stool had been analyzed with a newly acquired mass spectrometer, which found it contained an ample amount of uranium.

It hit Sun like a slap. Now it finally made sense. What she'd been searching for in Red 3. How Bub had been buried in Panama. Why it took him so long to wake up. His spaceship, the hieroglyphs . . . "The hot rock," Sun said.

Andy looked up at her from the file cabinet.

"It's uranium. Bub's got such a highly advanced genetic structure, he's very sensitive to radiation. Radiation destroys DNA, it kills cells. The ancient Mayans probably covered him in uranium ore when he was sleeping. That's the hot rock they were referring to."

"It put him in a coma, and they buried him," Andy said. "It fits with the glyphs."

"But there's more. The capsule, his spaceship, had lead in it. To protect him from the iridium in deep space. That's why he's been in a coma so long—it took him that long to get all of the uranium out of his system. The radioactivity slowed his metabolism down to a crawl. And being here made it even worse."

"How?"

"Look around," Sun said, picking up a handful of files. "X-rays. Thousands of X-rays. The X-ray machine was invented before the turn of the last century. They bombarded Bub with radiation on a continuous basis up until the 1970s. I'm surprised he didn't glow in the dark."

"Why'd they stop in the '70s?"

"Two guys took over, Meyer and Storky. They did other tests on Bub. But not anything involving radiation. I wonder why . . ." But Sun realized she already knew.

Dr. Meyer had died of cancer. Kaposi's sarcoma. A malignancy of the skin. He continued to work at Samhain through his illness, getting radiation therapy at the compound. Radiation in cancer treatment had to be carefully monitored. Meyer couldn't have worked on Bub if there was radiation involved. The human body could handle only so big a dose without getting sick, or dropping dead.

"Is the X-ray machine still here?" Andy said. "Maybe we could use it as a weapon."

Sun shook her head. "We've got something even better than that. Let's find those blueprints."

"It was a green folder?"

"Brown."

"Like this?"

Andy held up the folder full of blueprints. Sun hurried over and spread the folded document out over the floor.

"There," Andy said, pointing at some faint gray lines. "In Green 11. See the wall there? The lines continue beyond that. I'll bet that's the tunnel."

"How thick is that wall?"

"Got me. Probably eight-inch cinder block. Could be even thicker."

"Let's go," Sun said, folding up the blueprints.

They left Red 3 and hurried down the hallway. Sun tried not to look at the bloodstained walls and tried not to breathe the smell of violent death. Poor Rabbi Shotzen. There were bits of him everywhere.

Andy bent down and picked something up. A disposable lighter. He flicked it once, and the flame shot up two inches.

"Want to break for a smoke?" Sun asked.

Andy put it in his pocket. "Might come in handy."

In Red 14 they cleared off a desk and pushed it out under the ceiling air vent in the hall.

Sun went first, hiking her shirt up over her face to

make breathing in the dusty duct bearable. It was slow going, and to get to the Green Arm they had to pass over the Orange Arm, the ominous *CLANG* from below becoming louder and more frightening.

When Sun crawled over the grating she looked down, nervous to see what was making so much noise. It made her catch her breath.

The creature was simply massive. Those titanium gates wouldn't be able to hold up to a monster like this. This demon looked like it could eat a tank. How many of these things would Bub be capable of making if he escaped Samhain?

"What is it?" Andy whispered behind her, touching her leg.

"Shh!"

The awesome beast stopped in midcharge and lifted an ear to the ceiling. Sun held both her breath and her bladder as the monster stared up at the vent she was perched over. One of its enormous eyes inched closer, squinting into the darkness of the duct. It got so close Sun could count the dark blood vessels that squiggled around its black cornea, each the width of a pencil. The demon blinked, then turned away and resumed its attack on the gate.

"Are you okay?" Andy nudged her.

Sun exhaled. "Yeah. Don't look through the grille."

Sun continued forward, making the decision that if she did have to die, she wasn't letting Bub or this giant loose upon the world.

"Holy shit."

Andy had apparently looked through the grille.

"Keep moving."

"We're in hell, aren't we? We're actually trapped in hell."

"Let's just hope Frank found those shovels."


Dr. Frank Belgium opened the door to Green 5. He knew Green 6 and 7 contained medical equipment, Green 8 was the freezers, and Green 9 was the dry goods storage. This was the only room left to check.

Luckily, he hit the jackpot.

It was a large closet, and the overhead light didn't work. But stacked in the corner, gathering dust, was the excavation equipment. Picks, shovels, axes, hoes, and even a sledgehammer.

"Frank?"

Belgium spun around, looking for the voice.

"Up here."

Sun was poking her head down through the ceiling vent. He helped her climb through, and then they both assisted Andy.

"I found the equipment," Belgium told them. "Where's the cavern?"

"Green 11," Andy said. "Let's move."

"I want to check on Bub," Sun said.

Andy checked his watch. "We've only got sixty-two minutes to dig out of here and get a safe distance away."

"We need to see what he's doing."

Belgium watched Sun and Andy exchange a meaningful glance. He wished he had someone who looked at him like that.

Maybe, if he lived through this, he'd join a dating service.

If he lived through this.


Sun walked down the Green Arm toward the Octopus. She stopped at the titanium bars and pressed her cheek to them, looking left.

*CLANG!*

The ramming beast was almost through the Orange Arm gate.

She switched cheeks and stared at the Yellow Arm. Bub had his hands on the bars. His yellow eyes locked on hers.

"No meeeeercy for yoooooou." *CLANG!*

The giant demon burst through the Orange gate and went barreling into the Octopus, knocking over tables, chairs, and millions of dollars in computer equipment. Then it sat in the center of the Octopus and stared at its master, awaiting direction.

"You're neeeeeeeeext."

Sun tried to focus. They needed time to break through the wall and escape, and couldn't do that if Bub was on their tail.

When in doubt, tell the truth.

"There are four other titanium gates blocking the exit to the outside. You don't have time to come for us."

"I have tiiiiiiime," Bub hissed.

"No, you don't. Since the nuke didn't go off, they're going to drop one on us. A big one."

Bub sneered, his horrifying features becoming even more revolting.

"Liaaaaaaaaar," he spat. "You will beg for deaaaaaath."

The ramming beast pawed at the floor, then launched itself at the Green Arm gate. The shockwave jolted Sun backward.

*That didn't work out as I'd hoped*, she thought.

Sun flew into Green 11. Andy was attacking the concrete wall with a sledgehammer, awkwardly holding it with his left hand, and Belgium was having a time trying to figure out the proper swing of a mining pick. They were both sweating, and for their labors they'd made only a few cracks in the cinder block.

"I need help. Fast."

"What's wrong?"

"Defense," Sun said, thinking about the demon breaking into the Green Arm.

"We're about to have company."

# CHAPTER 36

Bub believed Sun. Her government would have a backup plan. He stared at the four sets of bars preventing his escape and felt anger welling inside him.

Anger, and an emotion he hadn't known in millennia of existence.

Fear.

Strong as the beast was, it wouldn't be able to get through all of these gates in time. Which meant it was within the realm of possibility that Bub might actually die.

The thought was horrifying. At the epicenter of a nuclear explosion the temperature was hotter than the sun. There was no way he could protect himself from that.

*Humans.* How had these miserable hunks of carbon gotten so smart so fast?

Sun had hurt him with her poison. Hurt him almost as much as those filthy Mayans did with their uranium ore. Bub could no longer alter himself to fit into the air duct—his body was busy trying to heal. Now, to add to his injury, he might actually have to comprehend his own death.

He concentrated. Was the Yellow Arm really the only way out?

Andy had been close to spilling his guts, but then Sun attacked him with the poison needle. That opportunity was lost, but perhaps there was another . . .

The demon walked down the hallway to Yellow 4. The door was locked, and there was a keypad on the wall next to it.

Bub didn't bother with the keypad. Regular doors he could handle. He turned around and gave it a quick kick with his massive hoof. The door burst inward.

General Race Murdoch was a hunk of dead meat, cooling in a pool of his own bodily fluids.

Bub had just enough of his essence left to suit the purpose.


Race had been dead. He was sure he'd been dead. He could even remember the moment his heart stopped pumping. His point of vision had become smaller and smaller, darkness enveloping him, until there was nothing.

So how could he be thinking? Race opened his eyes, amazed that his wounds were healed and his pain was gone. He soon realized why.

"Raaaaace. How was deaaaaath?"

"Quiet," Race answered the demon. The words felt sour in his mouth, like he'd just eaten some bad ham. "What the hell do you want?"

"Why is everyone in the Greeeeen Arm?"

"They're having a tea party. You weren't invited."

Bub gave Race's arm a swift tug, dislocating the shoulder.

"Tell meeeeeee."

The general winced. "I can see where this is going. You torture me until I talk. If I die, you bring me back."

"Yesssssssss."

Race hurt, but his level of annoyance was even greater. He'd been looking forward to death, had actually achieved it, and this smug son of a bitch had taken that from him. First Helen, now this.

Race wasn't going to tell him a damn thing.

"Well, I'll let you in on a little secret," the general said. "Any minute now we're going to be radioactive. I'd be tickled pink if you stayed here with me, so I could watch you bake like a cow pie on Georgia asphalt."

Bub tugged Race's dislocated arm and broke it at the elbow. Race cried out.

"Is there another way ooooooooout?" Bub asked.

"Please . . ." The general winced.

"Another waaaaaaaaay?"

"Please . . ."

"Pleeeeease what?"

Race grinned. "Please kiss my lily-white Southern ass."

Then the man actually began to laugh. His pain must have been excruciating, but he was laughing right in Bub's face.

And Bub was afraid.

He picked the general up and threw him against the wall as hard as he could. Race left a bloody spot there, then slumped to the floor, broken and unmoving.

Bub hurried out of the room and went to the Octopus. With a shrill shriek, he commanded the beast to begin breaking down the gate to the Yellow Arm.

There had to be another exit in the Green Arm. There had to be.

Bub would be damned if he lost his life because of some poorly trained pets on a fourth-rate planet.

*CLANG!*

He would see for himself what they were doing. And then he'd slaughter them all.

# CHAPTER 37

"What the hell is it?" Andy asked.

"It's a linac. A medical linear accelerator. A very unique one. Get behind it, let's push it into the hall."

Andy stared at the piece of medical equipment. It was white, about five feet high and four feet wide, and sort of resembled a large kitchen faucet. Attached to a rectangular base was a curved arm that could rotate. On the end of the arm was a lens kind of thing. The lens pointed down at a fancy table.

Sun explained, "A cancer patient lies down on the table, and then their tumors can be bombarded with either electrons or photons from the collimator here."

She tapped the spout of the faucet.

Andy nodded, getting it.

"Radioactivity."

"Right. It kills cancer cells. Actually, it kills all cells, but it's made to target cancer cells."

Andy got his shoulder behind the base and shoved. It barely moved.

"It's heavy as hell," he grunted.

"It's actually about half the size of a normal model. They must have custom made it to fit inside the compound's entrance."

Andy and Sun both put their weight into it, getting the machine to slide a foot.

"This is what Dr. Meyer used to fight his sarcoma." Sun groaned, pushing as hard as she could. "Skin cancer can cover a large surface area of the body, so this particular model is modified for TSEI—total skin electron irradiation. Instead of a thin beam, it showers the entire body with electrons."

"More powerful than an X-ray?" Andy asked.

Sun stopped pushing and sat down, breathing heavily. "An X-ray machine gives off two hundred thousand electron volts. This little baby can do about twenty-five million."

"But if it's used to cure cancer, how can it hurt Bub?"

"Are you ready for a mini lecture?"

Andy nodded. Sun brushed the hair out of her face.

"Radiation is measured on the gray scale. Let's say Meyer's cancer required a dosage of thirty-six gray to complete treatment. Even though it's an electron shower—electrons don't penetrate deeply like photons—thirty-six gray would make him sick or even kill him. So it's broken up into ten weeks of treatments, a single thirty-six-centigray dose a week."

"But if we give Bub a big dose at once . . ."

"It will destroy massive amounts of tissue. But it gets better. This machine can produce electrons and photons. Photons penetrate much deeper than electrons. So if we do a wide photon penumbra—a large beam width for a full-body target—at twenty-five million electron volts, it could really cause some grievous damage."

Andy said, "Nice. Let's do it."

They got up and finished pushing the linac out of

Green 6 and into the hallway, cables trailing behind it. Sun directed Andy to help turn the machine so it faced the Octopus.

"Anything else?"

"It'll take a moment to set up. Go help Frank with the wall."

He gave her a quick kiss on the cheek and ran down the hall.

Sun detached the treatment table and pushed it aside, and then used the control box to rotate the collimator on the gantry—the big counterweighted arm. She stopped it when the lower defining head was pointing straight down the hallway, aiming at the door to the Octopus.

That was the easy part. The hard part would be figuring out the settings. Sun had taken a solitary class in radiotherapy over ten years ago. She didn't remember much.

There was a computer control console in Green 6 near the far wall. She went to it and turned it on, hoping it would all come back to her.

One of the reasons Dr. Belgium had chosen science as a career was his distaste for manual labor.

"So much for that," he muttered, swinging the pick at the concrete. For all the oomph he put into it, the potato chip–sized piece that flaked off the wall was hardly satisfying.

"How's it going?" Andy asked, walking into Green 11.

"How much time do we have left?"

"About fifty minutes."

"In that case, not good. At this rate we won't break through until next Tuesday."

*CLANG!*

The noise reverberated down the Green Arm.

"Uh-oh," Belgium said. "It looks like that ramming beast has found a new target."

Andy picked up the twenty-pound sledge and hefted it to his shoulder. The bandage around his wrist had become dark red.

He gripped the hammer and let the wall have it.


The computer program that ran the linac had presets, calibrated to Dr. Meyer's dosage. Sun found a way to manually change them, but couldn't remember any dosage calculations. She had to deal with beam energy, field size, distance, filtration, quality, and a dozen other parameters. She decided the smartest thing to do was just shoot for the maximum on everything.

Dr. Meyer's beam energy was set at 6 MeV—six million electron volts. She changed it to 25, and went from there.


Andy and Frank developed a chain gang rhythm with their swings, one alternating with another. Slowly, gradually, they cracked through a single 8" x 16" cinder block, and were able to knock it into the wall.

Andy bent down and used his lighter to peer through the opening. He couldn't see a damn thing, but the flame on the lighter bent and blew inward.

"We found it," Andy said.

* * *

CURRENT SETTINGS WILL EXPOSE PATIENT TO LETHAL DOSES OF RADIATION the screen blinked at Sun.

"Good," she said.

Sun saved the settings in memory and started the program to charge the beam. She hurried out of the room to see how the guys were doing.

Not too well, it turned out. Both Frank and Andy were drenched with sweat, and they'd knocked only a single cinder block through. Blood was dripping down Andy's right hand. He'd popped several stitches.

"Give me a try," Sun said.

Andy handed over the sledgehammer, which was too heavy for her to properly wield. She tried Belgium's miner's pick. It weighed about ten pounds, and Sun found it much easier to handle. After five minutes of swinging, she managed to put the eight-inch pointed head through a second cinder block.

Andy and Frank helped her pry the rock away.

"One more, and we may be able to squeeze through," Belgium said.

There was a sudden *CRASH!* and the ground shook.

The trio ran into the hallway and watched as the giant ramming creature burst into the Green Arm.

It slowly backed out, and in crawled Bub, triumphant, his eyes burning with malevolent glee.

"Stay here," Sun told the others, and headed for the linac by Green 6. She immediately knew she wasn't going to make it in time. Bub was going to reach the machine before she had a chance to turn on the photon beam.

So she changed tactics and forced herself to stay calm.

"Well," she said, "it looks like you've won." Bub grinned.

"I alwaaaaaaaays win."

Sun considered her slim options. If she couldn't find a way to switch on the beam she was dead, Andy was dead, and possibly the entire human race was dead.

"I have one question to ask before you kill me," she said, getting closer. The linac was ten steps away.

"Yessssssssss."

Six steps. Five. Four.

"Do you know what a hertz donut is?" Sun asked.

The demon cocked its head to the side. "A heeeertz doooooonut?" Sun walked calmly up to the linac and put her hand on the control box.

"Watch," Sun said.

She hit the ACTIVATE button.

The linac hummed like a stock car and Bub immediately thrust his hands out in front of his eyes. He fell backward, his exposed skin mottling and turning brown.

"Hurts, don't it?" Sun said.

The demon opened his wings and attempted to shield himself, but only something with the density of lead could shield 25 million volts of X-rays. Every inch of his body seemed to bruise and mush like overripe fruit, weeping clear fluid.

He rolled backward, but his retreat did little good. There was no beam stopper, and photons travel in a straight line at the speed of light. They tore millions of subatomic holes in his body, ripping through membranes, ionizing atoms, and bursting cell walls, breaking down his DNA into base pairs.

As Bub rolled away, large sections of dead tissue were sloughing off his body in strips. Sun watched as he spewed blood along the walls and ceiling. He was screaming, a sound not dissimilar to the cries of the many sheep he'd gutted and eaten.

"Beg for death, my ass," Sun said.

Momentum took Bub through the Green door and into the Octopus, but from what Sun could tell he was no longer moving. The hallway was empty. The giant demon cowered off to the side, out of the beam's invisible perimeter.

Belgium came up and said, "Good good good. Leave it on and we'll get back to work.".

"Won't that beam run out of power?" Andy asked.

"It doesn't use any radioactive isotopes," Belgium explained. "A linac uses high-frequency electromagnetic waves to accelerate charged particles, such as photons, to high energies through a linear tube."

Sun said, "I thought you were a biologist."

"Minor in nuclear physics. Fun fun fun stuff."

"How much time do we have?" Sun asked.

Andy looked at his watch. "Forty-four minutes."

"Okay, Mr. Physics, assuming we can break down that wall, how far away do we have to be from here when the nuke is dropped?"

Belgium rubbed his chin. "I'd assume they'd use a simple fission mechanism in the lower kiloton range, maybe ten to thirty kilotons. A uranium-235 or a plutonium-239 bomb would vaporize metals for a kilometer in all directions. We'd need to be two to four miles away to escape the thermal effects. The blast effects would send hundred-mile-an-hour winds up to the two-mile mark."

"How about radiation?" Andy asked.

"If we're two miles away, we'd only absorb a minimal dose, maybe twelve centigray, but if they used a fusion weapon rather than a fission one, say a lithium deuteride core with a uranium jacket, then it would be a thermonuclear neutron bomb with the same explosive power, but thirty times the radiation. I'd guess that—"

The lights went out, plunging the entire complex into total darkness.

"This isn't a good development," Dr. Belgium said.

"The bastard cut the breaker."

"The linac is off!" Sun yelled. "Bub can get in!"

Andy's lighter cut through the darkness, and the trio shuffled back to Green 11. Sun knocked over a metal shelving unit, and she and Belgium pushed it in front of the door.

"SUUUUUUUUUUUUN!"

Bub's voice was hoarse and sickly, but it still carried with tremendous force down the hallway and caused Sun's knees to knock with fear.

"Look what you did to meeeeee!" he roared. "To MEEEEEEEEEE!"

"Give me your shirt," Andy said to Sun. "Mine's too wet."

She complied, stripping to her sports bra. Andy wound the shirt around an ax handle and lit it like a torch.

"Frank, where's the pick?"

"I think I dropped it in the hall. Want me to get it?"

"Here I coooooooome!"

"Perhaps not," Belgium said.

The doorknob turned. Sun held tight to the metal frame of the shelves and braced herself.

"Help me!" she said. Frank and Andy put their weight on it. The door exploded inward, sending the shelf skittering across the room.

Bub filled the doorway. His skin was blistered and peeling, brown and black rather than the normal red. A horn had fallen out, exposing a raw sore. His teeth had shredded his lips, and when he breathed bits of flesh fluttered out like streamers. He was missing his left eye; in its place was a gooey, dripping blob. His animal smell was now a roadkill smell, a stench of decay and death.

Before, Bub had been taunting and clever. His evil was sadistic and calculating.

Now he was simply a mad dog.

This scared Sun even more.

"Hey, Bub."

The voice came from behind the demon, in the hallway.

Bub spun around. "Yoooooooooooooou," he hissed.

Andy held up the torch and they watched as the vent grating fell from the ceiling and a figure crawled through.

"Race," Sun whispered.


General Race Murdoch landed hard, but without pain. Before crawling up into the air-conditioning vent he'd stopped at the med supply room. Besides shooting himself up with various painkillers and stimulants, Race had also made a weapon. He taped the largest scalpel he could find to a broomstick, and then wrapped the tape in a quick-setting fiberglass cast.

He stood up and gripped the makeshift spear in his good hand, pointing it at Bub's head. Race felt like he'd lost a fistfight with a lawn mower. But Bub looked even worse.

"Block off the door," Race told the trio. "Escape."

"What about you?" Sun asked.

"A little while ago I died with my tail between my legs. Bub injected me with that same stuff he used on Helen. God only knows what I'll turn into. I'm not going quietly this time. This time I'm going down swinging."

"Good luck, Race," Andy said.

Race winked. "I'll take training over luck any day. Now, get going." Sun nodded her good-bye and slammed the door to Green 11.

The hallway was enveloped in absolute darkness, save for a single thing.

Bub's glowing red eye.

"I can seeeeee you in the daaaaaark," Bub whispered.

"Not for long," Race said.

He put everything into the lunge: his rage over Helen, his frustration at wasting forty years being Bub's caretaker, his pure hatred for being forced back to life. The spear went into Bub's eye, through his brain, and stuck in the back of his unholy skull.

The demon fell, screeching.

Race sensed movement behind him. He turned and saw the huge glowing eyes of the giant gate-breaking demon draw nearer.

"Well, ain't you a big sonuvabitch," Race said.

He felt along the floor and found his spear, yanking it out of Bub.

"You hungry, big boy? I got something for you to chew on."

Race smiled, and when the monster opened its mouth and bit down on him, Race jammed in the spear as far as it could go, his very last thought of dancing cheek to cheek with his beloved Helen.


Andy and Sun threw everything they could find in front of the door while Belgium banged away at the wall.

Strangely, nothing tried to get in.

"Maybe he's finally dead," Andy said. He yelled, "Race!" No answer.

Sun rushed to Dr. Belgium and began to strip off his lab coat.

"The torch is dying."

He shrugged out of it and Sun ripped the garment in half, winding one part around the dimming flame.

Andy took the sledgehammer from Belgium and pounded away at the blocks until he could no longer lift his arms. Then Frank took over, breathing like an asthmatic. Sun had the next crack at it, struggling with the heavy weight but able to swing it underhanded.

The cinder block broke in half, leaving an L-shaped opening in the wall.

"It's not big enough," Belgium said.

"Yes, it is." Sun tossed the torch through the hole and then squeezed herself into it. The cinder block scraped her bare shoulders and back, but she made it through intact.

"Go on, Frank," Andy prompted.

The biologist had to tilt his shoulders, but he managed to fit his upper body in the opening. Sun helped pull him the rest of the way through.

"C'mon, Andy, let's go!" Andy looked at the opening and knew it was too small. Belgium was a thin man, 150 pounds max. Andy was 180, with a broader chest and shoulders.

"I won't make it."

"Try," Sun pleaded.

He stuck his head and one arm through the opening, but he couldn't get the other arm in.

"Go on," he said. "Go ahead without me."

"No. Just get your other hand through. Then you can make it."

Andy was wedged so tightly in the space that there was no way he could get his other hand through. The corner of the L was digging into his breastbone. "I can't. I'm going to try to widen the hole."

"There's no time!" Sun screamed at him.

Dr. Belgium said, "Exhale."

"What?"

"Your lungs are full of air. Breathe all of your air out and your chest will contract."

Andy blew out air, blew until his lungs were empty, blew until he was seeing spots. It freed up just enough space to force his other wrist through. Sun and Belgium grabbed it and pulled like crazy. The skin on Andy's arm scraped against the cinder block, and his chest felt as if he were pinned under a dump truck, but it was coming . . . coming . . . He was through.

They yanked him the rest of the way and Sun held him, even tighter than it had been squeezing through the hole.

"I can't breathe," Andy croaked.

She released her grip.

"The cave leads off this way." Belgium picked up the torch. "What's our time?"

Andy looked at his watch.

"Twenty-eight minutes."

They ran.

# CHAPTER 38

This was the scariest part of all for Andy. Everything that happened prior had been beyond his control, but this last attempt at survival was completely up to him. If he ran fast enough, he'd live. If he didn't, he'd die.

The natural limestone caverns they ran through were completely dark. Sun led the way, carrying the torch, keeping it low to illuminate their footing. The ground was sometimes hard jagged rock and other times loose gravel that sucked at their shoes like hungry fish. They ran past natural stone columns and underground pools, razor-sharp walls and stalagmites, alongside steep drop-offs that fell into oblivion.

Sometimes the cavern widened to the size of an auditorium, other times it was as thin as a hallway. They were following the original trail the excavation crew had made one hundred years prior, when Samhain was born. It surprised Andy to occasionally see a boot print in the ground, the mark of someone who helped build the compound, someone long dead.

They ran as fast as safety allowed. When there was an open area ahead, Sun picked up the pace, and they sprinted until their lungs were bursting and their stomachs clenched.

There was a bad moment, at the fifteen-minute mark, when the trail couldn't be found and they hit a dead end. All of them began to panic, Sun almost to the point of tears, when Dr. Belgium found a fork in the cave a hundred yards prior. They backtracked and took the fork, but precious minutes had been lost.

Andy fought the fatigue. He fought the many pains he'd incurred. But he couldn't fight his own mind, which kept telling him that this was the end, it was all over, his existence was about to be snuffed out forever.

"Please," he begged the universe, "don't let this happen. Don't let my life stop here. There's so much I haven't done, haven't seen."

The universe didn't answer. But surprisingly, his mind focused on something he'd long ago memorized, when he was just a boy.

*Pater noster, qui es in coelis, sanctificetur nomen tuum. Our Father, Who art in heaven, Hallowed be Thy Name.*

The Lord's Prayer.

He ran on, repeating it over and over in his head.

Sun was in better physical shape than her male companions, and she knew it. But she couldn't slow her pace, even when they began to fall behind. She had to be the goal for them, the one in the lead who forced them to catch up.

Belgium surprised Sun. He was thin and long limbed, and on the sprints he lacked breath control, but for the most part he kept up.

Andy was the problem. He was in fair shape, but he'd suffered so many injuries. The batling attack, his wrist, all the blood he lost—it was surprising he could even stand up. Still, Sun couldn't slow down for him. If she did, they all might as well give up.

Sun stopped only once, when the torch was dying and she had to wrap the other half of Belgium's lab coat around it. The rest of the time she ran as fast as her little legs could move.

The cavern was cool, and the air was good, two things that surprised her. Her conception of caves had always been of the mining type, cramped and choked with coal dust. These caves were pleasant, even tranquil. She could see how she might enjoy exploring them one day, possibly with Andy.

It was the first time she'd considered her future since Steven died, and it opened up a floodgate of emotion. Suddenly there was so much she wanted out of life. She wanted to be married, have kids, get her medical license back, buy a little house someplace—things she'd given up on ever doing. She thought about how many times she'd worried about money, and of how little importance it actually was.

If they lived through this, she promised herself she'd be different. More open. Less worried. More fun. Less angry. More loving.

If they lived.


Dr. Belgium was playing tricks with himself so as to not give in to exhaustion. He recited the periodic table of the elements, then he gave himself quadratic equations to solve.

But the cave kept interfering with his ploy.

It was the most eerily quiet place Belgium had even been in. Their heavy breathing seemed to echo and amplify in the silence, sometimes chasing them through the dark.

Several times Belgium lost his train of thought, trying to gauge if the cavern was actually heading upward like it felt. Or calculating twists and turns and puzzling over whether they had gone 180 degrees and were actually running back to Samhain.

Once, he lost aural contact with Andy running behind him, and stopped to find the man on his hands and knees, vomiting. Belgium didn't bother with inspirational speeches or voiced concerns. He yanked Andy up by his shirt and pulled him back into formation.

Frank didn't think they seriously had a shot at surviving. The odds against them having made it this far were astronomical. But he still ran, and this was curious to him. Only a short time ago, he would have been content to sit at his desk and wait for the bomb to drop. Perhaps he had finally learned to accept himself. To forgive himself.

Maybe someday he might even like himself.

If he lived to see someday.


With five minutes to go on Andy's watch they ran out of cave.

They'd come to an open area, large enough to drive

around in. Sun checked all of the walls and couldn't find any other tunnels. There was no place left to go.

"How far away are we?" Sun heaved.

"A mile and a half," Belgium said, hands on his knees. "Maybe two. We have to get out of the cave."

Andy leaned against a limestone wall. "Wouldn't it be safer down here?"

"Samhain is an underground target. The nuke they use will go down deep. A lot of the blast effects will happen underground and could travel through these caves. The surface would be better."

"I can't find the damn exit." Sun's voice was beginning to crack.

Then the bats swooped down.

Sun lost it. She swung the torch like a club, screaming at the bats, determined to burn them all to cinders.

Belgium held her back.

"They're bats," he said. "Plain old bats. If there are bats, there's an exit nearby."

He took the torch and held it up, illuminating the high ceiling, following the path of the flying rodents until they disappeared into a crack in the wall.

"There's the exit." Belgium pointed to a tiny sliver of light, twenty feet or so above them. The wall was so simple to climb it was almost anticlimactic. Even Andy, with his injured wrist, had no trouble with the large hand- and footholds. At fifteen feet up, the tiny splinter of light had opened up into a large crevice amid an outcropping of rocks.

Sun climbed onto the floor of the desert and hugged it like a lover.

Andy dropped to his knees and said, "Thank God."

Dr. Belgium looked around and tears streamed down his cheeks.

"This is the first sky I've seen in twenty years. I've forgotten how beautiful the world is."

"Look!" Andy said, pointing up.

Sun noticed the telltale trail of jet exhaust and followed it back to the area they'd just fled from.

"Get down, behind these rocks," Belgium said. "Put your fingers in your ears and close your eyes as tight as you can."

"Are we far enough away?" Andy asked.

"We'll know in just a moment." They huddled down together and waited.

*Beep beep.*

Andy's watch had counted down to zero.

Sun held her breath. She could feel the cool desert air on her face, and wondered if it would be the last thing she ever felt.

The moment stretched.

Andy said, "Maybe they—"

The light hit them first. Intense, superbright light, blinding their eyes even though their lids were closed.

Then the sound overtook them, the slap of an angry God, louder than the loudest thunder, and at the same time they were bowled over by a hot wind, spitting dust and debris into their faces, knocking them off their feet.

The wind died suddenly, bringing absolute stillness.

Andy opened his eyes. A breeze hit them from the

opposite direction, lasting a few seconds, but not nearly the strength of the blast wave.

"Negative phase," Belgium yelled. "The blast happened so fast it created a partial vacuum. This wind is the result of suction."

Andy wasn't listening. He was staring at the fireball. It was bright, almost too bright to look at, mostly red and violet with portions of pure white.

The giant fire column plumed at the top, becoming the recognizable mushroom cloud, gray and purple smoke billowing out in an expanding ball.

"Spectacular," Belgium said.

Sun was also taken in by its destructive beauty. The apex of mankind's scientific endeavors. The secret of the atom, on display in all of its kiloton glory.

"We weren't burned," Sun said. "How do we know about our radiation exposure?"

"It doesn't look like too big of a nuke, so it probably isn't a fusion bomb," Belgium said. "We won't know until later, but I think we're far enough away. Our radiation exposure should be minimal."

The mushroom cloud continued to expand, spreading open like a flower.

"Nothing could live through that, right?" Andy said. "Bub couldn't . . ."

"Nothing can survive a nuclear blast at ground zero."

Andy frowned. "But what if all of that outer space crap was just that—crap? Isn't the devil supposed to be a liar? What was it that Father Thrist said? *'Satan's greatest feat is to convince us he doesn't exist. Lucifer is the Master of Lies.'*"

"Trust me, Andy." Belgium patted his shoulder. "Even if Bub really was Lucifer, he doesn't exist any longer."

Andy thought about it. "So we did it," he said. "We actually beat the devil." The voice came from behind them, low and hoarse.

"I'm not beaten yet."

They spun around and watched in horror as Bub crawled out of the crevice. He looked even worse than before. One wing was missing, and the other dragged behind him, broken and bloody. Several holes in his flesh were so big that the bones showed through. Both eye sockets were empty, but he'd grown a tiny third eye in the middle of his forehead.

The demon glanced away from the trio and looked at the fireball, the plume still rising. He dropped to his haunches and vomited blood onto the desert sand.

"I am immortal . . . I was heeeeere before your species began . . . and I'll be heeeeeeere to lead you to extinctioooooooon!"

Bub stretched out his claws and raised them to the heavens.

"YOU CAN'T KILL ME!" he screamed, his voice spreading out over the expanse of the desert.

He pointed a misshapen claw at them, accusing.

"All you diiiiiiiiiid," Bub snarled, "is make meeeee angry."

Sun looked around for any kind of weapon—a rock, a branch, anything at all. She saw Belgium pick up a handful of sand, and Andy ball up his fists.

Then Bub did something that none of them could have possibly expected.

He exploded.

The demon burst into dozens of pieces with a splatting sound, like a giant water balloon had popped. Andy, Sun, and Frank dove to the ground and hid their faces from the blast.

But nothing touched them.

The trio looked, and saw that each of Bub's parts had sprouted wings and remained airborne. He had become a swarm of demons, each no larger than a tennis ball.

Perfect replicas of Bub.

They circled, briefly flapping around the trio in quick figure eights. Then they all flew off in different directions, scattering into the distance, as if each had a specific destination in mind.

Eventually they faded out of sight.

Andy reached for Sun's hand and held it. She squeezed it tight. They looked at each other, and then at Dr. Belgium.

The biologist made a long face and verbalized what each of them was thinking.

"Uh-oh."

*Turn the Page for an Exciting Preview*

# WELCOME TO THE RUSHMORE INN

The bed-and-breakfast is hidden in the hills of
West Virginia. Wary guests wonder how it can stay
in business at such a creepy, remote location.
Especially with its bizarre, presidential decor
and eccentric proprietor.

## ONCE YOU CHECK IN . . .

With the event hotel for the national Iron Woman
triathlon accidentally overbooked, competitor Maria
is forced to stay at the Rushmore. But after checking
in to her room, she quickly realizes she isn't alone.
First her suitcase isn't where she put it. Then her
cell phone has mysteriously moved. She hears an
odd creaking under the bed. Confusion quickly
turns to fear, then fear to hysteria when she
discovers the front door is barred and the
windows are bricked over. There is no way out.

Now, four new female athletes have become
guests of the Rushmore Inn. Will they meet
Maria's terror and her horrifying fate?

## . . . YOU'LL BE DYING TO CHECK OUT

## —IF YOU LIVE LONG ENOUGH

# ENDURANCE
by bestselling author
J. A. KONRATH

*Coming in May 2019,
wherever Pinnacle Books are sold.*

Maria unlocked the door to her room and was greeted by Abraham Lincoln.

The poster was yellowed with age, the edges tattered, and it hung directly over the queen-size bed where the headboard would normally be. The adjoining walls were papered with postcards, all of them boasting various pictures and portraits of Lincoln. The single light in the room came from a floor lamp, the shade decorated with a collage of faded newspaper clippings, all featuring—big surprise—Lincoln.

*So that's why the crazy old proprietor called it the Lincoln Bedroom.*

Maria pulled her suitcase in behind her, placed the room key on a scarred, old dresser, and turned the dead bolt. The door, like the lock, was heavy, solid. As reassuring as that was, this room still gave her the creeps. In fact, everything about this bed-and-breakfast gave her the creeps, from its remote and impossible-to-find location, to its run-down façade, to its eccentric decorations and menagerie of odd odors. But Maria didn't have a choice. The hotel in town had overbooked, and this seemed to be the last room available in the entire state of West Virginia.

Iron Woman had become quite the popular event, with worldwide media coverage, and apparently they'd given her room reservation to some reporter. Which was ironic, because Maria was a registered contestant, and without contestants, there wouldn't be any need for reporters. The reporter was the one who should have been staying in the Lincoln Bedroom, with its bizarre decor and its strange smell of sandalwood mixed with spoiled milk.

Maria sighed. It didn't matter. All that mattered was a good night's sleep after more than twelve hours on the road. She'd missed her late-night workout—this inn didn't have an exercise room—so the best she could hope for was a five-mile run in the morning before getting back to the event hotel, which assured her it would have a room available tomorrow.

*Actually, the hotel room will be ready later today.*

A glance at the Lincoln clock on the nightstand showed it was past two in the morning.

She had promised to let Felix know when she got in, and pulled her cell phone out of her jeans, her thumbs a blur on the keyboard.

F—U R probably asleep. I M @ a creepy B&B,
not the hotel. Long story, but it's free. That = more
$$$ to spend on our honeymoon. J WTL8R.
TTFN, H2CUS, luv U—M.

Maria circled the room, holding her cell over her head, trying to find a signal while the floorboards creaked underfoot. When a single bar appeared, she sent the text message and walked to the poster. She placed her cell on the nightstand as a reminder to charge it before she went to sleep, hefted her suitcase onto the bed, and dug inside, freeing her makeup bag and taking it to the bathroom. She flipped on the light switch and was rewarded with the sight of President Lincoln's face on the toilet seat cover.

"I'll never look at a five-dollar bill the same again," she said, but her tone was without mirth. Rather than amusing, she was finding this whole Lincoln thing creepy.

Maria shut the door behind her—more out of habit than modesty—lifted the lid, undid her jeans, and sat down, the cold seat raising goose bumps on her tan thighs. She yawned, big and wide, as the long day caught up with her.

The bathroom, like the bedroom, was tiny. The sink was crowded next to the shower stall, and if Maria were a few inches taller her knees would touch the opposing wall. Hanging on that wall was a framed painting of Lincoln. A head-and-shoulders portrait of his younger years, before he had the famous beard.

His ultrarealistic eyes seemed to be staring right at her.

"Pervert," Maria whispered.

Lincoln didn't reply.

Voices came through the wall. The same two men Maria had heard while checking in, arguing about some sports game, repeating the same points over and over. She listened to the floorboards creak and wondered if they'd keep it up all night, disturbing her sleep. The thought was quickly dismissed. At that moment, Maria was so tired she could have dozed through a Metallica concert.

She finished peeing, flushed, then turned on the faucet. The water was rust-colored. Last week Maria had read an article about waterborne bacteria, and she elected to brush her teeth with something safer. She turned off the water and set her toothbrush on the sink. Then she opened the bathroom door, picked her suitcase up off the floor, and placed it on the bed. Maria pulled out a half-empty bottle of Evian and was two steps to the bathroom when she froze.

*Didn't I already put the suitcase on the bed?*

A flush of adrenaline made Maria turn, her heart racing. She stared at the suitcase like it was a hostile creature, and then she hurried to the front door and eyed the knob.

Still locked. The key was where she'd left it, on the dresser.

Maria spun around, taking everything in. A small desk and chair were tucked in the corner of the room. The bed had a beige comforter and a matching dust ruffle, and it seemed undisturbed. The closet door was open, revealing an empty space. Tan curtains covered the window on the adjacent wall.

The curtains were fluttering.

*Almost like someone is hiding behind them.*

Her first instinct was to run, but common sense kicked in. She was on the second floor. It was doubtful someone had come in through the window and moved her luggage. A more likely explanation was she'd put the suitcase on the floor herself and was too tired to remember it. The curtains probably jerked because the window was open and a breeze was blowing in.

"You're exhausted," she said aloud. "You're imagining things."

But Maria was sure she put the suitcase on the bed. She'd put it on its side and unzipped it to get her makeup bag. She was *sure* of it.

*Maybe it fell off?*

*But how could it fall and land perfectly on its wheels? And why didn't I hear it fall?*

She stared at the suitcase again. It was heavy; packed alongside her clothes was an entire case of bottled water, a result of her recent germ phobia. The suitcase would have made noise hitting the floor. But all Maria heard from the bathroom was those men arguing, and . . .

"The creaking," she said aloud. "I heard the floors creaking." *What if the creaking didn't come from the room next door?*

*What if the creaking came from her room—from someone walking around?*

Maria felt goose bumps break out on her arms.

*What if that someone is still here?*

She paused, unsure of what to do next. Her feet felt heavy. Her mouth became so dry her tongue stuck to her teeth. Maria knew the odds were high that her paranoia was the result of exhaustion. She also knew there was practically a zero likelihood someone had come into her room just to move her suitcase.

*And yet . . .*

Maria clenched and unclenched her hands, eyes locking on the curtains. She made a decision.

*I need to check.*

She took a deep breath, let it out slow. Then she crept toward the window. The curtains were still, and Maria wondered if she'd imagined the fluttering. No light came through them even though they were thin. Not surprising—the inn was way out in the boonies, not another building for miles, and the tall pine trees obscured the moon and stars.

*Either that, or someone is crouching on the windowsill, blocking the light.*

Maria swallowed, knowing she was psyching herself out, feeling the same kind of adrenaline tingles she got before a race.

Upstairs, the arguing abruptly ceased, midword. The room became deathly quiet, the only sound Maria's timid footfalls, creaking on the hardwood floor.

The smell of rot in the room got stronger the closer she got to the window.

*Could someone really be behind the curtains, ready to pounce?*

Maria felt like she was nine years old again, playing hide-and-seek with her younger brother, Cameron. He loved to jump out and scream *Boo!* at her, making her scream. For an absurd moment, she could picture Cam behind that curtain, hands raised, ready to leap out and grab her. One of her few pleasant childhood memories of Cam.

Then she pictured something else grabbing her. A filthy, hairy, insane maniac with a rusty knife.

Maria shook her head, trying to dispel the thought.

The thought wouldn't leave.

"Get a grip," she whispered. "There's nothing there."
She was two feet away when the curtains moved again.

And again.

*Like someone was poking them from the other side.*
Maria flinched, jerking backward.

*It's just the wind.*

*It's got to be.*

*Right?*

"It's the wind," she said through her clenched jaw.

*The wind. Nothing more. Certainly not some creep climbing into my room.*

*But, what if . . . ?*

She thought about the pepper spray in her suitcase. Then she thought about just getting the hell out of there. Maria wished Felix were here with her. He'd find this whole situation ridiculously funny.

*You compete in triathlons and you're too chicken to check a window?*

*No. I'm not chicken. I'm not afraid of anything.*

But she got the pepper spray anyway, holding it out ahead of her like a talisman to ward off evil. She paused in front of the window, the curtains still.

"Do it."

Maria didn't move.

"Just do it."

Maria set her jaw and in one quick motion swept back the curtains—revealing bricks where the glass should have been.

She stared for a moment, confused, then felt a cool breeze on her arm.

*There. In the corner. A hole in the mortar, letting the air in.*

Maria let out an abrupt laugh. It sounded hollow in the tiny room. She gave the bricks a tentative push, just to make sure they were real and didn't swing on hinges or anything. They were cold to the touch, as hard as stone could be.

Only a ghost could have gotten through that. And Maria didn't believe in ghosts. Life had enough scary things in it without having to make stuff up.

She let the curtain fall, and thought of Cameron again. About the things he'd gone through. That was real horror. Not the wind blowing some curtains in a run-down, hillbilly bed-and-breakfast.

Maria hadn't seen Cam in a few weeks, because of her training regimen. She promised herself she would visit the hospital, right after the event. Maybe Felix would come with, even though Cam seemed to creep him out.

*He'll do it anyway. Because he loves me.*

Again, she wished Felix were here. He promised to be at the race on Saturday. Promised to rub her sore muscles afterward.

She glanced down at her left hand, at the pear-shaped diamond on her ring finger. Yellow, her favorite color. Sometimes hours would go by and she'd forget it was there, even though she'd only been wearing it for less than a week. Looking at it never failed to bring a smile.

Maria walked past the bed, glanced at the knob on the front door to make sure it was still locked, and mused about how she'd gotten herself all worked up over nothing.

She was heading back to the bathroom when she saw movement out of the corner of her eye.

The dust ruffle on the bed was fluttering.

Like something had disturbed it.

Something that had just crawled underneath.

Maria paused, standing stock-still. The fear kicked in again like an energy drink, and she could feel her heart in her neck as she tried to swallow.

*There is* NOT *some man under my bed.*

And yet . . .

Far-fetched as it may be, there was probably enough room for someone to fit under there. The bed was high up off the floor on its frame, with plenty of space for a man to slip underneath. *A filthy man with a rusty knife?*

Maria gave her head a shake.

*It's the wind again.*

*No, it can't be. This side of the bed isn't facing the window.*

*A rat?*

*Could be a rat.*

"I came in fourth in Iron Woman last year. I'm not afraid of a little rat." Maria got on her hands and knees and began to crawl over to the bed.

*What if there's a man under there?*

*There won't be.*

*But what if there is? What if he grabs me when I lift the dust ruffle?*

"Then I'll squirt him in the eyes and kick his ass," she said to herself.

Maria reached for the fabric, aiming her pepper spray with her other hand.

*I'll do it on three.*

*One . . .*

*Two . . .*

*Three!*

Maria jerked up the dust ruffle.

No one grabbed her. The space under the bed was vacant, except for a small plume of dust that she waved away. Maria let the ruffle drop, and her shoulders drooped in a big sigh.

"I really need to get some rest."

Maria got to her feet, wondering when she'd last slept. She quickly calculated she'd been awake for over twenty hours. That was probably enough to make anyone a little jumpy.

She padded back to the bathroom, reaching for her toothbrush on the sink, picturing her head on the pillow, the covers all around her.

Her toothbrush was gone.

Maria checked under the sink, and in her makeup bag.

It was nowhere to be found.

She stared at the Lincoln poster. He stared back, his expression grim.

*This isn't exhaustion. Someone is messing with me.*

"Screw the free room," she said, picking up the bag. "I'm out of here." Maria rushed to the bed, reaching for her cell phone on the nightstand.

Her phone wasn't there.

In its place was something else. Something small and brownish.

Maria let out a squeal, jumping back.

*This can't actually be happening. It all has to be some sort of joke.*

She stared at the brown thing like it would jump up and grab her.

*Is it real? It looks shriveled and old.*

*Some stupid Halloween prop?*

Then she smelled it. An odor of decay that invaded her nose and mouth and made her gag.

"It's real. Oh my God . . . it's real."

*Someone put a severed human ear in my room.*

She ran to the door, and the knob twisted without her unlocking it. Maria tugged it inward, raising her pepper spray to dose anyone standing there.

The hallway was empty. Dark and quiet.

She hurried to the stairs, passing doors with the names Theodore Roosevelt, Harry S. Truman, and Millard Fillmore. Over the winding staircase was a gigantic poster of Mount Rushmore. Maria took the stairs two at a time, sprinting as soon as her feet hit the ground floor. She flew past the dining room, and the living room with its artificial fireplace, and ran up to the front door, turning the knob and throwing her weight against it.

Her shoulder bounced off, painfully. Maria twisted the knob the other way, giving it a second push.

*No good. The door won't budge.*

She tried pulling, with equal results.

Swearing, Maria searched for a dead bolt, a latch, a doorstop, or some other clue why it wasn't opening. The only lock on the door was on the knob, and that spun freely. She ground her molars together and gave it another firm shoulder-butt.

It was like slamming into concrete. The door didn't even shake in its jamb.

*"Hey! Girly!"*

The words shook Maria like a blow. A male voice, coming from somewhere behind her. She spun around, her muscles all bunching up.

*"Yeah, I'm talkin' to y'all, ya pretty thang. We gonna have some fun, we are."*

The voice was raspy and mean, dripping with country twang. But she couldn't spot where it was coming from. The foyer, and the living room to the right, looked empty except for the furniture. The overhead chandelier, made from dusty deer antlers, cast crazy, crooked shadows over everything. The shadows undulated, due to the artificial fireplace, a plastic log flickering electric orange.

"Who's there?" Maria demanded, her pepper spray held out at arm's length, her index finger on the spray button and ready to press.

No one answered.

There were many places he could be hiding. Behind the sofa. Around any number of corners. Tucked next to the large bookcase. Behind the larger-than-life-size statue of George Washington, holding a sign that said WELCOME TO THE RUSHMORE INN. Or even up the stairs, beyond her line of sight.

Maria kept her back to the wall and moved slowly to the right, her eyes sweeping the area, scanning for any kind of movement. She yearned to run, to hide, but there was nowhere to go. Behind her, she felt the drapes of one of the windows. She quickly turned around, parting the fabric, seeking out the window latch.

But like the Lincoln bedroom, there was no glass there. Only bricks, hidden from view on the outside by closed wooden shutters that she'd thought quaint when she first pulled in.

*This house is like a prison.*

That thought was followed by one even more distressing.

*I'm not their first victim. They've done this before.*

*Oh, Jesus, they've done this before.*

Maria clutched the pepper spray in both hands, but she couldn't keep it steady. She was so terrified, her legs were trembling—a first for her. A nervous giggle escaped her lips, but it came out more like a whimper. Taking a big breath, she screamed, "Help me!"

The house carried her plea, bounced it around, then swallowed it up.

A moment later she heard, "*Help me!*"

But it wasn't her echo. It was a male falsetto, mocking her voice.

Coming from the stairs.

"*Help me!*" Another voice. Coming from the living room.

"*Help me!*" This one even closer, from a closet door less than ten feet away.

"*Help me.*" The last one was low-pitched. Quiet.

Coming from right next to her.

*The statue of Washington.*

It smiled at her, its crooked teeth announcing it wasn't a statue at all.

The incredibly large man dropped the WELCOME sign and lunged, both arms outstretched.

Maria pressed the button on the pepper spray.

The jet missed him by several feet, and his hand brushed her shirt.

She danced away from his grasp and then barreled toward the stairs as the closet door crashed open and someone burst out. Someone big and fat and . . . *Sweet Lord, what was wrong with his body?*

Maria pulled her eyes away and attacked the stairs with every bit of her energy. The hundreds of hours she spent training paid off, and she climbed so quickly the man—*Don't look at his horrible face*—on the second floor couldn't react in time to grab her. She ducked past, inhaling a stench of body odor and rot, heading for the only other room she knew to be occupied, the two men arguing sports.

And they were still arguing, behind the door labeled THEODORE ROOSEVELT. Maria threw herself into the room without knocking, slamming and locking the door behind her.

"You've got to help—"

The lights were on, but the room was empty. Maria looked for the voices, which hadn't abated, and quickly focused on the nightstand next to the bed. Sitting on top was an old reel-to-reel tape recorder. The voices of the arguing men droned through its speakers in an endless loop.

A trick. To distract her. Make her feel like she wasn't alone.

*Or maybe the purpose of the recording was to lure her into this room.*

Then the tape recorder, and the lights, abruptly went off.

Maria froze. She heard someone crying, and with no small surprise realized the sound was coming from her. Dropping onto all fours, she crawled toward the bed.

This room was laid out the same way as the Lincoln room, and she quickly bumped against the dust ruffle, brought her legs in front of her, and eased underneath on her belly, feetfirst, keeping her head poking out so she could listen.

At first she couldn't hear anything above her heart hammering in her ears and her own shallow panting. She forced her breathing to slow down, sucking in air through her nose, blowing it out softly through her puffed cheeks.

Then she heard the footsteps. From the hallway. Getting closer. First one set, slow and deliberate, each footfall sounding like a thunderclap. Then another set, equally heavy, running up fast.

Both of them stopped at the door.

*"I think the girly is in here."*

*"That's Teddy's room. We can't go in."*

*"But she's in there. It's bleedin' time."*

Maria heard the doorknob turn. She scooted farther under the bed, the dust ruffle covering her hair.

*"You shouldn't do that. You really shouldn't do that."*

The door creaked, inching open. Maria saw a beam of light sliver through the crack. It widened until she could see two huge figures silhouetted in the doorway. They each held flashlights.

*"The one that catches her, bleeds her first. Them's the rules."*

*"I ain't goin' in. You shouldn't neither."*

*"Shuddup. This girly is mine."*

*"It's Teddy's room."*

*"Shuddup!"*

The man dressed in the George Washington outfit

shone his light on the other man's face. Maria put her hand in her mouth and bit down so she didn't scream. His face was . . . *dear God* . . . it was . . .

*"Watch my eyes!"*

*"I said shuddup!"*

*"I'm tellin' on you!"*

*"Hey! Don't!"*

The door abruptly closed, and both sets of footsteps retreated up the hall, down the stairs.

Maria's whole body shivered like she was freezing to death. Terror locked her muscles and she couldn't move. But she had to move. She had to find some kind of way out of there.

Were all the windows bricked over? Maybe some of them weren't. Maybe she could get out of a window, climb down somehow. Or get up on the roof. The roof sounded a lot better than waiting around for those freaks to come back.

Maria heard something soft. Faint. Nearby.

Some kind of scratching sound.

She concentrated on listening, but couldn't hear anything above her own labored gasping. She took a deep breath, held it in.

And could still hear the breathing.

Raspy, wet breathing.

Right next to her.

*Someone else is under the bed.*

"I'm Teddy."

His voice was deep, rough, and hearing it that close scared Maria so badly her bladder let loose.

"I'm gonna bleed you, girly girl. Bleed you nice and long."

Then something grabbed Maria's legs, and she screamed louder than she'd ever screamed in her life, screamed louder than she'd ever thought possible, kicking and clawing as she was dragged down through the trapdoor in the floor.

"W hy don't you go with your grandmother?" Mom said, wiping the sweat from her forehead and replacing it with a streak of grime. "Take JD for a walk."

Kelly Pillsbury frowned at her mother, who'd been trying to change the flat tire for more than ten minutes now. The last nut refused to come off. Each of the women had taken a turn with the tire iron, but the nut was rusted on tight. Grandma was the one who suggested a squirt of WD-40. Now they were all waiting around for the lubricant to soak in, loosen the nut up, so they could get back on the road.

"I'm cool," Kelly said.

She took a furtive glance at the wilderness around her. More trees than she'd ever seen, covering the hills and mountains in every direction. It was gorgeous, and being out here made Kelly forget her established role as a sullen tween.

Make that *teen*. She was turning thirteen in only three days.

Something caught her eye at the tree line, alongside the winding road. A quick streak that looked like a man.

A man darting behind some bushes.

But it had been too big for a man. A bear, maybe?

*No. Bears don't wear overalls.*

Kelly squinted into the woods, but the figure didn't reappear. She listened for a moment, and heard only the faint *click click click* of the wind spinning the rear wheels of their three bikes, bolted to the rack on the Audi's roof. After a moment, Kelly believed she'd imagined the figure, that her eyes were playing tricks on her after such a long road trip.

*Who would be way out here in the middle of nowhere anyway? We left modern civilization two hours ago, the last time we stopped for gas.*

She looked back at her iPod and unpaused her game, *Zombie Apocalypse*, on level 64, with only one quarter of her health left. Kelly had never beaten level 65, and she'd been playing the game for more than a month.

"Kelly?" her mom said.

"Huh?"

"That wasn't a suggestion."

"What?" Mom was seriously breaking her concentration.

"Go help Florence walk the dog."

Kelly flicked the touch screen, pausing again. Mom had her bare arms folded, her muscles popping up like a man's. Kelly subconsciously checked her own arms. She prided herself in being strong, but she never wanted to look like that. *Never.* Muscles on women were gross.

"Grandma's doing fine."

The women both looked at Grandma. The sixty-five-year-old was tugging on JD's leash. JD was sitting on the road, licking himself between his legs. At over a hundred pounds, the German shepherd weighed about as much as Grandma did.

"Kelly. Don't make me say it again." Mom lowered her voice. "Give her a chance. Please. For me."

Kelly sighed loudly and rolled her eyes, even though Mom never said *please*. Then she tucked her iPod into her fanny pack and stalked over to Grandma and the dog. It was bad enough that Grandma was coming to live with them after the Iron Woman race, but Mom had also insisted Kelly give up her room and move into the much smaller third bedroom.

*Totally unfair.*

Kelly didn't understand why Grandma was moving in anyway. She and Mom had some kind of falling-out years ago, after Dad died, and Kelly hadn't seen her grandmother since she was six. She had no idea why they'd been out of touch for so long, but now here they were, pretending to care about each other.

One big happy.

"Stubborn, isn't he?" Grandma let the leash go slack. Like Kelly, she was dressed in jogging shorts and a loose tee, though even at her ancient age, Grandma filled the clothes out better. "I don't think he likes me."

"He only walks for me and Mom. If he didn't like you, you'd know. He'd be growling and the hair would stand up on his back. C'mere, JD."

At the command, JD's ears pricked up and he pranced over to Kelly, the leash pulling out of Grandma's hand. He bumped his massive head into Kelly's hip and gave her arm a lick. He then switched to licking the scab on her knee—a training injury from a few days ago.

Grandma walked up to them. She wasn't as muscular

as Mom, and just a bit shorter, but the resemblance was amazing. When the three of them stood next to each other, it was like looking at the same woman at different stages of her life. Each of them also wore their blond hair the same way, in a ponytail, though Grandma's was mostly gray.

"Want to go north?" Grandma said, pointing her chin over Kelly's shoulder.

"I hear a waterfall. We could go check it out."

"I don't hear anything."

"You will, as we get closer. Come on."

Grandma moved at an easy jog, cutting across the road, into the thick trees. Kelly lived her whole life in southern Illinois, flat as a bowling alley with no flora taller than cornstalks. West Virginia, with its mountains and forests, seemed like a different country. It was beautiful, but Kelly refused to admit it aloud, sticking her nose back in her iPod whenever Mom or Grandma pointed out something pretty during the long drive. She didn't want to give either of them the satisfaction, still sore about the bedroom thing, which Mom sprung on her when they picked Grandma up at the airport yesterday.

*Why didn't Mom give up her room to Grandma? It was all a bunch of BS.*

*No, not BS. It was straight-up bullshit.*

Just thinking about the swear word made Kelly feel older. She frowned, then followed her grandmother.

Ten steps into the woods, Kelly felt like she'd been swallowed. The trees were everywhere, and she lost all sense of direction. Grandma weaved through the forest like a jackrabbit, her pace increasing, and Kelly began to fall behind.

"Slow down! JD can't keep up!"

In fact, JD was doing fine. Kelly was also doing fine, at least in the stamina department. She'd trained for seven months for the triathlon and was enormously proud to be the youngest contestant this year. But Kelly was used to running on asphalt, not rocky wilderness. Her steps alternated between jagged outcroppings and soft dirt that sucked at her gym shoes. Kelly spent so much time watching her footing she was afraid Grandma would get too far ahead and disappear.

"Don't look at your feet."

Kelly startled, coming to a stop. Somehow Grandma had materialized right in front of her.

"I'm gonna break my ankle."

"Look into my eyes, Kelly."

Kelly did as instructed. Grandma's eyes were blue, like hers and Mom's, but set in a valley of deep wrinkles. Kelly couldn't remember Grandma ever smiling. Not that she was a mean woman. But she was serious all the time.

"Can you see my hand?" Grandma asked.

Kelly glanced down at Grandma's wriggling fingers.

"No, Kelly. Keep looking at me while you do it." Kelly sighed, then stared at Grandma again.

"Keeping your eyes on mine, can you see my hand?"

Kelly couldn't see it, at least not clearly. But she could make out an indistinct blur.

"I guess."

"What am I doing?"

"Wiggling your fingers."

"Good. Now watch me."

Grandma took a step back and stood with her legs apart, her hands at waist level, one in front of the other. She quickly raised her arms up over her head, then brought each hand around in a circle. They met again at her beltline, palms out. The entire time, her gaze was locked on to Kelly.

"What's that?" Kelly asked.

"The beginning of a kata called *Kushanku*. It helps improve your peripheral vision. The goal is to be able to see your hands while looking straight ahead."

"What's the point?"

"To be aware of everything around you and not just what's in front of you."

"So?"

"So then you'll know if someone does this."

Kelly felt wind on her cheek. She looked, and saw Grandma's palm an inch away from slapping her ear. Kelly hadn't seen Grandma's hand move at all.

JD growled, baring his teeth.

"Shush," Grandma said. "Be nice."

The dog whined, then sat down and began licking himself again.

"Can you teach me how to do that?" Kelly asked. "To hit that fast?"

"It's up to your mother. She never really warmed up to the martial arts."

"Show me that kata thing again."

"Kushanku."

Grandma repeated the move. Kelly handed over the leash and tried it. She could just barely make out her hands at the very edge of sight.

"I can see them."

She also thought she saw something else. Something moving in the woods. Kelly remembered the man she'd seen earlier, but kept her eyes on Grandma, as instructed. Besides, if there was a man in the forest, JD would be barking.

That is, if JD could keep his snout out of his own crotch for more than ten seconds.

"Good. Now use your peripheral vision when you're running over the rocks, so you don't have to keep your head down. Keep your eyes ahead of you, but not your entire focus."

"I can try."

Grandma took off, JD running alongside her. Kelly trailed behind, doing as Grandma said, and found she could move much quicker. She looked around for the man in the overalls, but saw only foliage.

Kelly smiled, relaxing a little. The summer breeze smelled like pine trees and wildflowers, and she enjoyed the stretch and pull in her hamstrings and quads. It was a brief run, barely even a warm-up, before Kelly caught up to Grandma on a crest.

"Hey," Kelly said. "JD let you walk him."

Grandma wasn't even out of breath. "Can you hear it now?"

"What?"

"Listen."

Kelly heard it. A hissing, splashing sound.

"The waterfall?"

Grandma nodded. "Which direction is it in?"

"I can't tell."

"Close your eyes. Open your ears."

Kelly shut her eyes and listened. The sound seemed to be coming from no particular direction.

"Try turning around. Tune out everything else."

Kelly shifted slightly. She spun in a slow circle, eventually locking in on the direction of the water. When she opened her eyes, she was grinning.

"It's this way," Kelly said, bounding off into the woods.

She jogged down a hill, around a bend, and then to a clearing, skidding to a stop because the ground simply ended. Kelly felt her stomach sink, staring down off the side of a sheer cliff. She wasn't good with heights, and even though she could swim three hundred laps in the school pool she was terrified of diving boards. Standing on ledges just wasn't her thing.

Then she saw the waterfall.

It was gigantic, at least fifty feet high. The vertigo made her back up two steps.

"Lovely," Grandma said.

Kelly hadn't even heard the old woman come up beside her.

"I don't really like heights."

"Your eyes can make you afraid of things you shouldn't be afraid of. Are you standing on solid ground?"

"Yeah."

"What do you think you should trust more, your eyes, or the solid ground?"

"The ground."

"So trust the ground and let your eyes enjoy the view."

Kelly trusted the ground and stared at the waterfall.

A fine mist hovered overhead and made a double rainbow in the rays of the setting sun. It was prettier than a postcard, and not so scary anymore.

"Is this what Vietnam looked like?" Kelly asked. Then she immediately regretted it. According to Mom, Grandma never talked about the war. Kelly knew she was there for four years as a combat nurse, but that was all.

"Parts of it. Parts of it were so beautiful it hurt."

"Is that where you learned that kung fu stuff?"

"It's karate. And no, I learned that after my tour ended. Let's go back, see how Letti is doing with that tire. Can you find the way?"

"I dunno. I don't think so."

"Try it. Maybe you'll surprise yourself. If you get confused, see if you can spot any of our footprints. The ground is soft and we made quite a few." Grandma's eyes were serious, but kind.

"How come you never smile?" Kelly asked. She watched Grandma's eyes get hard again and regretted the question.

"It happened during the war," Grandma said. "They shot my smile off."

*What? They shot her smile off?* Then Grandma winked.

Kelly grinned, took a final, unsteady glance at the waterfall, then bounded back into the woods. Nothing looked particularly familiar, but she managed to spot a footprint so she knew she was on the right track, even though the footprint seemed rather large. Then she recognized a big tree she'd passed earlier, and she altered her course, picking up speed and growing more confident.

Abruptly, something snagged her shoulder, pulling her off her feet. Kelly landed on her butt, hard, and someone covered her mouth before she could yell out.

"Shh." Grandma was kneeling next to her, her hand over Kelly's face. "Stay calm."

Kelly didn't understand what was happening, and she was about to protest, when she noticed JD. The dog was crouching down, ready to pounce, his teeth bared. All the hair on the dog's neck stood out like spikes. Kelly followed the animal's gaze and saw—

—trees. Nothing but trees.

Then something moved. Ever so slightly, but enough for Kelly to distinguish the body from the surrounding foliage.

It was a man, hiding behind a giant oak. The man she'd seen earlier, the one in the overalls. He was incredibly tall, wearing a plaid shirt and a baseball cap. There was something wrong—something horribly wrong—with his face. And his eyes . . .

*His eyes look red.*

The man stared right at Kelly, and she'd never been more frightened in her life.

JD barked, making Kelly jerk in surprise.

"Hello," Grandma said to the stranger. "We were looking at the waterfall. I hope we're not trespassing on your property. If so, we're sorry." Grandma didn't sound sorry. She sounded tough as a barrel of hammers.

The man continued to stare. He didn't move. He didn't even blink.

*What happened to his face?*

"We'll be on our way."

JD barked again, then began to growl.

"Easy, boy. We don't want you biting any more strangers."

JD had never bitten anyone. But Kelly understood why Grandma said that; it might scare the man off.

But the man didn't look scared. He simply shifted from one leg to the other, revealing something he was holding in his hand.

*Oh shit.*

*That's a shotgun.*

"Let's go," Grandma whispered. "Fast."

Kelly didn't have to be told twice. The two of them sprinted, JD alongside, down the hill in a zigzag pattern. Kelly kept expecting to hear a gunshot, and could almost feel a cold area between her shoulder blades where she was sure the bullet would hit. Mom had what she called a varmint gun, a small .22 she used to scare off the raccoons who liked to get into the garbage cans. Kelly knew the damage that could do.

This man's gun was a lot bigger.

Not soon enough, they broke through the tree line and were back on the road.

Kelly looked left, then right, and couldn't see their car.

*Had the man gotten Mom?*

"This way," Grandma said. "Over the crest."

Grandma's strides were long, and Kelly matched her. On the asphalt she had a lot more confidence, the hard road under her feet solid and familiar. She sprinted ahead, feeling her muscles stretch, JD easily matching pace as he galloped alongside. The hill was a gradual incline, tough on the shins, and after two hundred meters her breath came faster.

*Is this the right way? What if Grandma is wrong? What if Mom isn't over the crest?*

She took a quick glance over her shoulder, but the strange man wasn't behind them.

*What was wrong with his face? It was all messed up.*

They were almost to the top of the hill now. Ten steps. Five steps. Kelly willed her mom to be there. Not only there, but with the tire already fixed so they could get the hell away from here. Kelly pulled even farther in front, reaching the crest, staring down on the winding road and—nothing. Mom and the car weren't there.

Then JD took off, pulling the leash out of Kelly's hand, jerking her forward and almost making her fall. He tore ahead, running around the bend, out of sight.

Kelly glanced at Grandma, who was matching her pace. The old woman stared back, her face solemn.

"The car . . ." Kelly sputtered.

"It's ahead."

"JD . . ."

"Ahead."

Kelly felt like crying. "I'm . . . scared."

"Use it. Everyone gets scared. Don't let it paralyze you. Your body, or your mind."

Kelly lengthened her stride again; a dangerous move since they were going downhill. If she hit some loose gravel, or stumbled somehow at this speed, it would cause more damage than just a skinned knee.

"Kelly. Slow down."

But Kelly didn't slow down. Her feet pressed against the street faster and faster, and Kelly became off-balance on the decline. She pitched forward, envisioning her chin cracking against the pavement, her face scraping down to the teeth and cheekbones, her knees breaking and head bursting—

"Kelly!"

Grandma caught Kelly's shirt, steadying her. Kelly took a few more unsteady steps and then slowed down enough to keep her balance.

They pushed through the turn, Kelly hoping she'd see Mom and the car and JD, fearing she'd see the strange man with the gun.

But there was nothing ahead but empty road.

"We went . . . the wrong . . . way," Kelly said between pants. She began to slow down even more.

"Keep running."

Kelly wished she'd paid more attention on the car ride up. None of this seemed familiar. The road. The woods. The mountains. It all looked the same.

"Is this . . ." she gasped, "the right road?"

"Yes."

"But . . ."

"Don't talk. Run."

Grandma pulled in front. Kelly fell back five paces, thinking Grandma was wrong, thinking about turning around and going the other way.

Then they rounded another turn and Kelly saw their car.

JD left Mom's side and came sprinting over to Kelly. He knew not to jump on her and instead doubled back and ran with her until they reached the car.

"I changed the tire. Did you and Grandma enjoy—" Mom squinted at Kelly. "Babe, are you okay?"

"There was a man." Kelly huffed and puffed. "His face was messed up. He had a gun."

Grandma coasted to a stop alongside them.

"Florence? What happened?"

Mom hadn't called Grandma *Mom* since Dad died.

Grandma blew out a deep breath. "I'm not sure. Could have been a hunter. Could have been some hillbilly protecting his whiskey still. Scary-looking fellow, wasn't he, Kelly?"

"Did he threaten you?" Mom asked.

Grandma shook her head. "Kept his gun down. Didn't say a word. Might not be used to talking, though. He had a severe harelip, probably a cleft palate. Talking would be difficult."

"Should we call the police?"

"For having a gun in West Virginia? They'd laugh us off the phone."

"Are you okay, Kelly?"

Kelly felt like crying, and Mom showing concern made the emotion even stronger. But she sucked it in, got her breathing under control.

*I'm almost a teenager. Teenagers don't cry.*

"I'm fine."

"Are you sure?"

Grandma folded her arms. "She said she's fine, Letti. Kelly's almost a teenager. Quit treating her like a child."

Kelly matched Grandma's pose, taking strength from it. "Yeah, Mom. Now can we get going?"

Mom made a face, then looked at her watch. "We've got another forty minutes before we get to the bed-and-breakfast. Do you need to pee?"

Kelly rolled her eyes. "No."

"Are you sure?"

"Geez, Mom." She walked over to the car and climbed into the backseat.

Surprisingly, Grandma got in next to her.

"Let's let JD ride shotgun. I'd like to see that game you're playing on your iPod."

"Uh, sure."

As Mom pulled back onto the road, Kelly showed Grandma *Zombie Apocalypse*.

"It's really hard. I can't get past level 65."

"Sure you can," Grandma said. "You just haven't yet."

Kelly attacked the level with a frenzy. For some reason, more than anything, she wanted to prove Grandma right.